· HONEY MOUNTAIN SERIES ·

ALWAYS
Mine

· HONEY MOUNTAIN SERIES ·

ALWAYS
Mine

USA TODAY BESTSELLING AUTHOR
LAURA PAVLOV

Entangled Publishing, LLC
644 Shrewsbury Commons Ave., STE 181
Shrewsbury, PA 17361
rights@entangledpublishing.com

Amara is an imprint of Entangled Publishing, LLC.

Visit our website at www.entangledpublishing.com.

Edited by Sue Grimshaw
Cover design by LJ Anderson, Mayhem Cover Creations
Edge design by LJ Anderson, Mayhem Cover Creations
Stock art by Olga Grigorevykh/Gettyimages, jcarroll-images/Gettyimages,
Mimadeo/Gettyimages, and Studio LoveLens/Gettyimages
Interior design by Britt Marczak

ISBN 978-1-64937-778-4

Manufactured in the United States of America

First Edition November 2024

10 9 8 7 6 5 4 3 2 1

ALSO BY LAURA PAVLOV

HONEY MOUNTAIN

Always Mine
Ever Mine
Make You Mine
Simply Mine
Only Mine

MAGNOLIA FALLS

Loving Romeo
Wild River
Forbidden King
Beating Heart
Finding Hayes

COTTONWOOD COVE

Into the Tide
Under the Stars
On the Shore
Before the Sunset
After the Storm

Dear Lisa, Julie and Jen,
Thank you for being the best sisters around!
Love you, Laura

"A sister is a gift to the heart, a friend to the spirit,
a golden thread to the meaning of life."
– Isadora James

Chapter 1

Vivian

I made my way up the path of my childhood home. On Sunday nights, no matter where we were, if we were in Honey Mountain, we attended family dinner. The crisp fall air surrounded me, and I was thankful that I'd pulled out my warmest down jacket this morning. I loved that the mountains were in view here no matter where you were. Honey Mountain was a small town right on the border of Nevada and California, and it surrounded a giant lake which was a huge tourist attraction. But it was the tall peaks that I was most drawn to. A white dusting covered all the tips, always the first sign that temperatures were dropping.

"Hello," I said when I stepped inside.

I'd grown up here. It was an old farmhouse that my parents had restored over the years with a backyard to-die-for—seriously, you could have the party of all parties here, and we usually did.

"Vivi?" Ashlan yelled as she came barreling around the corner. She'd come home from college for the weekend, and even though we FaceTimed practically every day, hugging her in person always made me feel better.

"Hey, Ash," I said as I wrapped my arms around her. It had only been a few weeks since she'd gone back to school, but my sisters were everything to me.

"Don't make me dry-heave from all this gushing. The girl has not been gone *that* long," Dylan said as she came around the corner and her head fell back in laughter.

"Humans have actual feelings." Charlotte chomped on a carrot and chuckled. "Or didn't your alien leaders teach you that?"

Ashlan was the baby of the family. Dylan and Charlotte were twins and two years older than her, two years younger than me. Our oldest sister, Everly, was two years older than me. She was currently living across the country out east while finishing a fellowship program as a sports psychologist for a professional NBA team. My oldest sister was the most driven person I'd ever known, and I was so proud of her. But I missed her as I didn't get to see her often.

My mother had been an only child and wanted a big family, but I didn't think she'd expected to end up with five daughters. She'd left this earth far too soon and we'd all rallied around our father ever since. The thought still made a lump form in the back of my throat, even all these years later.

"Bite me, Charlie," Dylan said. "Come on. We need to get the plates out. Everyone will be here soon, and Dad's having a conniption that nothing is done. Remind me why we decided to live at home again?"

I laughed. The twins had just graduated from college a few months ago, and they were back at home until they had enough money to live on their own. Charlotte taught kindergarten at the local elementary school, and Dylan was attending law school with plans to take over the world, her words not mine. She commuted to Bridgewood University three days a week, which was an hour away, and the other two days she was allowed to attend remotely. They were both saving a ton of money by living at home, so it was worth it.

However, they were both living under our father's roof again, which meant lots of family dinners and their fair share of chores.

Dad was the Honey Mountain fire chief, and he'd always been strict but fair. He was my favorite person on the planet next to my sisters and my best friend, Niko, depending on the day... because they all drove me crazy as well.

"Well, I'm out of here in a few months. As soon as I save up enough for a down payment, I'll be buying my own place like Vivi," Charlotte said, winking at me over her shoulder.

"Girl, you know I'm moving in there the minute you find a place. If Vivi's house wasn't the size of a postage stamp, I'd be living there right now." We all followed Dylan into the kitchen, and as she pulled the plates out, I went to the drawer to get the silverware. The smell of my dad's famous mac 'n' cheese baking in the oven had my mouth watering.

"Hey, water views come with a price. I'll take my postage stamp all day long." I laughed. It wasn't a lie. I'd found a small cottage on the lake, and I wouldn't trade it for anything. Between the small business loan that I'd taken out to open Honey Bee's Bakery and my mortgage, I was happy to just be surviving at this point.

"I'm not complaining. I just wish there was room for me." Dylan shrugged.

"I'll be right back. I'm going to get the mail," Ashlan called out as she jogged out the front door.

"Please let her get that internship. She's been checking the mailbox all day and I keep telling her that Beatrice is delivering later and later in the day now," Charlotte said of our mail lady as she pulled glasses from the cupboard and set them on the counter as she counted out twelve.

Whichever firefighters weren't working on Sundays always came to dinner.

I peeked my head out the back door. "Hey, Dad."

"Hi, sweetheart. Did those slackers get the kitchen ready?" he asked as smoke billowed all around him. The man loved his grill, and my stomach rumbled as the smell of barbecue chicken wafted around me.

"I assume you're referring to your daughters."

"Sure am. One of the wonder twins has a big attitude about helping out lately."

I laughed. "She mentioned that. I'll get the salad ready."

When I came back inside all three of my sisters were huddled together, which was never a good thing.

Dylan looked up and shook her head. The girl had never been good at hiding her feelings, especially when she was angry. I walked to the fridge and pulled out a head of lettuce, some cucumbers, and two large tomatoes, and started rinsing them off in the sink.

"What's wrong?" I asked, glancing over my shoulder as I dropped the lettuce in the salad spinner and plunged down a few times while they all gaped at me.

Dylan yanked something from Ashlan's hand and hissed at her. Charlotte was shaking her head and glaring at Dylan, as they clearly disagreed about telling me something.

"Listen, if you two think keeping secrets from Vivi is a good idea, you're on your own. I'm a no-bullshit type of girl." Dylan flicked at the card and didn't hide her disdain.

"No kidding. And it's not called no bullshit, it's more like you have no couth." Charlotte rarely got mad at her domineering twin, but when she did, I knew she meant it. The joke in town was that the twins looked nothing alike, and everyone thought Ashlan and I held the strongest resemblance.

"Couth is for the birds. Shit happens. I don't believe in sugarcoating. And I never cared for that too-prim-and-proper, shady ex of yours." Dylan extended her arm and handed me the card as I pushed down one final time on the salad spinner before drying off my hands.

"FYI, I make a living by sugarcoating things," I said with a brow raised as I pulled the card out of the envelope.

I took a moment to process what was in front of me. A wedding invitation to Jansen Clark's wedding. He'd been my one and only boyfriend as we'd dated our last year of high school, and then we'd been long distance all through college. He wanted a life outside of Honey Mountain, and I didn't. So…I'd surprised him with a visit to San Francisco to end our relationship in person, only to find him in bed with his co-worker, Katie…aka the future Mrs. Clark.

There was a pang in my chest as I took it all in. I didn't know her outside of what he'd told me about her over the years. Not sure how much weight I could put on that considering he said she was bossy and irritating, yet he slept with her and was now walking down the aisle with her.

My chest squeezed. It wasn't sadness or heartache. Those were the things I should have felt the day I drove hours to have a face-to-face with him and found them together. It didn't hurt the way it should have. Sure, I'd felt betrayed. But relief was the most dominant feeling I had when I got back in my car and drove all the way home. I'd rehearsed the breakup speech all the way there and then cursed his name as I drove back to Honey Mountain that day. But I wouldn't lie and say it didn't sting.

All in all, I would have appreciated a phone call or a text giving me a heads-up before he invited my entire family to his wedding. And the truth was—it hurt to be so easily replaced. Hell, he replaced me before we were even done. And this only happened six months ago. Since then, I'd gone on two horrible dates and not so much as kissed a man since Jansen. Yet he'd managed to date his mistress, get engaged, and plan a wedding. How was that even possible?

"Her name is irritating as all get-out, and it'll be worse after she marries him," Dylan hissed, taking the invite back from me. "Kathryn Clark?" She groaned. "She sounds like a haughty, uptight politician's wife. And she's a skanky, cheating ho. So, there you go. You were way too good for him, and we all knew it."

"Her name is actually Katie," I corrected her, and she rolled her eyes.

I didn't blame her for what happened. Obviously, I wasn't a fan, but I didn't know her. Jansen was the one who hadn't had the decency to just end our relationship. He'd sent a few texts trying to apologize, but it was too little, too late. I hadn't heard from him in months, and I was fine with it. But I certainly wasn't expecting a wedding invitation to come in the mail.

"I liked Jansen before he cheated," Ashlan said before slapping a hand over her mouth.

"He was never good enough for you." Charlotte grabbed the cucumber from my pile and started peeling. "You deserve better."

"It's fine. He showed me his true colors six months ago. I guess I just didn't expect to hear this way."

"Oh, really?" Dylan oozed sarcasm. She claimed it was her second language and I could attest to the fact that she'd been fluent in angry sarcasm from the moment she'd said her first words, which were: *I got it.* "You didn't expect a wedding invitation in the mail after wasting years of your life on that cheating jackass? That would require him having any amount of decency, which he doesn't." Dylan shook her head and tossed the invitation on the counter.

"What's Grumpy Smurf ranting about now?" Niko walked into the kitchen with his niece, Mabel, in his arms. My best friend was all gruff and intimidating on the outside, but he was all sweetness when it came to Mabel. He adored his little niece so much.

"Oh, you know. That…" Dylan walked over to Niko and placed her hands over Mabel's ears as she kissed her cherub cheek. "That asshole Jansen is getting married to the skank Vivi found him in the sack with. And he had the audacity to send an invitation here, to the *Thomas family.* He's lucky he doesn't live here anymore. I wouldn't mind a minute alone in a dark alley with that wimpy, scrawny…"

"Okay. We get it. You don't like him," I groaned. I wasn't in the mood for a Dylan life lesson and when the girl got on a tangent, there was no end in sight. "It's fine. He's known us his entire life, so it's not that shocking that he invited us."

Niko studied me as Ashlan pulled Mabel from his arms and took her out to the living room probably to pull out the toys that we kept there for her. His shoulder-length hair was tied back at the nape of his neck, and a few pieces fell out around his face. He was almost a foot taller than me at six foot four, with broad shoulders and piercing gray eyes. Every girl in town fawned all over him, but he'd always just been my best friend. My rock. He despised most people, but for whatever reason, we connected when we were young, and it had never changed. He leaned down and studied my eyes.

"Stop. I'm fine. I'm not even upset."

"Bullshit, Honey Bee." His voice was deep, and his warm breath tickled my cheek, which made me chuckle. "I told you that dude wasn't good enough for you. I knew it and he knew it too. And he best not show his face around here for a while."

Niko had been calling me *Honey Bee* since we were kids and I'd ended up naming my business after the silly nickname.

"Who needs to be hiding from Niko?" Dad said with a laugh as he came through the back door.

Before anyone could answer, all the guys started filing in one by one. There was Big Al, my dad's best friend who also worked at the fire department, and his wife, Lottie, followed by three more firefighters, Rusty, Samson, and Tallboy. Everyone always got nicknames at the firehouse aside from Niko. They briefly called him Hero after he saved an elderly woman who'd been trapped in her attic bedroom two years ago during a house fire, but he'd put the kibosh on that immediately.

"Where's Jace?" I asked. Jace King was a firefighter too and he was Niko's closest guy friend.

"Karla's out again. He's home with the girls." Niko looked over his shoulder to make sure no one was listening. Jace's wife was a train wreck, and everyone knew it.

"She's unbelievable," I whispered. "He could have brought the girls."

"He wanted to spend some time with them and get them to bed early. But stop deflecting. We're not done with this Jansen conversation. You want to go to Beer Mountain tonight?" Niko asked as he bumped me with his shoulder and popped a tomato in his mouth.

"Sure. But I'm fine," I said with a shrug. Beer Mountain was our favorite bar in town. I wasn't much of a drinker, and I had to be up early for work, so I wouldn't normally go out on a work night.

But maybe blowing off some steam wouldn't be such a bad idea.

"You're always fine, Honey Bee."

I nodded. Because he was right. I'd been through worse than Jansen Clark cheating on me and inviting me to his wedding.

I would be fine.

I had to be.

Chapter 2

Niko

I dropped Mabel at home with my mom and my sister, Jada. I tried to get her out of there on the nights I wasn't working at the firehouse. My sister thought I was doing it to give her a break, but the truth was, I was doing it to give Mabel a break. My mom and Jada were too much for me on a good day. My mother hadn't been coping with reality since my dad went to prison, and my sister was far too young to be a mother, so together they weren't a strong combination.

"She needs a bath. She painted over at the Thomas' house, so you'll need to clean her up."

"Oh, man. I need to train you to bathe her too," Jada said as she lay on the couch with a tub of ice cream resting on her chest.

I rolled my eyes. She knew I had my limits and naked babies was one of them.

"Mama, I want some scream," Mabel said as she made her way toward my sister with her rosy cheeks and her curls springing

LAURA PAVLOV

out of her ponytail. The girl was so damn cute it was painful.

"Didn't Uncle Niko give you some dessert? Vivian always has the best treats," Jada said.

"I don't think so." Mabel looked at me with wide eyes.

"She had a cookie and half a cupcake already. She's going to get a bellyache if she has any more." I scooped Mabel up in my arms. "Don't you be fibbing, little girl."

Her giggles flooded the space around me just as my mother came out of her bedroom with a cigarette in her mouth.

"I thought we agreed you wouldn't smoke in the house?" I hissed as I dropped into the oversized chair and held the little munchkin on my lap.

"Mabel wasn't home."

"Well, she's home now," I said, and my mother rolled her eyes and walked toward the back patio.

"Fine. I'll be out here."

I pushed to my feet and set Mabel down, holding her hand while she stabilized herself. The girl was a tiny little thing with a cute round belly that seemed to throw off her center of gravity. I kissed the top of her head. "Love you, Mabel girl." I pointed at my sister. "Up. Get her in the tub and cleaned up. And don't let Mom smoke in the house."

"I'm too old for this," Jada groaned as she pushed to her feet.

"You're nineteen years old." I barked out a laugh.

Yes, my sister had Mabel when she was only fifteen years old. I'd tried my best to keep her on track, but some things are just out of your control no matter how hard you try. Needless to say, the baby daddy, Joey Black, wasn't interested in a kid. A loser my sister was better off without.

I swung my keys around my finger and made my way out to the patio where my mother sat puffing on her cancer stick. Her skin was tinted slightly gray, and she had no meat on her bones. Another family member who'd just given up.

"Did you hear any updates about parole?" I asked as I came outside and dropped in the chair across from her. I knew my father's hearing was coming up soon if it hadn't already happened, and there was a chance he'd get released. I hadn't seen the man in six years, and I was in no hurry for him to return. He was the reason I was still here after all. His choices had robbed me of many of my own.

"His lawyer thinks he has a good chance of getting out in a few months."

I nodded before scrubbing a hand down my face. The courts suddenly took on a leniency that I was not in favor of, especially since it involved my father. "And what does that mean for Mabel? Are you going to let that asshole back in this house?"

She inhaled her smoke stick before turning her head to blow it away from me. "He wasn't all bad, Niko."

Here we go.

"He's in prison for getting yet another DUI and nearly killing Tony. Or have you forgotten about that?"

"Tony wasn't exactly sober either," she hissed. This was my mother's MO. Defend. Deflect. Deny.

If there was an award for the best enablers, she would get the gold medal.

"He wasn't behind the wheel. Dad made that choice. He never stops to think about how his actions will affect everyone around him." I pushed to my feet because even talking about the asshole enraged me.

"No one made you give up that scholarship, Niko. That was your choice. You can't blame him for that."

Yeah, my father had gone to prison right before I graduated

high school. I'd planned to go play Division 1 football for a top school in Michigan, when the shit hit the fan. But my mother had checked out and at the time, my sister was only thirteen years old. I couldn't leave her to fend for herself. Couldn't leave them. So, I'd given it all up and stayed in this shit town to help my family. My sister had resented me for trying to parent her and ended up knocked up a couple years later, only reminding me more that I'd failed.

I shoved the sleeve of my hoodie up my arm and held it out to her. "Can I blame him for this? Or is this my fault too?"

Her eyes scanned the cigarette scars running up my arms and she looked away quickly. "He had a drinking problem."

I nodded. There was always a justification for his abuse.

And I would not allow Mabel to be subjected to it. He'd never laid a hand on Jada for whatever reason, and I'd been happy to be his punching bag back then. But who would he pick on if he came back here now? It wasn't going to happen on my watch.

If he laid his hands on that sweet little girl, I wouldn't stand by. Not a chance in fucking hell. I was bigger and stronger than I'd been when that piece of shit used to take out all his frustrations on me.

"If you let him back in this house, I'll be moving Mabel and Jada out of here."

She stubbed out her smoke in the ashtray. "How are you going to do that on a fireman's salary, huh?"

"You see, that's the difference between you and me, Ma. It doesn't matter. I'll do whatever it takes to keep them safe. That's what you do for the people you love. You just must have missed the memo."

"Niko," she called out, and I turned away as I moved to the doorway leading back in the house. "I do love you. I've just never been as strong as you."

Fuck. She always played the same card, and I couldn't muster up the empathy to care for her excuses anymore. When you chose to have kids, it was your fucking job to keep them safe. She should have left him. Walked away. Stood up to him. Whatever it took.

"I know, Ma." I knocked on the doorframe in frustration and made my way toward the front door.

"I love my Neek, Neek, I love my Neek, Neek," Mabel sang from the bathroom and my chest squeezed. She called me Neek, Neek and even though I despised silly names, I didn't mind it coming from her.

I shut the front door and checked my phone. Vivian had texted, asking if I'd pick her up after I dropped off Mabel. That meant she was going to drink, which was a rarity. She tried to act like it didn't sting that that fucking loser Jansen had cheated on her and was getting married already. But I knew her better than anyone. She didn't love the dude, not even a little. He'd just fit in her pretty little box that she'd designed for her life, and she'd stayed with him far too long. I think the fact that they'd been long distance had actually kept her in the relationship longer, because she'd fallen into a comfort of being on her own, but she liked saying she had a boyfriend. The dipshit was perfect on paper. I'd never cared for him, and he'd been the one topic that had been off-limits for us. We talked about everything aside from our personal relationships. Or my lack thereof. Vivian knew who I was, just like I knew who she was. It was no secret that I liked to fuck, but we didn't talk about it because it wasn't her thing. I mean, I knew she'd lost her virginity to that little pussy, and I knew he'd been the only dude she'd ever been with, and that was as much as she'd tell me. But I wanted more for her. She deserved more.

She deserved everything.

Vivian Thomas was the best person I knew. There weren't many people that I loved deeply...but she was one of them. Hell, she was at the top of the list next to my sister and Mabel.

I'd given her the name Honey Bee when we were kids because we'd learned about them in school. I'd always been amazed at the way the girl would buzz around spreading all her sweetness from one person to the next. Deep inside her lived a queen...but she hadn't tapped into that shit yet. But I saw it. I saw the fierceness behind her dark gaze when it came to protecting her sisters. Her father.

Just not herself yet.

I pulled up in front of her little cottage on the water. She'd dreamed of having a place on Honey Mountain Lake since we were kids, and even though it wasn't huge, maybe 900 square feet at best, it was all hers and I was proud as hell of her.

I turned the knob and walked in as she came out of her bedroom holding a glass of wine. "What did I tell you about locking your damn door?"

"It's Honey Mountain. Who's going to break in? They'd all be welcome even if they knocked. Thanks for picking me up."

Her words were slurring, which was a first. I'd never seen Vivian drunk before. She was always in control. I recognized it because it was something that we shared. My need for control was born out of anger, while Vivian's came from a place of loss. After losing her mother, she'd kicked into gear and stepped up for her younger sisters, while her older sister, Everly, went off to chase her dreams.

I guess we had that in common—but neither of us cried about it.

"Of course. How many glasses have we had?" I asked as she

grabbed her purse. Her black jeans hugged her tight little ass perfectly, and I always forced myself to look away. I'd spent the night in Vivian Thomas' bed dozens of times growing up and never had an issue. But these past few years, she'd grown up in more ways than I wanted to admit. Her body was sexy as hell, and she was the most beautiful girl I'd ever laid eyes on. Dark eyes, long, light-brown waves cascading down her back, and full, pouty, pink lips that I'd avoided looking at lately.

"Two glasses, *Dad*. I'm cutting loose tonight. Hence the ride," she said, raising a brow in challenge. "It was *your* suggestion we go out."

I put my hands up. "Got it. No judgment."

She flipped off the lights and made her way to my truck, climbing in. I leaned over and started to buckle her seat belt and she burst out in laughter before slapping my hand away. "I'm not Mabel. I can buckle myself."

I rolled my eyes before getting behind the wheel and heading to Beer Mountain. It was only a couple blocks away from her house. She lived close enough to walk to town, which was where her bakery was.

"Niko, my man," Joey Black said as he clapped me on the back when we stepped inside.

"Get the fuck out of my face. I'm not your man, nor am I your friend." I stared hard at him, and Vivian slipped her hand in mine. Our fingers intertwined, which instantly calmed my nerves. She'd always been the one to calm me.

"Easy, brother. Just saying hi." He tipped his head back to look up at me.

Short, shady fucker.

"Yeah, go find yourself a new friend," I hissed before walking away. The dude had knocked up my sister and run for the hills.

He'd signed off on his rights to Mabel and if I thought I could beat the bastard to death without any ramifications, I'd do it.

"Okay, you need to tone it down a little," Vivian said as she dropped my hand and hopped up on the barstool.

"He's like a little gnat. I have zero tolerance for men who duck out of their responsibilities," I said, dropping on the stool beside her.

"Says the guy who's never had a relationship that lasted longer than one night in bed." She reached for a handful of peanuts.

"Hey, I'm upfront about who I am, and I wrap my shit up. But if anything ever happened, I would not abandon my own kid. Not that I ever want one, but if I fucked up, I wouldn't duck and hide. And for the record, I don't spend the night with the ladies I grace with my impressive skills," I said, wriggling my brows. "So, I guess we could say my longest relationship lasted a couple hours." I held my hand up for Tanner the bartender.

She rolled her eyes. "Spare me the gory details."

"I always do."

"Are you guys eating or just drinking? Water for you?" he asked me and turned to look at Vivian. Most people in town knew that I didn't drink. Hell, my father drank enough for all of us.

"We already ate. I'll take a water. What do you want, Honey Bee?"

"I'll do a..." She scanned all the bottles behind the bar. "You know what, Tanner? I'll do a shot of tequila and whatever beer you have on draft."

"Oh. We're going big tonight, huh?" he teased.

"I guess so," I said, scrubbing a hand down the back of my neck.

"Listen, Jansen was not the guy for me. Thankfully, we found that out before it was too late. He's moved on and it's time I do the same." She picked up the little shot glass that Tanner set in front of her and tipped her head back. She winced and gagged, and it was impossible not to laugh.

"Pace yourself, Honey Bee. You've got to work tomorrow."

I thought about the first time I ever called her by that nickname. The first time I realized Vivian Thomas was my best friend. The first time I crawled through her window craving all her goodness…

"Niko?" she asked as she opened the window. "Did he hit you again?"

"Yeah. Can I sleep here for a few hours? I don't think I can sleep at my house tonight."

"Of course," she whispered.

I climbed through the window, and she moved back to her bed and held the blanket open for me. I moved in beside her. Vivi was a tiny little thing and there was plenty of room in her full-size bed.

I used my hand to muffle my moan when I rolled on my side. I was fairly certain my ribs were broken or bruised.

"You okay, Niko?" she whispered.

"Not right now, but I will be."

"Why can't we tell my mom and dad? They could help you."

"I told you, Vivi. It'll just make things worse. Last year when I went to the school nurse when he broke my arm, he was pissed off that I'd gone to her for help. He beat me where she couldn't see it and warned me that if I ever talked about it to anyone, things would only get worse. I just have to make it until I'm eighteen and then I'll go far away to school."

Her hand found mine, as she rolled on her side and faced me. Warm breath tickled my neck. "Don't ever go far from me, okay?"

"I won't. You'll keep my secret?"

"Yes. You're my best friend. Your secret is safe with me."

"And you'll always be safe with me."

"You didn't need to punch Boone Harrison today. I'm sure your dad wasn't happy you got a detention," she whispered.

"He slapped you in the chest. The jerk had it coming."

"Thank you. Night, Niko."

"Good night, Honey Bee."

Chapter 3

Vivian

"I'll be fine for work. Don't you worry," I slurred.

"Hey there, handsome." Two hands moved over his shoulders and squeezed. Niko set his water down and turned to face Sabrina Hobbs. I knew they'd slept together a few times because this town was small, and people talked. But Niko didn't do relationships, and everyone knew that.

"Hey." He crossed his arms over his chest, and it was clear that he didn't want to talk to her right now. Niko could be an intimidating guy. He never had been to me, but I'd seen him freeze people in place with just a look. Sabrina did not acknowledge my presence.

"Hi, Sabrina." My words slurred. "I wasn't sure if you saw me sitting here or if you were intentionally ignoring me?"

Niko chuckled, because I was definitely more confrontational when I was intoxicated. I liked the sound of his laugh. It didn't happen often, and mostly just when we were alone. My best friend was as broody as they come.

"Oh. I saw you. I just came over here to talk to Niko and had no desire to acknowledge your presence, Vivian." Sabrina raised a brow in challenge. I noticed Niko's shoulders stiffen at her words and he looked at me before turning in her direction.

"You can go. We're done here." He stared hard at her, and she giggled like it was all a joke.

"I'll call you later?" she asked.

"Lose my number," he hissed, and she walked away.

"What is her deal? She's always been a royal biotch to me when I'm with you. But when I see her on my own, she's nice. She clearly has a problem with our friendship."

"A lot of people don't understand our friendship. But I don't give a shit what anyone thinks."

"*They hate us 'cause they ain't us*," I said over a loud hiccup, and he barked out a laugh.

"Damn straight, Vivi. They can all go fuck themselves." Niko held up his water glass and Tanner walked over to refill it.

"I'll take another shot and one more beer," I said, and they both chuckled.

"You really are cutting loose tonight, huh?" Niko asked as he bit down on the lime slice that was in his water.

"Damn straight." I reached for the glass after Tanner set the shot down and let the cool liquid run down my throat. I rested my cheek in my hand.

"I just can't believe that he cheated on me and then decided to get married to her so quickly," I finally said, because the thought was weighing on me heavily.

"He's an asshole. He never deserved you in the first place." He shrugged. "You can do much better."

I sipped my beer and touched my lips to make sure they were

still there because I couldn't feel them anymore. "How do you know?"

"Because I know you. And you deserve the best."

"Maybe I should try the Niko West way of life for a while," I said, and I laughed because my words sounded funny, but Niko's gaze hardened.

"Drink this." He pulled the beer away from me and handed me the glass of water that Tanner had set down for me with my shot. "What are you suggesting?"

"I don't know." I shrugged. It was embarrassing to even discuss this with him. We talked about everything outside of our personal relationships. It had just always been off-limits. "Maybe I should play the field a little bit."

He sipped his water and watched me for a long moment. "I don't think that's your style."

"It could be. I mean, I've only been with Jansen, and it hasn't been…" I paused and took another sip of water. "I don't know, Niko. I've heard people talk about sex like it's the best thing in the world. I haven't found it to be all that great."

He coughed hard and set down his glass. He reached for a napkin and wiped his mouth. "You don't like sex, Honey Bee?"

I covered my face with my hands. "Forget it. I'm not talking to you about this. I'll talk to Everly."

"You know you can talk to me about anything. I'm obviously not an expert on relationships, but I can tell you that sex should feel fucking fantastic. If you haven't felt that way about it, it just means you've been with the wrong dude, which is what I've thought from the start."

"What if *I'm* the problem?" I asked as I reached for my beer and took a long pull. The topic was making me nervous, but I actually wanted to know. Niko was an experienced guy, so who better to ask?

"You're not." He cleared his throat and pushed the water glass in front of me again and motioned for me to drink.

"How do you know?"

"Trust me. I know this shit. Let me guess. Your dick of an ex-boyfriend probably went down on you once a year on your birthday but expected you to suck his dick often."

My mouth gaped open at his words. "No. No, that is not the case."

He barked out a laugh as Teddy Tarbo, a guy we'd grown up with, yelled out Niko's name and told him to come play pool. Niko shook his head and completely ignored him.

My best friend did not like many people, and I'd always been honored to be his favorite.

"Really? He went down on you often?" His voice sounded a bit strained, which made me laugh.

"No. Never. But in his defense, I never did either. He said he wasn't into that whole thing," I leaned closer to him, and whisper-shouted. "You know...oral sex."

His tongue swiped out to wet his bottom lip. "I know what it is, Vivi. And he's an asshole for not teaching you all the ways he could please you. Unless you didn't want to do it? That's a different story."

"No. I was curious. I am curious. But he said it was dirty, so I never asked again."

His gaze narrowed as he took me in. "There's nothing dirty about it. I can promise you that. Did the asshole even make you orgasm?"

"Um, that's a hard no." I hiccupped and laughed. "No pun intended. Maybe it's a soft no. Anyway, we were long distance for so many years. So, when we'd see each other, it was always pretty fast and uneventful."

He cursed under his breath. "You deserve better."

"So...you like sex, huh?" I asked, and I covered one eye because there were three Nikos in front of me.

"I do. And you should too," he said as he tossed some money down on the bar. "Let's get you home."

He wrapped an arm around my waist as we made our way out to his truck and this time, I let him buckle me in after he picked me up and set me down on the seat. When he climbed into the driver's seat, he pulled out of the parking lot heading to my house.

"Do you ever get tempted to have a drink?" I asked as I scooched closer and leaned my head against his arm. He was so big and muscley. And he smelled like mint and sexy man.

It wasn't the first time I'd ever asked him this, but the answer was always the same.

"Never."

I nodded. "I'm sorry your dad was such an asshole."

He chuckled. "I'm sorry your boyfriend never made you come."

I fell forward laughing. "I shouldn't have told you that. I'll never live it down."

"You know you can tell me anything. Just makes me happy that you didn't end up with that selfish prick."

"He wasn't all bad," I said as I threw my hands in the air. "I mean, aside from the bad sex and the cheating."

"You need to make sure that the next guy you date knows what he's doing." He pulled into my driveway and jumped out of the car. He unbuckled me and placed a hand beneath my legs and the other around my neck.

I sighed as my head nuzzled against his chest. "Maybe you

should have sex with me."

He nearly tripped over the step leading to the front door. "You're drunk, Vivian."

He only said my name when he was mad or serious. I guessed he was serious this time.

I handed him the key and he unlocked the door and carried me in and walked me back to the bedroom before dropping me on the bed.

"I'm not that drunk. Doesn't it make sense?" Suddenly, having sex with Niko didn't seem so strange.

"Doesn't what make sense?" he asked, yanking my boots off my feet.

"Well, we're best friends. You're clearly a very good lover, and I've been missing out. You could teach me a thing or two. Show me what to expect."

He left the bedroom and came back with two aspirin and a glass of water. "Take these."

"You don't want to sleep with me, Niko? I'm not wild enough for you?" I popped the pills in my mouth and guzzled the water, before busting out in a fit of laughter as I fell back on the pillow and the room started spinning.

"You're too good for me, Honey Bee. That's a line we can't cross." He kissed me on the forehead.

"Damn you. Now you've got me curious about this whole oral sex thing. I've always wondered what it would feel like to have someone, you know…go there."

He crossed his arms over his chest. "I'll bet you have. I blame your cocksucker of an ex for not showing you."

"So why can't you show me? Does the idea gross you out?" I sighed. My eyes were so heavy.

"Nothing about you grosses me out. I'll be on the couch. Get some sleep."

"You're sleeping over and you won't sleep in my bed?" I asked. "You used to sleep with me." I reached up and wrapped a hand around his neck and pulled him down to me. "I love your eyes."

He laughed and kissed my forehead again. "I'm not leaving you alone when you've had this much to drink. But after the conversation we just had, I don't trust myself in a bed with you. I'll see you in the morning. Sleep, Honey Bee."

I drifted off thinking of gray eyes and Niko's sexy smile.

And I wondered what it would feel like to have his face buried between my legs.

I was most definitely three sheets to the wind, because I'd never allowed myself to fantasize about my best friend.

But tonight, I'd let my mind wander.

Chapter 4
Niko

My dick throbbed against my zipper as I tossed a pillow and blanket on Vivi's couch. It wasn't my first time sleeping at her house, but it was definitely my first time doing it with a raging boner. Sure, I'd always found her attractive—hell, she was the most beautiful girl I'd ever laid eyes on. But I'd never allowed myself to go there with her, nor would I. She'd had the same boyfriend for years, and I'd been busy banging everyone in town.

Vivian had been the only good thing in my life for as long as I could remember. My only constant. I'd never fuck that up. Even if the thought of pleasing her was all I could think about now. That dip fuck ex of hers had never shown her pleasure. Never explored or tasted her sweet body. I wanted to beat him senseless, but at the same time, a small part of me was happy that he didn't get to share that with her.

Like I said, I'm a dark fucker.

A greedy bastard when it came to Vivian Thomas.

I wanted the best for her, and I knew without a shadow of a doubt that it wasn't me. But it sure as fuck wasn't that cheating asshole either.

I decided to go into the bathroom and take a cold shower, as it was my only chance of getting any sleep. I was on duty at the firehouse tomorrow, and I'd need to be rested as it had been busier than hell in Honey Mountain lately with fires and medical calls.

I let the cold water run down my back and I leaned forward and gripped my dick with thoughts of Vivi writhing beneath me as I made her come with my fingers and my mouth and my cock.

I wasn't proud.

It wasn't the first time I got off to thoughts of my best friend, but it was the first time I wanted to act on it.

And that could never happen.

I found my relief and dried off quickly, putting yesterday's clothes back on before slipping beneath the blanket. I finally found sleep.

The next morning, I woke up to the smell of coffee. I opened my eyes to see Vivi standing over me with a mug. I sat up and took it from her.

"Thanks. How are you feeling?"

She dropped to sit beside me on the couch. "A mix between relieved and wanting to die."

I barked out a laugh. "Well, you look good. Why are you relieved?"

"Because we had the sex talk. I needed that. I'd always thought it was me, but after talking to you, I think Jansen might have been the problem."

"He was definitely the problem." I cleared my throat because

I couldn't believe she was talking about this sober. And trust me—I had zero inhibitions when it came to sex. My problem was that talking about it with my best friend was causing tremendous issues for my dick.

And next to her, he was my best friend.

"So, you really don't think you could maybe, I don't know, rock my world? Go downtown and show me what I'm missing? Teach me a thing or two before I get into the next relationship."

I spewed coffee all over the table in front of me. "Jesus, Honey Bee. Prepare a man before you say it so casually."

"What? Aren't you the sex king? All you have is casual sex. Why is this a big deal?" she asked.

I pushed to my feet.

I needed air.

Space.

Another fucking cold shower.

"It's not happening. Crossing that line would fuck everything up."

"Because you're not attracted to me that way?" she asked, and the vulnerability in her eyes made my chest squeeze. This was exactly why this shit was dangerous. I was already hurting her, and I hadn't even touched her.

"Vivian. There isn't a man on this planet that wouldn't be attracted to you. You're fucking beautiful."

"So, what's the problem?"

"The problem is that you're the one good thing in my life, and I don't want to fuck it up. I don't have a lot of good, Vivi. You know that." I leaned forward and kissed the top of her head.

When I pulled back, she nodded. "Damn. Now you've got me all curious about the things I've been missing out on. I guess

I just need to find me a man to try it out with."

I groaned. "I'm leaving. Just give yourself a few days to recover before you do anything rash."

"I want you to remember that I did your calculus homework all of senior year. I think you owe me one," she shouted as I walked to the car.

"Who are you and what have you done with Vivian Thomas?"

"Her ex-boyfriend cheated on her and then got engaged shortly after. Oh yeah, and then he didn't bother to tell her, he just sent an invitation to his nuptials to her *entire* family. It's time Vivian Thomas had a little fun." She laughed, and she looked cute as hell standing in the doorway in just a T-shirt with her hair piled on top of her head.

"Go to work."

She waved and shut the door. The thought of Vivian with a random dude had me on edge. There'd been something safe about her dating the douchebag all those years. They'd been long distance, which meant her relationship never interfered with our friendship. When he'd come to town, I'd keep my distance. I hadn't cared for him in high school, and it had only worsened over the years. But now...she was single. Free to do what she wanted, and thanks to my sex talk, it appeared she wanted to do all sorts of shit.

Fuck me.

I pulled up to the firehouse and made my way inside.

"Tallboy's making bacon and eggs," Rusty said as I jogged up the stairs.

Rusty's hair was orange so at least his ridiculous nickname made sense. Tallboy, on the other hand, stood around five foot seven, so I wasn't sure why the fuck that was the name that stuck. But the dude could cook.

Cap, Viv's dad, was sitting at the table and motioned for me to take the seat beside him.

"The girls said Vivi was pretty upset about that dumbass wedding invite. I mean, what is that kid thinking? Hell, he hardly said a word every time he came in town. There just wasn't much there. Then, according to Dylan, he cheated on her. Vivian has spared me the gory details, but of course, Dylan couldn't resist taking a shot at the asshole. I don't think Vivi misses him at all from what I can tell. But that doesn't mean it doesn't hurt when someone betrays you and moves on that quickly."

"He's an asshole. I never liked him," I grumped as I filled my glass with orange juice.

"Tell us how you really feel," Big Al said over his laughter.

I rolled my eyes. I didn't mince words, and it worked for me. I told it straight. People could take it or leave it. I really didn't give a shit.

"That's how I feel," I said.

"So, the asshole is already getting married?" Samson asked.

"Yep," Jack said over a mouthful of eggs.

I scooped some food onto my plate and started eating.

"Who are we talking about?" Rook, short for rookie, asked. He was a new member of our crew, and he tried hard to keep up.

"Cap's daughter's ex-boyfriend is an asshole," Little Dicky murmured. He and Rook came out of the academy at the same time, but I'd quickly assessed that the kid was terrified of fire. Apparently, his name was Richard and the guys at the academy started calling him Little Dicky to fuck with him, and Rook somehow got lucky with a less offensive name, although he wouldn't be a rookie forever, so he may tire of it soon. "She's also Niko's best friend."

Gramps barked out a laugh. "What is this? Some goddamn reality TV show?"

Little Dicky looked up after he took a bite of toast. "Rusty told me it was important to know the dynamics of the station."

Rusty smirked. "It's just too easy."

You had to understand the firehouse dynamic. We needled, tricked, pushed, connived all in good fun—seriously. Push came to shove, and we had each other's backs.

"You were a rookie not that long ago," Hog said. He'd been here years and he didn't mince words either.

"Yeah, yeah, yeah. Anyway, Mandy just broke up with me last night. Maybe I should ask Vivian out?" Rusty said, and the entire room grew completely quiet.

"No," Jack and I said at the same time. Our voices equally harsh.

"Why not? What's wrong with me?"

"Well, for starters...Mandy broke up with you because she found you sexting Cheryl Smothers." Tallboy took a bite of bacon.

"Hey. She sexted me. That wasn't my fault. And Mandy and I hadn't been exclusive."

"Keep your dirty fucking paws off Vivi. It's not up for discussion," I hissed.

Samson whistled. "Such a protector." That got the guys snickering, until I looked around the room with my STFU glare which did as intended—shut them (all) the fuck up.

"You sure nothing's ever gone on with *you* and Vivian? You're awfully protective of that girl," Rusty said.

"No. Stop talking and eat your food before I shove your head in the shitter," I said, picking up my plate and dropping it in the sink.

I was in a foul mood today for reasons I couldn't grasp.

Because all I could think about was claiming Vivi's sweet mouth. Of burying my face between her thighs and tasting all that sweetness. Or holding her perfect tits in my hands.

Fuck me.

I heard the guys all laughing as I left the room. I wasn't in the mood for their shit.

"See you later, lover boy," Big Al shouted, and more laughter flooded the space around us.

I went up to stretch out on my bed and checked my phone. There was a text from my mother.

Mom: I heard from his attorney. He's getting out in a couple weeks.

Fuck me again. I knew this day was coming, I just didn't expect it to come so soon.

Me: Will he be living with you?

Mom: This is his home, Niko. We're still a family.

Me: Then Jada and Mabel need to move out. It's not up for discussion.

Mom: Will you be paying for that?

I scrubbed a hand down my face. The hits just kept coming. It's the way it had always been with my family. One disaster after the next. I was fucking tired of it. But I thought of Mabel, and I couldn't let her be exposed to that piece of shit.

Me: I'll figure something out.

I picked up the phone and dialed my sister.

"Hey, Niko. Did you hear about Dad?"

"I did. You can't let him around Mabel. You know that,

right?" I asked.

"I do. But how am I going to afford a place on my own? We're barely making it now and I don't pay rent, and you cover Mabel's preschool tuition."

"Can you get full-time work?" I asked. My sister worked part-time at a boutique in town.

"I was going to go talk to Vivian today. Mom said she had a sign up in her window that she was hiring."

I closed my eyes for a minute to process her words. I didn't like the idea of Jada working for Vivi because my sister did not share my work ethic. The girl had a hard time sticking with any job for more than a few weeks.

"Listen, Jada. If she hires you, you can't fuck around. The girl works her ass off at that bakery. It's no joke."

"Of course, I wouldn't do that," she said, even though it wasn't the first time she'd made a promise like that.

I let out a long breath. "Okay. We need to find you a place. I'd say you could stay with me, but you know I've just got the one bedroom, and with the two of you, it would be too crowded."

"I'll start looking for apartments. I might need a little help financially until I get on my feet," she said.

"It's fine. I've got plenty in savings to help you out." I'd been saving for a house of my own, but if that needed to wait, it wasn't the end of the world.

"Thanks, Niko."

I ended the call when the alarm sounded, and I was suited up and heading out to the firetruck in no time.

"It's a big one," Cap said as I climbed into the truck. "Apparently Callahan Ranch is on fire."

I nodded as we pulled out onto the road. I glanced down at my phone and saw a text from Vivi.

Honey Bee: I just want to throw this out there. I just made your favorite red velvet cupcakes. I set a dozen aside for you. How do you feel about a trade? <winky face emoji>

I barked out a laugh. The girl was relentless. And the thought of what she was offering had me struggling to focus on what was going on.

Because Callahan Ranch wasn't the only thing on fire at the moment.

My dick was on fire, but I'd have to deal with him later.

Chapter 5

Vivian

I'd been slammed all morning, and Dylan swept behind the counter while I cleaned up the kitchen. She'd been working for me ever since she graduated, and I had no problem working around her current school schedule. She usually came in one day a week, but if she was caught up on schoolwork, she could pull off two days when I was in a crunch. Jilly, who was Charlotte's best friend, was another part-time student that worked here as well, but we'd been so busy I was in desperate need of hiring someone new.

The bell on the door chimed, and I said a silent prayer that the lunch rush wasn't starting just yet.

"Hey, Vivian," Jada said as she stopped in front of the counter.

"Hi. Where's Mabel?" I asked.

"She was napping, so she stayed home with Mom. Did you hear about the fire at Callahan Ranch?"

My stomach dipped. It always did when there was a fire. The two most important men in my life would be at that fire, and the worry never went away. After my mom passed, the anxiety over my father's profession worsened. It's the reason I turned down my scholarship to go away to school and attended college close to home. And once Niko joined the fire department, my anxiety deepened.

I hurried to check my phone and Dylan breezed past me to get hers. Ashlan and Charlotte had sent several texts asking if I'd heard from Dad or Niko.

I responded quickly telling them I hadn't heard but would keep them posted. I regretted sending that joking text to Niko earlier when he'd probably been putting out a fire at the time.

"No. Have you heard from Niko?" I asked.

"No. Mom just heard from Busy Betty." Jada laughed. I wondered how she could be acting so casual when her brother was currently fighting a fire. Did she not know how dangerous it was? He provided so much for her and Mabel, and it frustrated me that Jada seemed to take it for granted most of the time. Niko gave up so much for his sister, and she never gave him credit for it.

"I'll text Lottie now and see if she's heard anything," Dylan said as she hopped up on the counter and her fingers frantically typed away on her phone.

"Okay," I said as I sent a text to my dad and Niko as well.

Lottie was our best bet, as she made it her duty to be in the know being Big Al's wife. Fire families always came together when there were fires, and we shared what we'd hear from the guys. Busy Betty had earned her name with everyone in Honey Mountain due to her gift for gab and her son, Rusty, worked at the department, so it didn't surprise me that she knew. She also lived down the street from Callahan Ranch.

"Lottie said they already have it under control," Dylan said, jumping down from the counter and heading for the kitchen in back.

I let out a sigh of relief.

"Oh, good," Jada said as she perused the pastries behind the glass case.

"Can I get you something?" I asked.

"I'll take four red velvet cupcakes. Hopefully Mabel won't eat Niko's before his shift is over later in the week." She chuckled.

"She's such a cutie pie. I'll drop a few boxes off at the firehouse on my way home, so I'll make sure he gets one." I slipped on some gloves and started placing the pastries in the box for her.

"I saw you were looking for help?" she said, and I looked up to see her cheeks flush. I liked Jada West, and seeing as she was Niko's sister, I'd always do what I could to help her. Niko didn't care for many people, and life hadn't always been kind to him— but he'd always been there for his sister and her little girl.

"Yeah, I am. We've been swamped lately. All the tourists will be coming for the ski season soon too, so things will only get busier," I said as I tied some string around the box.

"I work at the boutique three mornings a week, and I don't know if Niko told you, but my dad is getting released from prison soon." She said it like we were discussing the weather. Not the fact that a man who had terrorized Niko most of his life, and nearly killed his own brother because he'd been driving drunk, was going to be back in their lives.

"When did that happen?"

"Mom told Niko about it last night, and then his attorney called this morning to say everything looked good."

My chest squeezed. I wondered why Niko hadn't mentioned

it to me. Probably because I'd been too drunk last night to focus on anything but myself, and I felt horrible that he'd dealt with that news on his own.

"Wow. Time sure flew. I can't believe he's already getting out." Anger moved through my body, remembering all the times that Niko had snuck through my bedroom window as a kid. His dad never laid a hand on Jada, but Niko had sustained a lot of abuse for as long as I could remember. When it got really bad, my best friend would come in my window and sleep in my bed. I don't think my parents ever knew, and nothing ever happened between us. We just comforted one another the best we could. He stopped his nighttime visits once we were in high school, and he'd said that things were better. But I saw the bruises and the burn marks on his forearms, and he'd always just say the bruises were from football.

But I knew better. When we were young, he'd talked to me about being woken up to a swift kick in the gut or a cigarette being extinguished on his skin. I begged him to report his father, but he said it would only make things worse for him. Niko always planned to leave Honey Mountain when he graduated. God knows he had enough full-ride scholarship offers to go anywhere he wanted to play Division 1 football. But after his dad went off to prison and his mom fell apart, he chose not to leave her and Jada.

"Yeah. Niko doesn't want Mabel living at the house if Dad's going to be coming home."

My eyes bulged out of my head. "Your mom is letting him come back to the house?"

"Well, yeah. He is her husband."

I let out a long breath. I had no respect for Shayla West. She'd allowed her son to be abused for years. And she'd never done anything to stop it. She'd never protected Niko from the violence, and I'd tried hard to forgive her for that. She was my best friend's mom after all. My parents had confronted her with concerns about the bruises on Niko's body, as had many people in town—but she'd always brushed it off to him being a rough-and-tumble kid.

"So, you and Mabel are moving out?"

"Niko's going to help us. But I sure could use some more work. I love this place. I can't even imagine spending my days here," she said, glancing around.

I was proud of Honey Bee's Bakery. I'd worked hard to save up the money to open my business after I graduated from college. The logo was a giant honey bee with the name in the center. Black and white checkered floors and cute bistro tables and chairs filled the dining space. There were four crystal chandeliers hanging above, and a big pink neon sign hung on the wall that read: *Life is short. Lick the Bowl.*

I tried to always have fresh flowers on the tables, as Mrs. Winthrop, who owned the floral shop next door, always gave me a deal on the ones she didn't sell each day. We sat on the busiest street in town, and business was good. This bakery had allowed me to buy my first home, and I was proud of how quickly we'd grown. I was even getting online orders from the surrounding larger cities, which I would ship to both Reno, Nevada, and San Francisco, California. Jilly had been a lifesaver as she handled all the shipping and online orders. I needed more help if I wanted to continue to grow. But I knew Jada West hadn't held down a steady job, ever. She'd dropped out of high school and only received her GED because Niko had been relentless about her getting her high school degree. But she was my best friend's sister and there was nothing I wouldn't do for him.

If only he'd do a little something-something for me.

My cheeks heated at the thought. The things we'd talked about last night. Yes, a lot of the evening was fuzzy, but not the way Niko had looked at me when he'd dropped me on my bed.

However, if you were to look up the world's most unattainable man in the dictionary, there would be an eight by ten glossy of Niko West. His father had made it difficult for him to trust, and I felt fortunate to be one of the few people he trusted. But he didn't do relationships outside of our friendship. I'd lost count of how many times he'd told me he would never get married and he didn't want a family. He said that me, Jada and Mabel, and the guys at the firehouse were his family. But maybe we could just have a short-lived fling, he could teach me the ropes, show me what everyone was talking about, and then we could return to normal.

Was that not possible?

"Hello? Earth to Vivian," Jada said with a laugh.

"I'm sorry. I didn't get enough sleep last night." I laughed, trying to cover up the fact that I was currently fantasizing about her brother.

My best friend.

"So, would you consider hiring me? I could start tomorrow."

I glanced over her shoulder and Dylan was watching us with concern. I looked away, because the truth was…I had to give her a try. It would be helping Niko in the long run, and if it didn't work out, that would be on Jada.

"All right. Let's give it a try," I said. I spent the next half hour sitting with her at a table discussing her responsibilities and her pay. She hugged me tight when the door opened, and people started to file in.

"I won't let you down, Vivian. Thanks for giving me the chance."

I waved goodbye before hurrying around the corner.

The next few hours flew by in a rush, and Jilly, Dylan, and I both sighed in relief when the last person finally left. I locked the door once everyone was gone, and we started cleaning up.

"Do you seriously think Jada will be a good employee?" Dylan asked.

"Honestly? Probably not. But I need to give her a try for Niko."

"I can't argue that. And it would be helping you out if she can pull this off. I wish I could find me a good guy best friend. It's got to be hard spending all that time together, you know, with him being so..." She shook her head and laughed.

"Being so what?" I whipped her with a towel.

"Sexy. Come on, Vivi, I know you always deny it. But are you telling me you don't find him to be jaw-droppingly attractive? And he's so...big and muscley. I'm sure he's got a giant package." She wriggled her brows and laughed. "My god. That must be torture hanging out with him all the time. Although Jansen Clark was a scrawny little thing, so you obviously like them a little daintier."

We all burst out in laughter. "You've always hated Jansen. Even before he cheated. Why?"

"Because he's a selfish narcissist." She shrugged.

"Are you sure you don't want to go back to school to get your degree in psychology?" I asked as I moved to wipe down the last two tables.

"I should, right? I could be a fabulous sex doctor."

I barked out a laugh. "If anyone is capable, it's you."

"Well, I didn't know Jansen well, but I have to agree with Dilly about Niko. That man is so freaking hot," Jilly said as she wiped down the glass on the display case.

"Well, you weren't missing out not knowing Jansen. How was the sex with him anyway? You never talked about it," Dylan asked, and she yanked the towel out of my hand and waited for me to look up.

"It was...uneventful."

"I knew it." She threw her hands in the air. "Narcissists make terrible lovers. They chase their own pleasure and don't care about their partners. Good luck to his little missus. Perhaps we should send her a vibrator as a wedding gift. She'll need it." Dylan whipped around and wiped down the last table.

Jilly was laughing hysterically now. "I think that's a great idea."

"Have you talked to Dane again since you broke up with him?" I asked my sister as I moved behind the counter to grab us each a cookie, and we all three dropped to sit around the table.

"He's old news. It wasn't all that serious. But there's this hot guy in my class right now. Everyone calls him King, and let me tell you...he can rule over my kingdom anytime he wants." She burst out in laughter. "I don't even know his real name. But you guys, trust me when I tell you...he's so hot. I'm considering a little flingaroo. He's been texting me nonstop and I'll let him sweat it out for a while longer before I decide."

"What do you even know about him?" I asked. "You need to be careful."

"I know he's hot. He's charming. And he's friends with Glen Peters, so we know he's not a serial killer." She laughed. "You worry too much. You're young. You need to have some fun."

"I agree. This is your time to have some fun, Vivi," Jilly added.

"Says the girl who's been in a relationship for years," I teased.

Jilly had been dating Garrett Jones since high school.

"True. But you're single now. This is your time to go a little crazy. Break a few rules," she said, and Dylan nodded.

"Maybe I'll have a fling."

Jilly beamed, and Dylan clapped her hands together once. "For-fucking-sure! That's exactly what you need, Vivi. You've played by the rules your entire life. Let's find you a hot lover."

"I don't think it's a bad idea." Jilly smiled, popping the last piece of chocolate chip cookie in her mouth.

It wasn't a horrible idea. I'd never considered it because I'd been with Jansen for so long. "Maybe."

"Why don't you go on one of those dating sites?" Dylan asked as she picked up her phone.

"I feel like I know everyone my age in Honey Mountain." I broke off a piece of the oatmeal raisin cookie.

"Hey, he doesn't have to be your age. It's a fling. Let's call it a sexual awakening," she said as she wriggled her brows.

"I'm begging you...let's not give it a title."

"Why not hit Niko up for a little friends-with-benefits action?" she teased. "I can only imagine what he could do with those hands. Kara Kline said he made her orgasm three times in one night when we were in high school."

I pushed to my feet. The thought of Niko with other girls had never bothered me before, but it had also never been something we talked about. I didn't like hearing about it. "Okay, that's enough sex talk for one day, you little horndog." I moved behind the counter and started packing up two boxes full of pastries to drop at the firehouse.

"Ahhh...a fling with Niko West would be every woman's fantasy," Jilly said, gazing out the window.

Dylan barked out a laugh. "Agreed. We're not giving up on

you, girl. I'm on the lookout."

"Fine. Do not mention this to Charlie and Ashlan, please."

"Your secret's safe with us." Dylan winked and Jilly nodded in agreement, very unconvincingly. She and Charlie were very tight, and I highly doubted this conversation wouldn't be mentioned. I just didn't want to make it a bigger deal than it was.

"All right, I need to go. My brother's home for the weekend, so we're going to dinner tonight." Jilly reached for her jacket. Ledger was in my grade, but he'd moved to San Francisco after college and came back often to visit.

"Tell him I said hello." I moved back behind the counter as she waved goodbye.

Once Jilly left, Dylan slipped her jacket on as well.

"I need to get home and start dinner. Dad assigned nights for us to cook now. I seriously can't live like this much longer." She made her way to the back door. Considering law school was three years, she'd be living with him for a while or at least until Charlotte found her own place.

"I'll come over and eat with you guys after I hit the firehouse. Love you, Dilly," I shouted.

"Yeah, yeah, yeah. Love you."

I wrapped the boxes with twine and cleaned up a little bit more before setting the security alarm and locking up. I walked the two blocks down to the fire station which was on the way to my house anyway.

"Hey there, Vivian," Hunter Hall said as he came out of the veterinary hospital. He was a few years older than me and had opened his own practice in town just a few months ago when he graduated from vet school.

"Hi, Hunter." I paused as he locked the door. "Or should I

call you Dr. Hall now?"

"Oh, please don't," he groaned, and we both laughed.

"Okay. Hunter it is."

"You got cookies in there?" he teased. "I've been craving one ever since I ate a dozen at one sitting last Christmas."

I moved the twine and opened the top. "Take a few. I'm just dropping them at the firehouse."

"I would have stopped in to buy some, but as long as you're offering, I can't turn them down." He smiled. "I was going to stop by and talk to you anyway this week." His cheeks flushed just a little bit and my stomach dipped.

"Oh, really? What's up?"

"Well, you know, I heard you're single now, and I uh—" He broke off a piece of cookie and fidgeted. "I wanted to see if you would want to grab dinner sometime next week?"

I tried to hide my surprise. "Um, yeah. Is it a date? I thought you were engaged?"

"Well, I was. Until I found out Sarah was sleeping with my best friend from vet school. That'll ruin the wedding buzz pretty quickly."

My chest squeezed for him. Hunter had always been a really nice guy and the taste of betrayal was still fairly fresh on my tongue, so I knew how bad it felt. Maybe he could be a new prospect, after all, we did have something in common right now. "I'm so sorry. I'd love to have dinner with you. I am single and ready to mingle." I cringed as the words left my mouth and I imagined Dylan rolling her eyes at how not cool I was.

He chuckled. "Great. Hand me your phone. I'll text myself so I'll have your number and I'll message you in a little bit to see what works for you."

I handed him my phone and he shot himself a text and then

handed it back to me. His fingers grazed mine and I can't say I felt a spark, but I liked him well enough to hope for the best.

"All right. I better get these over to the firehouse. I'll see you soon, I guess," I said with a chuckle. I needed to work on my flirt game. I was definitely not smooth.

He winked. "Yes, you will."

I turned and walked toward the firehouse when my phone dinged with a text from Hunter. I glanced over my shoulder, and he was laughing. "Too eager?"

"Never," I called out and tried to hide my blush as I continued a block farther.

I made my way upstairs, pausing to give Big Al and Samson a hug as I walked by them.

"You guys all right?" I asked as I held up the boxes. "I brought you some treats."

"You sure keep us well fed," Big Al said. "Thank you, Vivi."

I dropped the boxes on the table just as my dad came around the corner. I hugged him tight, and he chuckled.

"It wasn't a bad one, baby girl. We're fine."

"Good. Where's Niko?" I asked.

"He went to grab a shower. Should be out by now." I made my way to the room where they slept, and thoughts of a naked Niko in the shower had my heart racing. I'd never seen him naked. Not even when we were kids.

I'd seen him in a bathing suit plenty of times, but not in a while.

When I made my way to the room, he rounded the corner wearing nothing but a towel. My eyes moved down his muscled chest covered in little water droplets, and I fought the urge to move closer. I continued scanning his body, and my mouth gaped open at the deep V that led to where his low-slung towel hung.

Holy hotness.

The man was even more chiseled than the last time I'd seen his bare chest, which had been a few years ago.

"Wow," I whispered.

He chuckled. His long, wet hair stopped just at his shoulders and was a disheveled mess as he pushed it away from his face.

He moved closer to me and grasped my chin between his thumb and finger, lifting it so my eyes met his. "You like what you see, Honey Bee?"

Hells to the yes.

His voice was gruff and strained, and I couldn't speak. I nodded. But then he chuckled and stepped away from me, just as Rusty and Jace entered the room.

"Thanks for the cupcakes, Vivi," Jace said as he walked toward the bathroom.

"Of course." I cleared my throat. I needed to get out of there before I made more of a fool of myself. "Glad you guys are okay. I'll see you later."

I looked up to see Niko's steely gray eyes watching me. And then he did the most surprising thing of all. He turned to walk toward the bathroom and dropped his towel. Flashing me his finely toned ass.

Rusty whistled. "There's a full moon out tonight, people."

I got the hell out of there and made my way home.

I needed to get thoughts of Niko as more than a friend out of my mind. I needed to forget the way his muscled abs led down to his chiseled happy trail. And don't even get me started on that fine ass of his.

Chili peppers.

Sick puppies.

The stomach flu.

Sex with Jansen.

That did it. At least I wasn't hot and bothered anymore. Nope. I wasn't even thinking about my best friend being naked right now.

Not at all.

Why am I sweating?

Chapter 6

Niko

After three long days at the firehouse, I was ready for a day off. I'd worked out this morning and spent an hour looking at apartments for my sister and Mabel. Shit was expensive in Honey Mountain because it was a beautiful mountain town, and you didn't have to deal with the traffic and the congestion of a big city. The tourists only made things worse with their long-term rentals. We had two busy seasons. Lake season in the summer and ski season in the winter. So basically, this town was buzzing more than half the year.

I'd agreed to meet Vivi after work to get out the canoe and eat dinner out on the lake. It's something we'd been doing since we were young, but now that she had a place on the water, it was even easier. I had a canoe, and she had a dock, so I kept it out at her place, and we snuck out every chance we got. I'd bring the pizza and she'd supply the best fucking baked goods on the planet.

When I arrived at her place, I tried the door, and it was locked. About fucking time, she actually listened. I knocked twice and she pulled the door open.

"See. I do lock it sometimes, although it's stupid because there's no one in this town that I wouldn't let in."

"That's shit reasoning, Honey Bee. You don't know everyone in this town, and I can assure you there are plenty of fuckers that lurk around the outskirts. Keep that door locked."

She wore jeans, a navy down jacket, a white turtleneck, and tennis shoes. She had a hat and gloves on the counter. Vivi was always colder than everyone else. I ran hot, so I had on jeans and a hoodie.

"Let's talk about it on the water. I want to get out before it gets dark." She grabbed the pastry box from the counter along with her hat and gloves, and we made our way out the back door.

I carried the pizzas and a six-pack of Cokes and set them in the canoe, holding it still as she climbed in before I followed suit.

"I don't know how you can get in here without rocking it and falling. God knows you're not small," she teased.

"It's called agility. I played football, remember?" I pushed us away from the dock, and the Bay Area leading out to the lake was overgrown with trees and shrubbery surrounding us. This was my favorite place in the world. It was peaceful and quiet, and it was the one place I felt most relaxed, next to the mountains.

"Do you ever regret that you didn't go away and play ball?" she asked. It's not the first time either. We'd talked about it a lot over the years, but I suppose she wondered if the answer would change as time went on.

"Nope. I mean, it's not like I kept Jada out of trouble," I said, using the paddles to get us out to deep water while my best friend lay back with her legs stretched out beside me. Not many people came out here this time of year, as the summer months on the lake would be packed this time of day. But the weather was changing, and cold temperatures tended to cut back traffic on the water. There wasn't a boat in sight. "She got knocked up, but I think had I not been around, she would have gotten more mixed up in drugs and alcohol, and who knows what that would have meant for Mabel. So, I still believe it was worth it. And you know I don't spend time looking back. I made a choice and I trust that."

"Do you think she appreciates the sacrifices you've made for her?"

"I don't give a shit if she does or not. I don't do things for praise. I do things because I want to." I opened the lid to the pizza box and handed her a slice, as she pulled out two plates. "How about you? Do you think your sisters appreciate the fact that you turned down Berkeley to stay close to them?"

Vivi had been accepted into the business school at UC Berkeley on a full-ride scholarship, but with her mother's passing and her older sister, Everly, across the country at NYU, she hadn't felt like she could leave her sisters or her father. She knew they needed her.

She took a bite and stared out at the water. "I do. I know my dad does. And I feel the same. I don't need the praise. They needed me and I wouldn't change a thing."

We came from two different worlds in so many ways...my heart hard and her heart soft and tender; yet we shared a lot of similarities as far as loyalty and loss and all the bullshit we'd both been through.

I took a large bite of pizza after setting the oars down and leaning back. "Has Everly decided if she's coming home after she finishes her fellowship?"

"Yeah, I think she'll be home in a few weeks. She's got

several interviews with some pro teams in California and one in Chicago, but she'll come spend a few weeks with us until she figures out where she's going."

Vivi never complained about the fact that her sister went off to school to fulfill her dreams, while she stayed here to deal with the fallout from her mother's passing.

"I know the anniversary for your mom is coming up. How do you feel about that?" I reached for another piece of pizza.

"I can't believe it's been nine years. In some ways, it feels like it was just yesterday and in other ways, it feels like forever."

I nodded. "Yeah. I get that."

"How about you? When were you going to tell me about your dad getting out of prison?"

I took a minute to think about her question. Fucking Jada. She couldn't keep her trap shut, and now that she was working for Vivi I'd have to deal with that shit.

"I didn't tell you because I knew you would worry. I don't give a shit about that fucker, as long as he stays away from Mabel."

"Of course, I worry about how it will affect you. I was thinking maybe when Everly comes back, you could talk to her. I know she's not technically a therapist, but she's a sports psychologist and she's helped a ton of athletes deal with trauma and different things they've experienced."

"It's only trauma if you allow it to be. What that asshole did to me does not affect me. I've told you that."

She nodded. "You don't have to be strong for me, you know."

I grabbed another slice of pizza and nearly tipped the boat with my jerky movement. She lunged forward, grasping on to my shoulders. I waited for the boat to steady before pulling back.

"We're fine. I'm fine. I'm not being strong for you or putting on a show. Shit happens. It won't happen to me again. I'd never give power to a piece of shit like my father. If you want to talk about it, we can talk about it. But I'm not talking to anyone else."

"Do you ever have nightmares about the things he did to you?" she whispered.

"No. I don't think about it." I studied her. "Do you have nightmares?"

"Yeah. About the day my mom passed. About those last few hours. Every year around this time I have bad dreams."

I leaned forward and took her hand. "I think that's normal. It's just memories coming back to you. There's no shame in that."

She nodded and rested her cheek against my hand. "Yeah. I still remember how you were there with me that day, and how you came and slept in my bed every day for a week after she passed. I'll be grateful forever, you know that, right? I don't think I would have slept, let alone pulled myself together if you hadn't been there."

"Nothing I wouldn't do for you, you know that." I leaned back, letting her hand slip out of mine.

"So, on a lighter note. I have a date with Hunter Hall tomorrow night."

"Hunter Hall? The dude with the lisp?"

She rolled her eyes and chuckled. "He doesn't lisp anymore. He's a veterinarian now. And he's super cute and really nice. And I don't know...maybe *he* could be my guy to try things out on."

I coughed as the pizza crust went down the wrong tube.

"The fuck he is. I don't like him."

Her jaw fell open as I reached for a napkin and wiped my mouth.

"You don't know him."

"I know enough. He clearly relates better to animals than people."

"What does that mean?" she hissed.

"It means he probably relates better to four-legged pussies than the one between your legs." I shrugged.

She fell back in laughter, and I grabbed the oar to keep the boat steady. "That's rich, even for you, Niko. Maybe it makes him an expert." She wriggled her brows.

Was she trying to be sexy? Because the way her honey-brown gaze shimmered with the last bit of sunlight shining down on us had my dick jumping to attention.

"Trust me. He's no expert."

"So, you're the only expert around, huh?"

"Maybe. It's a gift." I clasped my hands together and locked them behind my head.

"Well, I offered you first dibs and you turned me down." Her tongue dipped out to wet her bottom lip.

"Not because I don't want to, Honey Bee. Because I don't want to fuck up what we have. It's the one good thing in my life and I'd like to keep it."

"Why don't you do relationships? You say you aren't affected by what your dad did to you, so what's the reason for you refusing to let anyone in?"

My hands fisted at my sides, and I sat forward. "I let you in, don't I?"

"Sure. But you won't cross that line with me. And the women you have sex with you don't have relationships with. So, what's the reason?"

Was she trying to piss me off? Because she was succeeding.

"The reason is that I don't want one. I don't want to get married. I don't want to have kids. I don't need to be fucking responsible for anyone but myself. And I like the way my life is set up, so I'm not sure why you have a problem with it."

"I don't. It seems like you're the one that has a problem with me dating Hunter Hall."

"No problem here, Honey Bee."

She leaned back in the canoe and closed her eyes. "Fine. I'm going to rest for a bit. Do a little daydreaming about my date tomorrow night."

I lifted the oar and splashed water in her face, and she squealed.

Served her right.

"Damn you, Niko. You sure have been in a mood lately."

"It's water. You're fine. And I'm not in a mood. This is me. You know me." I raised a brow as she wiped her face with the towel that we kept out here.

"Well, you're grumpier than usual, which is saying something, because you're fairly grumpy most of the time."

"Thank you. I'll take that as a compliment. Now how about those cookies?"

She shook her head and smiled before digging in the box and handing me a few of her oatmeal chocolate chips.

"You're lucky I love you," she said as she lay back again in the canoe.

Don't I know it. I'm the luckiest bastard around.

Chapter 7

Vivian

"I'm all done sweeping up," Jada said, as she set the broom in the closet in the kitchen.

I was making some butter cookie dough for tomorrow that I would refrigerate overnight.

"Okay, thank you. You can head out. I'm just about done here." I placed the large ball of dough in a bowl and covered it with Saran Wrap before heading to the sink to wash my hands.

"I'll see you tomorrow," she called out as she walked toward the door.

"Don't forget the cookies for your mom and Mabel." I dried my hands as she thanked me again and left with the pink box in hand. I walked through the dining room and locked up before making my way to the back door.

I'd have about an hour to get ready for my date, so I wouldn't be stopping by the firehouse today with treats. I tried to go a couple days a week and they'd be just fine if I skipped today.

When I walked up my driveway, I saw Dylan's car there. She'd had class today, so she hadn't been at the bakery. The door was unlocked, and I stepped inside to find Dylan and Charlotte sprawled out on the couch watching something on TV with a plate of cookies on the table.

"Um...hello?" I said as I folded my arms over my chest and watched them.

"Shhhh...we've been waiting to see which brother she chooses." Dylan held her hand up to me.

I rolled my eyes and tried not to laugh when Charlotte jumped to her feet and clapped her hands together. "Yes!"

Dylan fist pumped the sky before reaching for the remote and turning off the TV. "We're here to help you choose an outfit for your hot date." Dylan laughed and moved to her feet.

"I told her you would be fine picking your own outfit, but we wanted to come sit with you while you get ready."

"Nooooo. We want you to skank it up a little bit. You've been in a relationship with the world's most boring guy for years... this is your chance to reinvent yourself. Be a little wild. And I'll be doing your makeup." Dylan moved to my closet and started coming out with all sorts of things I hadn't worn in a long time.

Her long blonde hair fell around her shoulders and her makeup was always impeccable.

I glanced at Charlotte and held my hands out at my side as if I didn't know what to do.

"Everly's FaceTiming me right now," Charlotte said as she held up the phone in front of both of us.

"Hey, girl," Charlotte and I said at the same time and laughed.

"Dilly told me you're going out with Hunter Hall tonight. Good for you. Time to be done with Jansen. I never liked the guy." Everly was sitting on her couch with her dark hair in a messy bun piled high on her head.

"If none of you liked him, why the hell didn't you ever tell me?" I hissed as my eyes doubled in size at the bodysuit Dylan was holding up. It had a deep plunging V in the front, which would mean no bra. It wasn't a huge problem as I didn't have a whole lot there, and pasties would work. But...I hadn't worn anything this sexy in forever.

"I wanted to tell you, but Charlie always made me keep it a secret. I couldn't stand the dweeb. He was so whiny too, right?" Dylan groaned, letting us all know she was disgusted. "I hate whiny little bitches."

Charlotte barked out a laugh. "This is why I told you not to say anything. Your delivery sucks."

"It's to the point. We're sisters. I would expect you guys to tell me if I was dating a sad sack in a fancy suit. Pffftt. And don't even get me started on the fact that he's a damn cheater. I have zero respect for the dude. You need to date a real man." She shook the black bodysuit in front of me. "Come on, Vivi. This will look amazing. With your jeans and booties. So hot."

"Hello, I'm still here. Let me see what you want her to wear." Everly studied the bodysuit as Dylan hustled to the closet and came back with my black heel booties. "I vote yes. She's got horrible people skills, but her style is damn good."

"I can hear you, Ev," Dylan hissed.

"I'm aware. I thought you liked a straight shooter."

I moved into the bathroom and slipped on the bodysuit and stuck the pasties over my nipples and shook my head. Was I really doing this? I shimmied into my jeans, and I was surprised at how good the top looked.

It made my girls look a little bigger than they really were, and seeing as there wasn't much cleavage, it really didn't look too hoochie. I moved to sit on the bed and slip on the booties before standing.

"Wow. Vivi. You look amazing," Charlotte said.

"You are smoking hot. If this doesn't get you a romp in the hay, nothing will," Dylan said as she lifted up one side of my top and peeked in to see the pasties. I slapped her hand away.

"What are you doing?" I gasped.

"Please. You don't have much to look at. Just making sure there's no chance of a nip slip. But those little cotton balls seem to be staying in place."

Everly and Charlotte were laughing hysterically as I rolled my eyes. "They're not cotton balls, you little tartlet. They're pasties."

"I wonder if Hunter will think your pasties are tasties," Dylan said in her deepest voice, and the room erupted in laughter again.

"You're so twisted, Dilly," Charlotte said, wrapping an arm over my shoulder.

Dylan's phone vibrated and she held it up and wriggled her brows. "It's Ash." She answered and held the phone up so we could see her. "Were your ears burning that the Thomas sisters were all together without you?"

Ashlan chuckled. "No. But I wanted to see if Vivi was ready for her date."

I'd talked to her this morning, and honestly, I'd learned at a young age that there was no keeping secrets from a Thomas girl. We were all in one another's business, and it had just always been that way.

Dylan turned the phone to show her my outfit as I sat at my little vanity in my bedroom, putting loose beach waves in my hair that added a little body to my normally straight hair. I pushed to my feet and did a little curtsy. "Dilly has me all sexed up."

"Girl." She whistled. "You look hot."

"We're going to dinner. I'm not sure this is really the look I wanted to go for, but hey, I'm living on the edge, right?"

"I'd say it's a curb, not an edge," Everly piped in, and I didn't miss the sarcasm. I was the steady Eddie of the group. The most cautious, although Charlotte wasn't far behind. "You're young. Come on, go for it."

"Yes," Dylan shouted. "Strut your shit. Okay, Ash, I'm handing the phone to Charlie. I need to do her makeup. We're going for a serious smoky eye."

"Don't forget to add some highlighter down that plunging V," Everly shouted. "I've got to go. One of the players is beeping in."

"They need to stick to work hours," Charlotte said, shaking her head as she took the other phone from Dylan and looked down at both screens.

"They're professional athletes and it's a fellowship."

"What does that mean?" Ashlan asked.

"It means she's their bitch," Dylan hissed, and Everly said goodbye over her laughter and ended the call.

I turned to face her as she applied my makeup, while Ashlan told us all about her journalism class. She was a junior and a great student, but she'd struggled with choosing a major. We listened and encouraged her to just be patient.

My mother had always been a believer that you should do what you were meant to do. She didn't believe in stressing out over things you had no control over. I wished I were that Zen about life. I never had been. But I'd tried hard not to pass my anxiety about making sure I did what I needed to do, to my sisters.

"My counselor said I better make a decision quickly if I want to make sure I graduate next year."

"What do you want to do after graduation? I knew I wanted to work with kids, so that helped," Charlotte said.

"I don't know, that's the problem. I mean, I see myself married with a family down the road, but I can't picture what job I'm doing."

Dylan barked a laugh after she turned me to face the mirror. She looked quite proud of herself so I couldn't wait to see what she'd done.

Wow.

My eyes looked sexy. Dark and smoky.

My lips looked much plumper than they already were, and they were plump to begin with. She'd used a liner on the outside, which made them appear even fuller.

"I love it. Thank you. And Ash, you're fine. You don't need to know. Pick something that you can do a lot with, like business."

"Yeah. Look how many times I changed my mind before I realized I wanted to go to law school. Pick something that allows some flexibility. You've got this." Dylan bunched her fingers and thumb together and pressed it to her lips before letting it open and making a kissing noise. She was happy with the way I looked.

"That's a good idea," Charlotte said before gaping at me. "You look so good, Vivi."

"Okay. I need to go. I told him I'd meet him there. I didn't want to drive with him in case it doesn't go well."

"We'll drop you on our way there," Charlotte said, as Dylan paused and put lipstick on her own lips.

"Yeah. And call us if it's a bust and we can pick you up after."

"I don't need my sisters driving me to and from my date," I said as I found my purse and reached for my long black trench coat.

"Well, too bad. This town has one main road, and we happen to be going home right now. We're passing Ricardo's, so stop your whining and get your fine ass in the car." Dylan swatted my behind and I squealed.

"Keep me on the phone. I want to feel like I'm with you guys."

"This is crazy. Drop me off a few doors down so he doesn't see me get out of your car," I said as we pulled out of the driveway. "I should just walk. It's literally a block away."

Instead, Dylan chose to pull up right in front of Ricardo's like the lunatic she was. I shook my head and whipped my door open. "Bye, Ash, bye, Charlie, suck it, Dilly!" I slammed the door, but the window came down after I walked toward the entrance of the restaurant.

She whistled. "Go get 'em, hot stuff. You're looking smoking, am I right, fellas?" A few guys walking by looked horrified and waved at me.

I held up my hand. "Oh, hey, Joey. Hi, Marcus."

I turned around and shot her a look and shook my head. "Paybacks are a bitch."

"Oh, that's a tough way to start a date." Hunter came up behind me and I wanted to die. Dylan was laughing her ass off as she sped away from the curb.

"I'm sorry about that. That was my sister just messing with me."

"Not much to mess with, Vivian. You look gorgeous," he said as he pulled the door open. "I would have been happy to pick you up though."

"No. I only live a block away. They were just at the house before I left."

He nodded and told the hostess his name and we followed her to the back of the restaurant. He pulled out my chair and then dropped to sit in the chair across from me. Our waiter came and took our order. We each got a glass of wine and I asked for a water as well.

"So, you and your sisters are still really close, huh? I remember always admiring that growing up. Everyone loved the Thomas girls." He smiled up at the server when she set our drinks down, and we both ordered dinner before she stepped away.

"Yeah. Too close sometimes. I love them, but they drive me crazy."

He nodded. "I get that. My older brother, Logan, is always hitting me up for money."

I laughed. "I just get hit up for baked goods and clothes."

"Do you still hang out with that big guy? I think his name was Nick?"

I took a sip of my wine and nodded. "Niko West. Yep. We've been besties since kindergarten."

"The guy always scared the shit out of me. I played football with him my senior year and he was only a freshman, but the guy was so intimidating."

"He's like an M&M. He's got a hard shell, but he's soft beneath. Just don't ever tell him I told you that." I smiled and took him in.

He was tall and lean, wearing a button-up and sweater, and his blond hair was perfectly gelled into place.

"Trust me. I won't say a word. That's how Sarah and I were. Best friends, you know?"

I smiled, but I doubted it was the same. Sarah wasn't from Honey Mountain. They'd met in college and dated. Completely different from me and Niko, but I wouldn't point that out.

"Oh, that makes it so hard."

"You have no idea. We did everything together. Movies.

Painting. Long walks. When we weren't together, we were FaceTiming. And the sex, don't even get me started. It was something." He looked up at the ceiling with this longing look in his eyes like he was actually there. In bed with his ex, making sweet love to her right now.

While on this date with me.

He swiped at a tear coming down his cheek, and I gasped.

"Hunter. I'm so sorry. That's awful. Truly it is."

"Have you ever just loved someone so much that you felt like you couldn't live without them?" he asked just as the server set our plates down in front of us.

I thought about his question. "Um...honestly, no. I haven't ever felt that kind of connection with someone I was dating."

"It's really hard, Vivian." His words broke on a sob and the server gave me an empathetic look.

It was okay. He was a nice guy, and he was hurting. I was just sorry I'd worn this sexy bodysuit because the highlighter in my cleavage was distracting me every time I looked down at my plate.

Damn you, Dylan.

"I'm so sorry. I'm always here if you need to talk." I forked a piece of meatball and popped it in my mouth.

"We had sex two to three times a day when we were together. So why would she cheat on me?"

I didn't have the answer, but the real question was...why was everyone on the planet having good sex aside from me?

I wasn't sure—but I did know that it was time to change that.

Chapter 8

Niko

Vivian had stopped all her playful texts about the things she'd like me to do to her since we'd taken the canoe out last night, and I didn't like it. Because she was on a date with Hunter fucking Hall. I played football with the dude, and he was the guy who cheated when we had to run two miles. He'd brag about how he lied to coach about cutting it short a lap and I never trusted the guy after that. I didn't like the idea of her being out with him, and I sure as shit didn't want him putting his filthy hands on her.

Me: Hey. How's the date going?

Fuck. I needed to leave her alone about this. Why the fuck did I care so much?

Honey Bee: Well, I just listened to two hours of stories about all the good loving he and his fiancée had before he walked in and found her and his best friend doing it doggy style. I kid you not. I just left.

I'm walking home. He's definitely not the guy. I guess
you were right on this one. I'm just going to die an old
spinster and the only person on the planet that never
experiences the good sex. Unless you want to revisit
my offer? <winky face emoji>

I barked out a laugh, and relief flooded. I didn't want her
out there hooking up with strangers—and I couldn't deny Vivian
Thomas anything. She was the one person I would walk through
fire for. The one person I would cross any lines for. But I'd need
to be clear. It would be a one-and-done deal. No sex. I couldn't
allow that to happen. But I could make her feel good. I owed her
that much, right?

And it's all I could fucking think about for the past week. She
knew I didn't like her walking alone and I didn't respond, I just
got in my truck and drove to her house. I didn't allow myself to
stop and think about what I was doing.

I knocked on her door, which I knew would surprise her,
because I hadn't told her I was coming. I knew she would beat
me here as she only lived a block from the restaurant.

She pulled the door open. Light-brown waves traveled over
her shoulder and down past her chest. Her honey-brown eyes
found mine. She had more makeup on than usual and she looked
sexy as hell. Pops of gold and amber made her brown eyes even
softer. Warm.

Home.

She wore a white robe, and it gaped open at the top and it
took all that I had not to yank it off of her right there.

"Hey. You didn't text me back. I was just getting in the tub."

Thoughts of a naked Vivian flooded my head.

"I got your text, Honey Bee. I thought you were done sexting
me?"

Her cheeks flushed pink, and she shrugged. "Hey, a girl can try, right? But it's okay. Dylan is going to get me set up on a dating app tomorrow at work."

"No," I growled. "Some strange fucker is not going to touch you."

She put her hands on her hips and lifted her chin. "Is that so?"

"That is fucking so." I leaned down and placed my thumb and pointer finger on each side of her chin and forced her to meet my gaze. "I'm not going to have sex with you, Vivian, because you and I see sex differently."

She cleared her throat. "How so?"

"I fuck. You make love. And you deserve that, but that isn't me. But I can sure as hell manage to rock your fucking world without sticking my dick in you. And I want to be the first one to taste you."

Her eyes doubled in size, and she blinked a few times, but she didn't speak.

I moved forward, crowding her. "You sure you want this?"

"I'm positive," she whispered.

That was all I needed.

I rushed her, scooping her up into my arms and carrying her across the room. I set her down on the couch, on the side with a chaise lounge, as if she were porcelain. Because in a way, she was. To me, Vivian Thomas was the most beautiful, delicate person I'd ever known.

I hovered above her, and my fingers grazed her collarbone.

"One time, Honey Bee. Then we go back to normal," I said against her ear, nibbling on her lobe before I could stop myself. Lavender and honey flooding my senses.

She nodded, and a breathy word escaped her lips. "Okay."

My fingers grazed her smooth skin. Our differences impossible to miss. My fingers were rough from fighting fires and working at the firehouse, and everything about Vivi was soft. Her skin. Her hair.

Her heart.

Her chest was pounding up and down and I hadn't even touched her. My dick was raging against my zipper because I'd never been so turned on in my life. My fingers moved down, pushing her robe open as I took in her perfect tits. I'd always admired her body, but seeing it in the flesh—I'd never seen anything more beautiful. I grazed each hard peak with the pad of my thumb, as her breaths came hard and fast. I reached lower and tugged at the belt, allowing the robe to fall completely open. All she had on beneath was white lace panties. I dropped to my knees beside her as my mouth crashed into hers, and my fingers continued to rub and tease her nipples. Her lips parted, allowing my tongue to explore her sweet mouth. Our tongues tangled, and I kissed her like I would die if I didn't. This wasn't part of the plan. I was just going to make her feel good. I needed to stay in control.

My hand moved down her taut stomach, grazing her silky skin as I found the edge of her panties. I pulled back to look at her and her eyes were wild with need.

"Can I touch you?" I asked because I needed to make sure this was what she wanted.

"Yes," she rasped, tangling her hands in my hair and tugging me back down to her mouth.

I slipped my hand beneath the lace and swiped across her most sensitive area. "Jesus, you're soaked."

Her hips bucked against my hand, and I started circling her clit. I kissed her harder as she continued to ride my hand.

Faster.

Needier.

She moaned and whimpered before she finally cried out my name against my mouth as I continued to move my hand just enough for her to ride out every last bit of pleasure. Her head fell back in a gasp and her eyes were closed.

"Look at me," I demanded. "I want to see you."

Her eyes opened, long lashes framing them. Her gaze locked with mine. Little pants escaped her mouth as I pulled my hand away and tucked the few hairs that had escaped her elastic band behind her ear.

"You okay?"

She nodded. "I'm great. Um. Thank you."

I barked out a laugh. "Happy to help."

Her eyes searched mine. Wondering what would happen next. But I wasn't done yet. I moved back and started kissing my way down her heated body. My hands massaging her breasts as my lips trailed down to her panties. I looked up at her and smiled. "Now I'm going to taste you, Honey Bee."

She nodded frantically and I tried not to laugh. I reached for the edge of her panties and slid them down her tanned legs, feeling her feminine muscles as I made my way down to her ankles. I dropped them on the floor and ran my hands up her thighs.

"Spread your legs, Vivi." My voice was so gruff I almost didn't recognize it.

Her legs fell apart and I licked my lips with anticipation. I kissed my way up her inner thigh, taking my time on one leg and then the next before I buried my face between her legs. I licked across her folds and looked up to make sure she was okay. Her breathing was frantic, but she watched me with trusting eyes.

"So fucking sweet. Just the way I knew you would be." My tongue teased and explored before I sucked hard on her most sensitive spot, while my finger found her entrance and slowly moved forward. "You're so tight, Vivi."

Her hips bucked and I swear it was the most erotic thing I'd ever experienced. Bringing Vivian Thomas over the edge was beyond my wildest fucking dreams. I applied more pressure with my mouth, sucking and licking and driving her mad, as my finger continued its torture, and she arched her back and nearly came off the couch as she cried out her pleasure again.

"Oh my god," she whispered over and over as I continued to move my hand and my mouth as she rode out her orgasm.

She fell completely still aside from her breathing, and I slowly pulled my hand away and pushed up to look at her. Her honey browns locked with mine, and I slipped my finger in my mouth, wanting to remember how sweet she tasted for the rest of my life.

"Oh," she whispered. "That was…"

I leaned down and found her panties on the floor, and I slowly slipped them back up her legs and she lifted her tight little ass up so I could pull them into place.

"That was what?" I asked, as I propped myself above her and cupped her perfect tit one last time. I made a mental note to memorize everything about this moment. The way she looked sated and relaxed after she'd come from my hand and my mouth. I couldn't even imagine what it would be like to have her come on my dick.

He wasn't pleased with the situation, but I'd take care of him in the shower when I got home.

"That was amazing. Do you want me to do something for you?" she asked, wide eyes and all that sweetness. My chest nearly exploded.

"No. This was about you. One time, and back to business as usual."

She chuckled. "Okay. *Business as usual it is.* I think I'll be good for the rest of my life actually."

I kissed her hard. One last kiss. My tongue dipping in for one more taste of all that goodness.

I pulled back and adjusted myself. Her eyes moved down to see my erection bulging out of my jeans. I had no shame. I was a sexual dude. I had an impressive dick, so what can I say? There was no hiding it.

"This is what you do to me. You're fucking beautiful, Honey Bee." I leaned down and kissed her forehead.

She didn't move from the couch. She didn't try to close her robe. She just lay there watching me. "Did you have dinner? Are you hungry?"

"I just ate," I teased, referring to the fact that I'd just had my head between her legs, and a pink hue covered her cheeks. "Sure. You know I can always eat."

It wouldn't be a bad thing to just get back to normal right away. Sure, I was tempted to go home and take a quick shower and rub it out to watching Vivi fall apart twice, crying out my name and writhing with need. But this way we wouldn't have to wait until tomorrow to make sure there was no awkwardness.

"I'm kind of hungry again too," she said, moving to sit forward and closing her robe. "All that crying from Hunter made it difficult to eat."

I barked out a laugh. "Sounds good. What are we making?" I followed her into the kitchen, and she opened the refrigerator.

"How about omelets?"

"Sounds good to me."

And just like that, we were acting completely normal. But being near her was challenging now. I wanted more.

And that couldn't happen.

Chapter 9

Vivian

It had been three days since Niko had come by the house and, well, basically rocked my world, literally and figuratively. I'd never experienced anything close to that and we hadn't even had sex. But to say I'd been floating on air ever since would be a massive understatement.

I'd had a taste of how good it could be, and now it was all I could think about. I never thought about sex before. Not really. It was more of a chore with Jansen. Something I was happy to get over with when we were together.

But now. I dreamed about the way Niko touched me. The way he made me feel.

I'd hoped if I acted normal after everything would be fine, but he'd been distant ever since. We'd eaten our eggs and made small talk and I thought everything was okay, but he hasn't been texting as often as he usually does, so clearly, we have an issue. I haven't seen him since as he's been on duty at the firehouse, and

I've gone by once to drop off treats and he was MIA. Jace said he was out on a run, but I had the feeling he ran out the minute I walked in.

I knew he was avoiding me, and it pissed me off. I hadn't freaked out or asked for more, so it made no sense why he was acting so weird. I hadn't told a soul even though Dylan was grilling me about why I was hesitant to get on the dating website with her. I couldn't tell her about what happened between me and Niko because she would never let it go, and I didn't want to risk her slipping and saying something to him.

Things were already weird between us, and I didn't want to make it worse.

It was Friday and the lunch rush had been busier than ever today. I was thankful that I had Dylan, Jilly, and Jada here to help. Dylan and Jada didn't seem to be the biggest fans of one another, but in a way, it was a good thing because they both just focused on work.

The last of the lunch rush had just left. Ever since we added sandwiches and quiche to the menu we'd been slammed. I was getting cookies ready for a pickup order for Maralee Rhodes, a sweet lady who owned a vintage bookstore up the street.

The door chimed and I looked up to see Ruby Rhodes stroll in.

"Hey, Vivian," she purred. She was a year older than me and oozed sex appeal. She was known as a bit of a party girl, and it always surprised me because her mom was so reserved.

"Hi, Ruby. Are you picking up the order for your mom?"

"Yep. She made me get out of bed. I'm seriously so hungover today," she said as she placed two hands on the glass casing and rested her head there. Did people not understand that we didn't want fingerprints all over the glass? And now she was laying her head there as well.

"Where'd you go last night?" Jada asked as she wiped down the last table in the dining area.

"Beer Mountain, of course. I saw your brother." She giggled, and my chest squeezed. "We hung out. Had a good time, if you know what I mean."

Maybe that's why Niko hadn't called me last night or even checked in the way he usually did when he finished a shift. He'd obviously been hanging out with Ruby. He and the guys from the firehouse went to Beer Mountain often and even though Niko didn't drink, he was a pool shark and he'd play for hours.

"That sounds fun. Although you look like you're paying for it today," Jada said.

Dylan came out from the kitchen and crossed her arms over her chest as she took in Ruby and Jada talking, and I had to fight to stop myself from laughing.

My sister stood out like a sore thumb in this bakery. Her sarcasm and disdain for some of the customers that came in did not jive with the vibe of Honey Bee's. But I loved her all the same. Jilly was busy in the kitchen filling online orders for me, which I appreciated.

"All cleaned up," she said.

"Oh, hey, Dylan. I didn't know you were working here."

"Why would you?" Dylan shrugged, and her attitude was impossible to miss. She squared her shoulders as she slipped on her black beanie which matched her black leather coat and military boots.

Ruby chuckled. "I see you're still all sunshine and rainbows."

"I'm just happy that your mom prepaid for the baked goods. Wouldn't want you stealing anything."

"OMG! This again?" Ruby shook her head and took the box

from me. "I did not steal your cell phone, Dylan."

Dylan raised a brow. "I tracked it to your house, and your ex-boyfriend admitted that you sold it to him. I may not be able to prove it in a court of law, but I know you're shady, Ruby Rhodes."

Ruby barked out a laugh. "You're such a character. Thanks for the treats, Vivian."

When she walked out the door, I rolled my eyes and stared at my sister. "Seriously? Can you not drop it? She's a customer."

"She's a thief," Dylan hissed.

"I'm with Dylan on this one," Jada said, glancing over at my sister with a smirk. "I'm certain Ruby Rhodes stole my iPad right out of her mom's bookstore last year. I had it on the table and went to the bathroom, and when I came back it was gone. Ruby was covering the store for her mom at the time, and she just said she didn't see it and I must have left it at home."

"She's a freaking kleptomaniac!" Dylan shouted and we all three laughed.

"I don't know why my brother would be messing around with her." Jada set the cleaner and the towel on the counter and reached for her jacket hanging on the wall.

"Because she's hot and a total skank," Dylan said.

"Oh my gosh. Take your hostility out of here, please," I said, but her words sank in. He was ignoring me and probably sexing it up with Ruby Rhodes, who really was hot.

Jada was hysterically laughing as she waved at both of us. "I agree. See you guys tomorrow."

"I guess she's not so awful," Dylan said about Jada after she left, before coming around the counter and grabbing a cookie. "So...remember how I told you I was setting us both up on that dating app?"

"Yes. I'm not a huge fan of the idea, but I'll give it a try." Why shouldn't I? Just because Niko was against it? He had no right to tell me who I could or couldn't date, just like I had no right to tell him who he could or couldn't hook up with.

"Well, you and I have a date tonight."

"With who?" I wasn't in the mood for a date. I wanted to go home and take a hot bath and zone out to Netflix.

"Two super-hot guys. They're from northern Cal and are in town for a few weeks looking at potential spaces to open a restaurant/bar. They are a little older than us, but both really good-looking. I totally stalked their profiles."

"Oh my gosh, Dylan, you know nothing about them."

"I know as much as you can know about someone on a dating app. And we'll be together. Come on. It'll be fun. We'll go to Beer Mountain. Maybe we can convince Charlie to come meet us too."

"Okay. I like the sound of that. Three of us and two of them. That makes it less pressure. More like a group of friends getting to know one another."

"Dating hot guys is not pressure, Vivi. It's supposed to be fun. Go out and flirt a little. Have a good time."

I nodded. "Fine. I'll meet you there."

"Yay," she sang out. "I expected that to be more of a fight. Okay, can I leave a little early? The rush is done, and I have a paper to write that's due tomorrow."

"Yes. I've got this. Love you."

She kissed my cheek and snatched one more cookie before heading out the door.

I got to work making butter cookies and red velvet cupcakes, and the next few hours flew by with only a few customers stopping in, which was easy to handle with Jilly and me. When I got home, I had time to take a bath and pinned my hair up, before I got ready for our odd double date. I'd texted Charlotte and she was going to meet us there too, so I was happy about that.

Temperatures were dropping, and I wore a heavy white turtleneck sweater and my skinny jeans and booties. As I walked to Beer Mountain, the chill in the air had me pulling my coat closed. We'd be getting snow any day now, and once it started, it wouldn't let up for a while.

When I stepped inside Beer Mountain, the place was buzzing. I said hello to a few locals that were regulars at Honey Bee's, and I pulled off my coat and made my way to the tall-top table my sisters were currently sitting at with two guys. They were definitely older. Maybe even early forties. But she was right, they were good-looking.

Charlotte jumped to her feet and hugged me as she whispered in my ear. "So glad you're here."

"Hi," I said, waving at Dylan and the two men who were now moving to their feet.

"Vivian, nice to meet you. I'm Donald and this is Lyle." He shook my hand and Lyle did the same thing.

There were cocktails on the table, and Dylan pushed a glass of Chardonnay my way. "We got this for you. Drink up, girl."

She wriggled her brows at me when they weren't looking, which made me laugh.

I scanned the bar and immediately spotted Niko in the back room playing pool. He'd be impossible to miss, as he stood much taller than everyone else. His long hair wasn't tied back, and he pushed it away from his face as his gaze locked with mine. I'd barely heard from him today aside from a text where he was just checking in. I forced a smile and then looked away. If he wanted to act distant and weird, that was on him.

Donald and Lyle told us all about the bar they were looking to open. They were nice guys, but there was no spark, and I didn't think my sisters felt one either. But they were nice enough, and now that the first glass of wine had set in, I didn't mind being out tonight. My gaze kept moving to the back room and it felt strange that Niko and I hadn't said hello when we were at the same place.

I picked up my phone and shot him a text.

Me: Why are you being weird?

Niko reached for his back pocket when the text went through and glanced over at me before typing into his phone.

Niko: Not being weird, Honey Bee. I'm not the one hanging out with random dudes.

No, you're just the one hooking up with Ruby Rhodes and acting distant.

Me: Whatever.

If he wanted to act like us not talking wasn't weird, I wasn't going to play along. I reached for a few tortilla chips in the middle of the table as Donald went on and on about the interior plans for the new bar. My phone vibrated and I looked down to see a group text to me and Charlotte from Dylan, even though we were sitting at the same table. This was typical Dylan behavior as the girl had no patience. When she wanted to say something, she was not going to wait until we were done.

Dylan: Donald has a tan line on his ring finger. I think the bastard's a player. I'm going to end this as soon as he stops talking about cherry wood and brass hardware and boring me to death. And Lyle looks like he's three sheets to the wind.

I laughed because my sister didn't miss a beat. Charlotte responded that she was tired and ready to go.

"I need to use the restroom and then I'm going to call it a

night," I said, pushing to my feet.

"We're all calling it a night. Thanks for the drinks, gentlemen." Dylan tipped the last of her wine back and then set it on the table.

"Yeah. We've got a big day tomorrow," Donald said as he waved the server over and paid the tab.

We thanked him and I hugged my sisters before heading to the bathroom. I made my way down the dimly lit hallway leading to the women's restroom, when a hand wrapped around my forearm.

"Who are those guys?" Niko said, his lips grazing my ear.

"Geez. You scared me." I whipped around and my back pressed up against the wall.

"Who are they, Honey Bee?"

I rolled my eyes. "They're guys Dylan met on a dating app. Why do you care? You're hardly talking to me. And didn't you just have sex with Ruby Rhodes last night?"

I hated that I sounded jealous, but I was. It had been eating me up since she left the bakery. I knew Niko slept around. Hell, he made no secret of his lifestyle. But he was acting weird about what happened between us, and he'd run off and hooked up with someone the first chance he got.

His gaze searched mine as he hovered over me. One hand was on my shoulder and the other came to rest on my cheek. "I didn't have sex with Ruby. I don't know what you're talking about. And of course, I care who you're with."

"Ruby said she hung out with you last night." I searched his gaze.

He smirked. "She was here, and I was here. She got sloppy per usual, and sure she hit on me, but nothing happened. She's a thief and a liar. I don't mess around with that shit. I haven't slept with anyone in several weeks, and I haven't touched a woman since I touched you."

"Okay. Well, you've still been distant since, you know, that night," I whispered because I didn't want to make things worse, but we needed to talk about it.

"I have been. I'm sorry."

Wow. That was the thing about Niko. He was a straight shooter if you asked him anything.

"Why? Do you regret it?" I asked and I closed my eyes and leaned into his touch. His warm hand was so comforting there, and I wanted more.

"I don't know, Honey Bee. I can't stop thinking about it and it's messing with my head."

My eyes flew open. "It is? Why?"

"Because I liked it. Liked making you feel good."

"Me too," I whispered. "And now I'm kind of mad at you."

His gaze widened and he moved even closer. His forehead almost touching mine. "Why are you mad? Do you regret what we did?"

"No. But you made me feel things I've never felt, and I'm still, you know, curious. I guess that makes you a tease," I said with a chuckle.

"No one's ever called me a tease, and I would never tease you. I'd be lying if I didn't say I wanted to do it again, but I don't want to do anything to hurt you. Don't want to take anything I don't deserve."

I groaned and put my hands on each side of his face. "Niko. I'm not a virgin. I've done it before. It just wasn't very good. You wouldn't be taking anything from me. You'd be giving me something."

His tongue dipped out to wet his bottom lip and I squeezed my thighs together to stop the throb that was currently taking up residence there.

"Oh, hey, is that you behind that hunky dude, Vivi?" Dylan said from behind Niko from the other end of the hallway. Niko moved back and I straightened.

"Yes. We're just talking. Are you heading out?"

"Yeah. Charlie and I are going home. Donald gave it one more shot and when I confronted him about his tan line on his wedding finger, he admitted he was married. The jerk." She laughed. "He said they were going through something. I told him he best go through that door and head home and lose my number."

"You need me to take care of him?" Niko said, stepping back, but his gaze never left mine.

"No. We're going to walk home."

"I'll drive you." He turned to look at me. "I'll take all three of you home."

"I'll bet you will," Dylan said under her breath once I moved beside her, and I shot her a warning look.

"All right, let me run to the bathroom," I said.

I used the restroom and then stared into the mirror. What was I doing? What did this even mean? I wanted to finish our conversation and I hoped he'd take the girls home first and me home after so we could talk about this some more.

He was struggling too and that made me feel relieved to know I wasn't the only one thinking about the other night.

When I came out of the restroom, they were waiting for me by the door. He handed me my coat and we all climbed in Niko's truck.

"I thought that guy would pee his pants when Dilly called him out about his wedding finger tan line," Charlotte said over her laughter as we drove toward my dad's house.

"Serves him right. What kind of married man goes on a dating app? I have half a mind to find out who his wife is and give her a heads-up about who she's married to."

"They also looked your father's age," Niko grumped as he pulled into the driveway at my dad's house.

"Yeah, they were definitely not twenty-nine like they claimed on the app. The lying bastards," Dylan said as she unbuckled.

"Thanks for the ride," they both sang out as they climbed out of the truck, and we watched them make their way inside the house.

We drove in silence to my house and the tension nearly killed me.

He wanted me.

I wanted him.

What was the problem?

Chapter 10

Niko

I pulled into her driveway and turned to face her. "What do you want, Honey Bee?"

"You," she said, raising a brow and daring me to challenge her.

"You know relationships aren't my thing. I don't want to fuck up what we have."

"Niko, I'm not asking you to marry me or promise me forever. We're best friends. You made me feel something no one ever has. I'm just asking for more. It's temporary."

"And you're sure you're okay with that?" My voice was gruff. I'd been struggling ever since I left her house. Fantasizing and dreaming about this girl every second of the day. I already loved Vivi, I had my whole life. Wanting her wasn't supposed to happen.

I shouldn't have crossed that line with her, but now that I had, I couldn't stop thinking about her.

"I'm positive. Nothing could ever come between our

friendship. Let's just enjoy this time together for a little bit. My only rule is that you can't be sleeping with anyone else if you're sleeping with me. I mean it, Niko. No hookups. No other women. And when you want to go back to that again, you just tell me, and we call this done. Fair?"

I wrapped a hand behind her neck and tangled it in her long hair before my mouth crashed into her. I'd been craving the taste of her ever since I left her. Her lips parted, allowing me access to her sweet mouth. I pulled her onto my lap, and she straddled me as I took the kiss deeper.

She was grinding her tight little body against mine and my cock was ready to explode from behind my zipper.

She must have felt it because she pulled back to look at me. "Should we go inside?"

Her head fell back in laughter, and I turned off the engine. "Oh, you think that's funny, huh?"

I was out of the truck with Vivi in my arms, her legs wrapped around my waist as I made my way inside.

"It's a little funny," she said, her lips grazing my ear as she spoke.

"This fucking door better be locked, Honey Bee," I said as I tried the handle and smiled when I found it wasn't open.

She reached in her purse and handed me her keys. "It's locked."

Once we were inside, I dropped her down to her feet and she tossed her purse on the counter. Her eyes were wild with need. Her hair mussed and falling all around her. I pushed her up against the door and dropped to my knees right there in her entryway.

"I can't wait to taste you again," I growled as I lifted her legs one at a time and pulled off her boots. I undid her jeans and tugged them down her beautiful legs, and she lifted them one at a time to help me pull them completely off. I pushed her legs apart and buried my face where I'd been dying to be since the last time I saw her. I breathed her in right over the lace that was the only barrier between my mouth and all her sweetness.

"Damn, you're so fucking perfect, Honey Bee. So fucking perfect." I licked and sucked right through the fabric as she ground up against me. I gently pushed her legs farther apart, allowing me better access. I glanced up to see her watching me, her honey browns glazed over with desire. Her fingers clutching my hair and driving me wild. I pushed the fabric to the side and swiped between her folds, moaning against her most sensitive area as I continued to tease her, as she bucked against my mouth.

"Niko," she whispered. "Please."

I couldn't deny her. Never had been able to. I covered her with my mouth and moved faster as she ground up against me.

Faster.

Needier.

She cried out my name and I stayed right there, letting her ride out every last bit of pleasure and enjoying every minute.

"Oh my gosh," she whispered as she tugged at my hair, forcing me to look up. "That was amazing."

"You're amazing." My hands trailed up her body as I pushed to my feet. Waiting for her to tell me what she wanted.

"No more waiting. Come on." She reached for my hand and led me to the bedroom. When we stepped inside, she raised her arms above her head for me to pull her sweater off, and I dropped it on the floor. I reached around and unsnapped her white lace bra and let that fall to the ground as well, as my thumbs grazed her hard peaks.

"God, I love your tits so much."

She smiled up at me and bit down on her bottom lip, not having a fucking clue what it did to me. No idea just how sexy she was. "There's not a whole lot there."

"They're perfect, Honey Bee."

She reached for the hem of my hoodie and pushed it up and I used one hand to yank it off and toss it on the floor. Her hands trailed over my chest as if she were memorizing every line. Every muscle. She moved closer as she reached for the button of my jeans, and her lips kissed my neck and down my chest as she did so. I'd never been so hard in my life, and she paused to look down at my swollen cock that was sticking straight out.

"Um. Wow," she whispered, and her tongue came out and swiped at her lush lips.

"Don't lick your lips when you're staring at my cock unless you intend to do something about it," I said, my voice gruff.

"Maybe I want to do something about it." She reached for the waistband of my boxer briefs and slowly shoved them down as she dropped to her knees. It was the sexiest, most erotic thing I'd ever seen. And I'd been sucked off plenty of times in my life, so it wasn't the first time a girl had dropped to her knees for me.

But it was the first time *this* girl had.

"Vivi, you don't need to do this tonight." The words were so strained, and my dick was throbbing at the thought of her sweet mouth being this close.

"I want to. You just need to help me."

I nodded. *Take it slow, asshole.*

"You can lick the tip and then just take me in as far as you're comfortable." My voice was barely recognizable as it took every ounce of restraint I had in me to speak.

She tipped her head back and her honey browns locked with mine, and I swear I nearly came undone just at the look in her eyes. She smiled and nodded as her tongue came out and traced the tip of my dick.

I'd never seen anything sexier.

"You can hold it with your hand," I grunted, and her hand wrapped around the shaft as she continued her slow torture before her mouth came down over my erection and she moaned.

She fucking moaned.

My hips started moving because I couldn't stop them. I tangled my hands in her silky hair, forcing myself to stay in control.

She took me deeper, and I closed my eyes and my head fell back at the feel of her mouth on me.

"Fuck, Vivi," I grunted as I pulled her head away and covered her hand with my own to keep stroking me as I came harder than I'd ever come in my life. "Fuck!"

I came all over both of our hands and she just stared in complete amazement. I continued stroking as I rode out every last bit of pleasure. I leaned down and grabbed my hoodie, wiping her hands first and cleaning myself up.

"Why'd you pull out?" she asked, her voice gruff.

"I figured you wouldn't be ready for all of that just yet. That was amazing," I said, placing my finger and thumb on each side of her chin and forcing her to look up at me.

She moved to her feet and smiled. "Good. I plan to practice plenty. I liked it."

My dick hardened immediately.

"What the fuck are you doing to me, Vivian?" I whispered as I pushed her back until her legs hit the back of her bed and she fell back. I hovered above her, staring down at her.

"The same thing you're doing to me. There are condoms in my nightstand," she said as she scooched back further on the bed and reached in the drawer and pulled out a foil packet.

I reached for it, but she held on to it. "Teach me. Jansen wasn't big on showing me anything, and I'd like to do it."

Jesus. Her desire mixed with her innocence is so fucking hot.

I nodded, taking the packet from her and tearing the top off with my teeth. I pulled out the latex and took her hand in mine, as I guided it over my erection. Her fingers moving slowly as she sucked in a breath.

"You sure about this?" I asked.

"Yes." It's all she said as she tipped back.

I teased her entrance with the tip of my dick and her breaths were labored. "I'm going to go slow. You're really tight and I don't want it to hurt."

"It's not my first time," she rasped. So determined to show me she wanted this.

"I know, Honey Bee. But you've clearly been with a pencil dick, selfish bastard, and this is going to feel different."

"How do you know?" she asked as I pushed forward just a little bit.

"Because my finger barely fit and I have a giant cock."

She chuckled and the look in her eyes was filled with heat, but I saw the fear even if she wanted to hide it.

"I'm not going to hurt you. If it doesn't work, we can do other things, okay?"

She nodded and squeezed her eyes shut.

"Open your eyes, Vivi. I need to see you." I pushed forward another inch and her eyes sprung open. "Does it hurt?"

"A little, but it feels good too. Keep going."

I did what she said, inch by inch, I invaded her. Needing to claim her. Consume her. When I was all the way in, I stayed perfectly still, allowing her a minute to adjust to the intrusion.

My dick was having a complete meltdown, begging me to move. Begging for release. He'd have to sit the fuck down, because we weren't rushing this, no matter how fucking good it felt.

She was so tight it felt like a goddamn vise was blanketing my dick. I hissed out a breath. "Are you okay?"

She smiled up at me. "I'm more than okay. I want this, Niko."

She arched up, letting me know she wanted me to move. My lips came down over her nipple and I made my way from one breast to the next as I started to move. Slowly at first. Her hands were in my hair, and she urged my mouth back up to hers and I kissed her hard as we found our rhythm.

Our perfect fucking rhythm.

It was melodic and wild all at the same time. And nothing had ever felt better in my entire fucking life. I pulled my mouth from hers as I could feel her pulsing against my dick. I wanted to watch her come undone.

Her nails dug into my shoulders.

Her body nearly arching off the bed. My hand moved between us finding her sweet spot, and all it took was a touch. She gasped and cried out in beautiful fucking glory.

"Niko," she shouted, and I pumped once, twice, and that was it.

I went right over the edge with her.

It was beautiful and terrifying all at the same time because nothing had ever come close to feeling this fucking good.

I fell forward, bracing myself so I didn't crush her. I rolled onto my side, taking her with me, struggling to catch my breath as she did the same.

"You're amazing," I said as I pushed the hair out of her face. My thumb finding her plump bottom lip and tracing it as her breaths started to slow down.

"Thank you," she said, and a tear ran down her cheek which startled me.

I swiped it away with my thumb and searched her gaze. "Are you upset?"

"No," she said, and her voice trembled. "I've just never felt that before during sex."

"Yeah, it's powerful shit, right?" I pulled her close, wrapping her up tight in my arms.

What the fuck was I doing? How the hell was I ever going to walk away?

"It is. And I'm just happy I get to share it with you."

"Me too," I said, kissing her forehead and pulling out of her slowly. I made my way to the bathroom and dropped the condom in the trash before coming back to bed. She was propped up on one elbow. The sheet pooled around her slender waist, exposing her perfect tits and gorgeous body. The moonlight made her tanned skin shimmer, and damn, if I didn't want to go back in for more.

"I want to do it again before you run for the hills, but I'm a little sore." She turned to sit up.

"I'm not going anywhere, Honey Bee. Not yet. We've got time. It'll be you who tires of this agreement." I knew it was the truth because she deserved more than I could give her.

She deserved everything.

Chapter 11

Vivian

"I highly doubt that. Hey," I said. "What if we soak in a tub for a little bit? That might help with the soreness and then we can go for round two." I wriggled my brows, and I could feel my skin heating with embarrassment.

"I'm not much of a bath guy. I don't think I've taken a bath since I was maybe four or five years old."

"Well, I've never had an orgasm before you...so there are firsts for both of us." I laughed. Niko was the only guy on the planet that I'd ever felt a comfort like this with. I could say anything to him, and I knew he wouldn't judge me or make fun of me.

"You want to take a bath, Vivi?" His voice was so deep, and he tucked his wild mane of hair behind his ears as he leaned down and kissed the tip of my nose. "I don't know if I'll fit, but if it helps you to not be sore, I'm willing to do it."

I hopped out of bed with the sheet wrapped around me, and

he smacked my butt as I hurried to the bathroom while he was putting that offer out there. I knew this wasn't his thing, but I'd always had a knack for convincing Niko to do things he didn't want to do. He'd gone to paint and sip classes with me, a few cooking classes, and even gone on a retreat to learn about local plants and flowers because I didn't want to do it alone.

I turned on the water and sat down on the furry bench I had beside the clawfoot tub. This was the one space that I'd renovated before I'd moved in, and I loved it. It had been stuck in a different time period when I purchased the little cottage, and I'd stuck with the vintage vibe of the home but updated every detail in my master bath. The marble flooring was gorgeous and screamed French farmhouse. The clawfoot tub was large because I wanted it to be as big as the space would allow since I was a bath girl. It was the way that I unwound every night.

"There is no way I'm fitting in there," he said, and I burst out in laughter. He was so big, in every sense of the word. His body was lean and cut, but his shoulders were wide, his arms muscled and even his hands were large, and I wouldn't even get started on his…package. He stood there buck naked with all the confidence in the world. His skin was tan and beautiful ink covered his arms and shoulders, and he leaned over and yelped at the temperature of the water.

"You will fit. You climb in first and I'll just find a way to fit in there after you're settled." I reached for an elastic and tied my hair in a messy bun on top of my head.

"The shit I do for you sometimes," he grumped.

"It's a bath. You aren't robbing a bank." I laughed as I watched him step in and hiss about how hot it was. "You fight fires. How can you be such a baby about taking a bath?"

He dropped to sit, and I wished it wouldn't be weird to take a photo of Niko sitting in a porcelain tub looking like an out-of-place Greek god. His arms rested on the sides and his tongue swiped out to wet his bottom lip. "Climb in, Honey Bee."

His gray eyes darkened, and I sucked in a breath as I dropped the sheet, held on to the edge of the tub and stepped in. There was just enough room between his legs for me to fit.

"See, isn't this nice?" I asked as I turned off the water.

"It's only nice because you're in here."

I rolled over on my stomach to face him. "You're sweeter than people think, you know that?"

"I'm not. Only with you," he said as he tucked a stray strand of hair that had sprung free behind my ear.

"And with Mabel." I loved how he was with that little girl.

"You're both fucking impossible to ignore," he said over a laugh and my chest squeezed. I loved when he put his guard down. Let himself be in the moment.

I stroked his arm with my fingers and kissed every burn mark with my lips. He had at least a dozen on each arm. He didn't say a word as I did it, taking my time not to miss one. We'd talked about his burns over the years, but he always brushed it off.

"Do they hurt anymore?"

"Nope."

I looked up at him, searching his gaze. "I hate your dad."

He stroked my hair as he studied me. "You're too good to hate anyone. I'll hate him enough for the both of us."

"Are you worried about him coming back?"

"I don't want to give it any energy. Am I worried for myself? Fuck no. I will destroy him if he comes near me. But do I worry that Jada will get into trouble with him? That he'll get near Mabel? That he'll beat the shit out of my mother again? Yes."

My fingers ran over the tattoos covering his upper arms.

Angel wings and fire all melded together.

"Are you having any luck finding an apartment for Jada?"

"I've found a few. But it's going to be pricey. She's shit with money, you know that. So, I'll cover it for now and we'll just have to see how things play out. I'm guessing the asshole won't last long out of prison. And they'll be watching him, so the first time he fucks up, he'll be going back."

"I hate that you have to cover everything for everyone," I said, resting my cheek on his chest. Niko's whole life he'd been sacrificing for his family.

"It's just money, Honey Bee. It'll come and go. I've got plenty saved for shit just like this. Jace and I have gotten lucky investing in the stock market lately, so I'm fine. I appreciate you giving her a job, but I want you to cut her ass if she isn't doing what she needs to be doing. I figured Dilly will put her in her place if she's slacking." He chuckled. Niko had always been close with my sisters, and he knew them well.

"She's been doing a great job, honestly. I'm impressed. I offered her more hours starting next week. I could use the help."

"Yeah? That's great. She's got lots of potential if she'd just stop partying. You'd think after growing up with a drunk, she wouldn't want to expose Mabel to that shit. And then she leaves her at home with my mother, and that won't fly when the asshole is back. She'll need to be home and take care of her kid."

I knew Jada went out a lot. Living with her mother allowed her a full-time babysitter, which made it easy to have that freedom.

"She's just young, I think. She had a baby at fifteen, so she feels like she's missed out on a lot in her life, you know?"

He pushed the hair back from his face and leaned back. "Life is all about choices. She made hers, so she needs to be a grown-up and do right by Mabel. End of story."

Niko wasn't that guy. He didn't whine about missing out on things or complain that life wasn't fair. He was a doer. If he wanted something, he went after it. He grew up with a drunk father who beat him, so he didn't drink, nor did he want a family of his own.

"You're so good with Mabel. I think you'd be a great dad," I whispered.

He stayed quiet for a long time before he finally spoke. "It's not for everyone."

I nodded and dropped the subject because we were having a good night and I didn't want to ruin it.

"Fair enough. So, you're off the next two days, huh? What do you have planned?"

"I've got to go look at a few more places for Jada and Mabel, and your dad has me leading some workouts for the new rookies on my off days, in hopes of toughening them up. Why? Did you have something in mind, Honey Bee?" he purred, and my lady bits literally almost exploded. Niko was the sexiest man on the planet when he shined his light on you, and the way he was looking at me right now had me squeezing my legs together.

"Well, maybe a repeat of tonight?" I chuckled.

"Fuck, you're cute when you aren't even trying to be." He licked his lips and ran the pad of his thumb over my bottom lip. "Sounds like a plan. And let me be perfectly clear. If I'm not fucking anyone else, you aren't going on any goddamn dates with your sister as long as we're doing whatever the hell we're doing for a little bit. Got it?"

"So, what do I tell Dilly? You know how persistent she is. But I can't tell her about this, or she'll never let it go."

He chuckled. Niko didn't care about keeping secrets. As long as I knew this was temporary, he was good with it. But I knew we needed to keep it between us because the town gossip would run rampant, and when it ended and I had to pick up the pieces, I didn't want anyone to hate him.

"You're fucking brilliant. You'll come up with something. But I would prefer your dad not know what's going on between us. I don't think he'd take too kindly to this agreement." Niko and my father were close. I think my dad was the father he'd always wanted. He respected him. But this was none of my dad's business. We were two grown-ups who could make decisions for ourselves.

"Fine. I'll think of something." I smirked.

His hand came up and caressed my cheek. He studied me like he was memorizing every curve on my face.

His mouth covered mine, soft and sweet this time, and I got lost in the moment again.

Because it felt damn good.

• • •

"Um, that hot guy that bought the cupcakes dropped a hundy in the tip jar along with his phone number," Dylan said, holding up the hundred-dollar bill and tossing his number in the garbage. This past week had been crazy busy at the bakery.

"I saw him out front and I don't think he planned to come in here, but he was staring at you through the window, Dylan," Jada said. "And then he beelined it in here and pretended he needed cupcakes."

"I've never seen him before. He must be a snowbird getting ready for ski season," my sister said.

"Are you going to call him?" Jada asked as she wiped down the last table.

"Hells to the no. A guy like that knows he looks good. He

knows where to find me now, so he'll have to make an effort."

"Or log onto the dating app," I teased.

"Yes. We'll see if he's resourceful. Ugh. After that bastard Donald last week, I think I'm tapping out of the app. And this one seems to have lost any desire to date again." Dylan flicked her thumb at me, and I rolled my eyes.

"You can't rush these things," Jilly said as she came out from the kitchen with a stack of boxes ready to get mailed off. "Okay, I'm off to the post office. I'm having dinner tonight with Charlie, so I need to get going."

"Have fun. Thanks for taking care of those packages," I said as I held the door open for her.

Jada grabbed her coat and waved at us. "See you guys in a few days. Thanks for giving me the time off to move into the new place."

"Of course," I said. I knew she was moving because Niko and I were up half the night as he'd spent every night at my house for the past week. And I was floating on air. He was moving her and Mabel into their new apartment today, and then he had to be at the firehouse for the next three days. "Good luck with the move."

"Thank you," she said as she walked out.

"All right, we're finally alone. You are acting so freaking weird lately. Like you're the happiest you've ever been, yet you're trying to act like you're not. What gives?" Dylan said as she followed me into the kitchen, and I started measuring ingredients to put in my KitchenAid mixing bowl.

"I'm going to make pumpkin cookies. Do you want to help?"

"Ummm, I want you to tell me what's going on. You aren't a good liar, Vivi. You never have been." She leaned against the counter and crossed her arms over her chest. "Is this about me finding you and Niko all cozy in a dark corner last week?"

I turned the mixer on high speed and laughed. She walked over and flipped the switch.

"Vivian Grace, do not make me sic Everly on you. She's home next week and she can sniff out a lie like no other."

I let out a long breath. "Please don't say anything, Dilly. Not to anyone, please. This is just for me, okay? I don't want to talk about it because it can't go anywhere, but right now, I'm happy. And I'm giving myself this time to enjoy and not overthink it."

She narrowed her gaze. "You're bumping and grinding with him, aren't you? Yes," she shouted as she fist pumped the sky.

"Dilly. Listen, I don't want anyone to know. It's temporary. You know this isn't his thing. I don't want there to be a fall out when it ends. And it will. He's my best friend. I know who he is, and I know how it will end. Okay? Can you just for once in your life not have an opinion? And not tell anyone else? Can this just stay between us?"

She held her hands up and then moved closer to me and hugged me. "Of course. I'm happy for you. I've wanted you two to hook up for so long. But I understand why you need to keep it a secret. At least no one will be suspicious because you've always spent so much time together anyway. But you've got to tell me, how is it?" She pulled back and rubbed her hands together.

I turned on the mixer again, and she slapped my arm and shook her head. She left the kitchen briefly and came back with four cookies, and she set two in front of me, as she hopped up on the counter and took a bite. I turned off the mixer and reached for the cookie.

"Come on. Spill. It's our secret. But you can at least tell me if it's great."

I nodded and took a bite of the oatmeal raisin goodness. I looked up to meet her gaze. "It's…really good. Like nothing I've ever experienced."

"Damn. I need to find me a lover like that. Someone to service my needs...although, living at Dad's house sure does throw a wrench in that plan. Can you feel Niko out and ask about the new firefighters?"

I laughed. "Yes. But you need to keep this a secret, no matter how much Everly grills you when she comes home."

My oldest sister always knew when we were up to something or keeping something from her. She'd be home soon for the holidays and with Niko's dad being released from prison soon, I knew things were about to change.

And for the first time in my life...I wanted to freeze time right here.

I didn't want anything to change.

Chapter 12
Niko

"Niko, breakfast is ready," Tallboy yelled from downstairs, and I pushed to my feet and reached for my hoodie. It had been a brutal three days as there'd been two house fires and a slew of medical calls that Cap and I had been called to. I'd barely slept, and I'd quickly realized that sleeping with Vivian was the best sleep I'd ever gotten in my life. I'd never slept with another person. Not when I was a kid or an adult, aside from her.

And there was a peacefulness that surrounded me when I was with her. Hell, it's the reason I'd hung on to this one relationship like my life depended on it. And here I was fucking it all up. And I didn't know how to stop. Now that I'd had a taste, I just wanted more.

I was a greedy bastard when it came to Vivian Thomas. Always had been. But this was next level. We'd been texting nonstop, which wasn't totally out of the ordinary, aside from the fact that we were missing one another in ways we'd never experienced before. And we weren't hiding it. A few of the texts had caused me to have to take a cold fucking shower in the middle of the night.

I couldn't wait to get out of here and go see her. She'd dropped off treats for us, but I'd been away at a house fire and hadn't gotten to see her.

My phone buzzed and I glanced down to see another call from my sister. Hell, I'd moved her in, but she wasn't doing all that well on her own. She needed to figure it the fuck out because my father would be home in a few weeks, and she needed to be settled and not relying on my mother for help with Mabel.

"What's up?" I grumped.

"I called you last night four times, Niko."

I scrubbed a hand down my face and dropped to sit back down on my bed. Everyone had gone down to eat but I didn't want to bring this conversation downstairs. I loved my crew, but they were a bunch of nosy ass hens who were always trying to figure out what I was doing. And they weren't sly about it.

"Jada, I told you we had a fire. I was out at a call. You've got your own place. You just need to get used to it."

"Well, it sucks. I have no *me time* anymore. I'm working two jobs," she said, as she started to cry. I didn't want to be a dick and remind her that she was working two part-time jobs. She barely got in thirty hours a week between the two of them. "And I haven't been able to go out since I moved in. Mom's suddenly making herself unavailable with Dad coming home."

"Mabel goes to school full-time. You have a little time each day to yourself, Jada. And guess what, this is parenting. You need to step up. I've done all I can to help you. I'll watch her one night so you can go out, okay? But you've got to figure this shit out. You can't be calling me fifteen to twenty times a day when

I'm at a fucking fire."

My sister was still a kid and I had to remind myself of that. Between my mom and me, she'd had a lot of support with Mabel, and I would continue to do what I could to help her, but she needed to grow the fuck up and be a mother.

She sniffed a few times. "Okay. It's just a lot. And Mabel keeps asking for you."

She knew how to get to me. She knew that little girl was my weakness. "I'll pick her up from school today and take her to dinner, all right? That'll give you a few hours to yourself." I knew Vivi wouldn't mind. She loved Mabel.

"Thank you, Niko. It's hard doing this all by myself."

I tried not to show my irritation because she'd never done it by herself. My mother watched Mabel often and I picked up the slack financially for her. She didn't have a fucking clue what doing this by herself would look like. But I didn't want her to run home with my father returning in a few weeks. I needed her to find her footing.

"All right. I've got to go. I'll drop her off to you around seven, okay?"

"Great. Love you," she said.

"Love you." I ended the call and made my way downstairs.

"I heard you up taking a shower long after we got home last night," Rusty said as he looked at me over a mouthful of eggs. "I'm guessing someone needed some one-on-one to slap the salami?"

Big Al chucked a buttermilk biscuit across the table, hitting Rusty right in the head. "No dick talk when we're eating. Jeez. I told you this younger generation has no manners." He looked at Jack, but he just shrugged and kept eating.

"Why don't you mind your own fucking business," I hissed.

Although he was right. I doubted it would be a good time to say that I was rubbing it out to Cap's daughter. I reached for my water and took a long sip.

"How about some fucking manners at the table," Jace said as he shot Rusty a look.

"You've been in a foul mood for days. What's going on?" Gramps asked Jace and I looked up to meet his gaze.

We were a family here at the firehouse, but some things were off-limits. Jace had opened up to me that the last few times that he'd come home from the firehouse, the babysitter was there, and she'd told him that Karla never came home and she'd spent the night with the kids. He was done trying to fix his wife. They'd only gotten married because she'd gotten pregnant, and the dude was a stand-up guy. But Karla was a train wreck. In all the years I'd known her, the only times I'd ever seen her sober were during her two pregnancies. But the minute she handed those little angels to Jace, she was sneaking out of the house and chasing her youth.

"I think Karla and I are calling it quits," Jace said, looking up at us before forking a bite of pancake. "And that's as much as I want to say about that."

Cap and Gramps both nodded in understanding, and the subject was dropped. No one would question his decision to call it done. He and Karla had had a one-night stand a few years ago, and out of it came Paisley. Jace had married her even though everyone warned him that she was trouble, but they gave it a shot. They had Hadley two years later, and things had gone from bad to worse.

"How about that fire last night," Rusty said, trying to change the subject.

"That was brutal. I'm fucking exhausted, and you bitches

have me cooking for you first thing this morning," Tallboy said as he barked out a laugh.

"You wear that pretty apron so well," Samson teased.

"Damn straight. You assholes can't cook for shit. One of us has to step up to the plate."

I chewed my food and chugged my orange juice before pushing to my feet. I paused beside Jace while everyone else was laughing about Tallboy. "Call me if you need me, brother."

"I will. Thanks." He nodded.

I dropped my dish in the sink. "I'm out. I'll see you in a few days." A few of the guys howled for reasons I didn't even understand.

"Someone's in a hurry today. Where you running off to, hot stuff?" Rusty shouted.

I flipped him the bird without looking back and I heard Cap and Big Al cackling behind me.

We gave one another shit, and I wouldn't have it any other way.

And they were right. I was on a mission. I saved plenty of room for my favorite baked goods. I knew Vivi would be alone at the bakery this early in the morning. Dylan and Jada didn't come in until the lunch rush, and Jilly was off today.

I parked behind Honey Bee's and knocked on the back door because I knew she'd be getting things prepped before the morning rush.

When she opened the door, I rushed her. She gasped over a laugh as I scooped her up. Her legs came around my waist and I kissed her hard.

"Damn, Honey Bee. I missed you."

"I missed you too," she said against my mouth, and I knew she was smiling. I set her ass down on the counter and my gaze locked with hers. Her hair was pulled back in a loose braid, and it fell over her shoulder.

"Damn, you look so fucking good." My fingers moved beneath the hem of her sweater, and I cupped both of her tits in my hands. I pressed my erection against her, and she gasped.

Her fingers were in my hair as she kissed me hard once more. The door flew open, and Vivian nearly fell off the counter, but I steadied her.

"Oh. My. I see I've interrupted something. I would call the fire department to put out this fire, but it appears you're already here," Dylan said over a fit of laughter.

Vivi straightened herself and adjusted her sweater before jumping off the counter. "You're early."

"I'm not. You asked me to come in this morning to help you make the holiday cookies."

I stepped back and leaned against the counter as I watched Vivi hurry into the refrigerator and pull out an enormous cart with trays on it. Dylan moved close to me.

"Well, aren't you the busy fireman?" she whispered with a mischievous smirk.

"Aren't you the busy cockblock," I said with my arms crossed over my chest.

She laughed and then straightened her face and leaned in close so only I could hear her. "I am sorry about that. You know I like seeing her happy. It's been a long time."

Dylan Thomas was a smart-ass most days, but she was salt-of-the-earth good to her core. She was a straight shooter, and she loved her sisters fiercely. But her words struck a nerve. Because this wasn't going to last forever. I nodded as Vivian pulled out several bowls of pre-made dough.

"Okay, Dylan, you start rolling. Niko, I'll see you later." She walked toward me and pulled the back door open and looked behind her to make sure no one was watching. "Sorry about that," she whispered.

"Don't be. You're mine tonight," I said against her ear, my lips grazing her neck just enough to make her squirm. I fucking loved it. Loved seeing the way she reacted to me.

"I'll be off around five today." She cleared her throat.

"Sounds good," I said, walking backward toward my truck. "Do you mind if we take Mabel to dinner to give Jada a break? She's been whining and complaining now that my mom isn't watching her, and she hasn't had any time to herself."

Something crossed her gaze, but she didn't say anything. But I knew Vivi. Something was up.

"Of course not. I'd love that."

I nodded and hopped into my truck. As I pulled away, I glanced in the rearview mirror and my gaze locked with hers and she waved. And my goddamn chest squeezed, which pissed me off. I needed to stay in control. I never allowed emotions to rule me, and I damn well wouldn't start now. Losing control was not an option.

• • •

I pulled up to Mabel's school and chuckled when they brought her to my car. Dropping off and picking up kids these days was like going through a drive-thru for a burger. And this girl was definitely a special order.

"Neek, Neek," she squealed when her teacher, Miss Adams, opened the back door. I was on the list and had picked her up a couple times this year, and I'd grown up with Janey Adams, so it made things easy.

"Hey, princess." I looked back at her as Janey buckled her in her seat.

"Hi, Niko," her teacher said.

"Hey. How was her day?"

"You know. She's an angel bug. She helped Abe who was missing his mama real bad today. She held his hand and kept telling him everything would be okay."

My heart expanded in my chest, and I nodded. "That's my girl. Always taking care of everyone else."

I'd noticed that about Mabel even at her young age. She was always checking on her mama and worried about her grandmother. It was her nature. She was a lot like Honey Bee as a young girl. Flying around spreading their sweetness to everyone else.

"Have a good night." She waved before closing the door.

"Where are we going? Is Mama okay?"

"She is. I just wanted to spend some time with my girl, is that all right?" I asked as I pulled out of the drive-thru and made my way toward town.

"Yeah. What are we going to do?"

"I thought we'd go meet up with Vivian and have some dinner. How does pizza sound?"

She clapped her little hands together and squealed. It was a sound I was certain I'd never made as a kid. It was the sound of pure joy. Of happiness.

I'd never felt that kind of safety or contentment in my life, as far as I could remember. I'd always been on edge as a kid, because my dad had hated me from my earliest memory. I never knew why, nor did I care to find out. He was a drunk, drugged-up, irrational, angry man. And being on the receiving end of that as a child didn't allow for a lot of squealing. I was thankful that Mabel wasn't tainted by life, at least not yet. And I'd do everything in my power to make sure it stayed that way.

"I get to see Miss Vivi two days in a row," she said, and I glanced in the rearview mirror to see a smile spread clear across her face.

"Did you and Mama stop by the bakery yesterday?"

"No. Mama took me to Miss Vivi's house last night. We painted a little bit and drank hot chocolate out by the water. I love Miss Vivi's house so much."

I gripped the steering wheel hard. My sister had dropped her off with Vivi last night after I hadn't taken her calls. Then she'd tried to guilt me this morning, knowing she'd gotten a break after all.

"Really? Did you have dinner over there?"

"Yeah. Mama took me to her house and then me and Miss Vivi picked up Mama from her playdate and she took us both to our new house that Neek, Neek got us. And guess what?"

She'd picked up my sister's drunk ass. It was all coming together now. Yet she hadn't mentioned it. Vivi knew I'd be pissed that Jada did that. She'd hoped I wouldn't find out. But thankfully the little munchkin couldn't keep a secret if her life depended on it.

"What?"

"Miss Vivi said she would make my room a real princess room. She likes to paint, and she told me and Mama she would paint the room for me." She clapped her hands together again.

I pulled into Vivi's driveway and came around the truck to get her out of her car seat that was permanently in the back seat now.

"That's cool," I said as I pulled her into my arms.

"Neek, Neek," she shrieked and looked up with her two hands out at her sides. "It's snowing!"

The first flakes fell from the sky. I'd grown up here. Snow didn't faze me anymore. It meant cold-ass days fighting fires, but seeing the way her gray eyes, which matched my own, danced with excitement, made me chuckle.

"It sure is, Princess. Let's get you out of the cold."

I pushed the door open because of course it wasn't locked. But I had bigger battles to fight Vivi on than that at the moment.

"Hey," I called out and she came out of her bedroom wearing a black turtleneck and black leggings and snow boots.

Her body was toned and tight and sexy as hell. She was small, but her slight curves had my dick going hard instantly.

"Hi," Vivi said, and Mabel squirmed out of my arms and ran toward her.

"I told Neek, Neek that I get to see you two days in a row." Mabel held up her two fingers for Vivi, who bent down and wrapped my niece in a hug.

"Yes. I feel very lucky about that." She looked up at me and bit down on her bottom lip and gave me an apologetic smile.

"Yeah, you didn't mention that when I saw you today."

"It must have slipped my mind," she said as Mabel ran off toward the back door to watch the snow falling on the lake.

"Maybe I should punish you later for withholding the truth," I whispered against her ear, and she shivered.

"I guess I have it coming," she said and pulled back and smiled at me.

"Oh, you'll be coming all right."

She smacked my hand and pointed at Mabel. "Save your filthy mouth for later."

"You can count on it," I said as we both made our way over to my niece to watch the snow fall with her.

As we sat there listening to Mabel giggle at the falling snow, I realized that this was where I was most content. Watching these two stare out the window as the large flakes fell on the water.

It was the most content I'd ever felt.

Chapter 13

Vivian

I placed two scones on the tray with two cups of coffee and made my way back to the bedroom where a naked Niko was just starting to stir. I took a moment to take him in. His backside was completely exposed as he lay on his stomach. His muscled, tattooed arms stretched beside his head, and his chiseled ass was a sight to see.

"You watching me, Honey Bee?" His voice was gruff, and I startled before breaking out in a fit of laughter.

"Busted," I said, coming around to the other side of the bed and setting the tray down on the nightstand before climbing back into bed. "I opened the curtains, take a look outside."

He rolled over and sat up, his long hair falling all around his face. He pushed it back and glanced out the window. My entire backyard, which was small because there was just a sliver of grass leading out to the gorgeous bay of Honey Mountain Lake.

"Wow. We got a lot, huh?" He turned to look at me. "But I

like this view much more." His large hand found my cheek and tangled into my hair.

"Oh yeah?"

He leaned over and pulled me down, and he settled above me as his gaze searched mine. "You're so pretty."

My breath hitched and I bit down on my bottom lip trying not to show how much his words affected me. "I'll bet you say that to all the girls."

He shook his head. "No. Just you. The prettiest girl I've ever seen. Not sure what you're doing messing around with me."

"You're the best person I know, Niko. You're the only one who doesn't know it."

It was the truth. He hated where he came from, and he thought that was a part of who he was. But it wasn't. It never had been. But he kept a shield around himself like a warrior going to battle. I hated it. Hated that he felt judged by the sins of his father.

"That's because you're pure sunshine, Honey Bee. And you deserve better than this," he said, his gaze searching mine.

"I don't think it could get any better than this." I chuckled, reaching up to stroke his cheek. "I'm good with what we have. But…"

"But what?"

"I have to get the pumpkin scones in the oven at work, so there's no time to lounge in bed with big daddy," I teased, rolling my hips up against his erection.

He barked out a laugh. "Big daddy, huh?"

I gave him a chaste kiss and shoved him off of me and he groaned. I handed him his coffee and his scone. "How about we eat quickly and take a fast shower. Together." I wriggled my brows.

He shoved half the scone in his mouth and spoke over a mouthful of pastry. "Let's do it."

I took a few bites and laughed before we hurried off the bed and made our way to the bathroom. Niko was buck naked, and I raised my arms, allowing him to pull his oversized hoodie over my head.

He stepped into the shower and turned on the water, reaching for my hand to tug me inside. He pushed me up against the wall and dropped to his knees with no warning. I gasped with surprise before my head fell back, and I groaned as he buried his head between my legs.

Not a bad way to start the day.

And I wasn't talking about the pumpkin scones.

. . .

The next two weeks had gone by in a blur. Niko and I had gone trick-or-treating with Mabel and Jada on Halloween, and I'd never seen anything cuter than little Mabel dressed up as a sunflower. Niko had carried her on his shoulders for blocks when her little legs got tired.

The days were gray and cold, and over a foot of snow had accumulated outside the bakery. I was thankful for the town plows and the people who kept the roads and the sidewalks clear. Thanksgiving was around the corner and my sister, Everly, was coming home today. Ashlan had been home for two days and she'd spent the night at my place both nights. Niko had been on duty at the firehouse, not that she knew he stayed with me every night that he wasn't working. And I missed him so much. He'd be coming over tonight for dinner, as my father was throwing a big feast for Ev's homecoming. But I wouldn't be able to touch him in front of everyone and after three days of being apart, that would be a challenge.

"I've barely seen my brother. Are you hiding that boy away?" Jada asked as I rolled out some holiday cookies. The Thanksgiving orders were the most we'd ever received, and I was drowning. Jilly was doing the best she could to keep up with the orders, and Ashlan was coming by today to help and earn a little extra holiday shopping money. Dylan was swamped with school, so we'd cut back her hours, and Jada had been working more; however, she'd been calling in sick every other shift, which left me to fend for myself.

I chuckled and made light of it. "You know Niko, he's probably hanging out with the firefighters at Beer Mountain."

"No. I've been there the past few nights. Mom finally decided to let Mabel spend the night because she knows her time is limited once Dad gets out next week."

I tried to hide my irritation. First off, that she needed a break constantly from Mabel, who was the sweetest kid on the planet. She was at school all day, and then she spent her nights with Shayla? And I knew Shayla well. That meant Mabel was parked in front of the television while she drank and smoked the night away. It's how she'd always been.

Completely checked out.

"I've seen him a few times, but I don't know where he spends his free time," I said, keeping my gaze down on the dough to avoid her being able to tell that I was lying. He spent every minute with me that he wasn't at the firehouse.

"He's probably skanking it up with Ruby Rhodes or one of his many ladies." The disdain in her voice made it difficult for me not to bite her head off. Her brother was the one person who always had her back, and she didn't hesitate to throw him under the bus every chance she got. It bothered me. Niko was the most loyal guy to the people he loved, and he deserved loyalty in return.

"I don't know. I think he's working a lot."

"Yeah. He'll probably work even more after Dad comes home. I don't know why he hates him so much."

I dropped the dough on the counter and wiped my hands on a towel as I leveled her with my gaze. "Seriously? Did you not grow up in the same house? I didn't live there, but I know what the hell went on."

Her eyes doubled in size and her mouth gaped open. I'd never been short with Jada nor shown her anything but kindness. But right now, she didn't deserve kindness.

"I mean, lots of kids get spanked, Vivi."

I nodded and fought back the tears that were building because her lack of empathy felt like a punch to the gut.

"Spanked? Have you seen your brother's arms that are covered in scars from cigarette burns? Do you not remember the black eyes and the bruises? Or how about the year your father wound up with a broken foot on Christmas morning after kicking your brother so hard in the back because *you* didn't clean up your toys? Is any of that ringing a bell?"

She held up her hands and I swiped at the falling tears. I hated thinking about the hell that Niko had lived through.

"I, uh, I guess I forgot about some of those things," she whispered and tucked her hair behind her ears.

"You forgot about them? I'll bet if they happened to you, you wouldn't forget, Jada. And as far as him working all the time, do you realize that a huge bulk of his income goes to covering Mabel's school and your rent? So instead of throwing stones, I'd be real thankful that you have a brother who would literally do anything for you. A brother who gave up his chance to play football and go away to school to stay and help take care of you."

It felt good to get it out there, but I was surprised by how emotional I was. She walked toward me and reached for my hand. "You're right, Vivi. Niko has been more like a father to me than a brother. I forget sometimes that he's not, you know?"

I squeezed her hand. "I know, Jada. But he's your brother. And he went through a lot as a kid, and I know he doesn't talk about it, but I remember. And I know you remember because you were there too."

"I do. I used to hide in my room and Niko would tell me everything was fine the next day, so I guess I just like to pretend that it was. Our family is so messed up, it's easier to pretend."

I wrapped my arms around her and hugged her. "Your family is not messed up, Jada. Your dad is an asshole, no doubt about it. But your brother has his shit together enough for everyone. And you have an amazing little girl who loves you."

"That's true. It's shocking that I made that little angel, isn't it?"

I chuckled as she pulled back. "She is a little angel."

"All right. Hey, do you mind if I take a box of cookies over to the firehouse? I kind of want to hug my brother right now." She swiped at the tears coming down her face and giggled nervously.

"Absolutely. Let me help you box that up. They like the cupcakes too."

· · ·

The house was packed by the time I made it over there. I swear every firefighter who wasn't on duty was here. They all loved my dad so much and he'd been bragging about his oldest daughter coming back home after working for the New York Gliders. I was so bundled up I could barely see as I made my way up the steps to the front door. When I stepped inside, I untied my hood and let it fall as Everly barreled toward me.

"Sissy, I missed you," she shouted as she wrapped me up in a hug.

"I missed you too."

"Oh gosh, this is a never-ending gush fest. I just can't with you people," Dylan groaned as I hung my coat on the coatrack near the front door.

"The Thomas girls are united." Charlotte came over and wrapped her arms around both of us, just as Ashlan hurried over.

"I want in," she said, and we opened our arms and huddled together like a football team getting ready to take the field.

"Get in here, Grumpy Spice," Everly said to Dylan as she leaned back and yanked her over.

My dad hurried toward us with his phone. "I need a picture. I think Dylan is actually smiling for the first time since she returned home."

My father snapped a photo, and I barked out a laugh when I glanced at his phone and saw all of us beaming up at him and Dylan giving him the bird.

"Why must you always ruin the photo?" Everly hissed.

"It's my civic duty to make sure nothing ever looks too perfect." She gave my dad a half hug and I looked up to see Niko watching me. His gray eyes scanning my body like I was his next meal.

I sure hoped I was.

I smiled and waved, and he tipped his chin up, but his heated gaze never left mine.

"Okay, let's eat," my dad shouted, and everyone made their way to the kitchen. We had a screened-in patio with heaters and two large tables set up, which is where most people would eat.

Me and the girls usually ate at the dining room table because Dylan claimed fireman talk was too disturbing for her taste.

I hugged each of the guys as I made my way to the kitchen island for a plate, and I pulled away quickly from Niko to not be too obvious. Rook was the youngest and every time I looked up, he was staring at me.

Rusty finally slapped him on the back of the head and kept his voice low so my dad, who was on the other side of the kitchen, wouldn't hear. "Dude, that's Cap's daughter. Put your eyes back in your head."

Niko looked up at his words and his gaze landed on Rook, and the poor guy winced. They weren't that far apart in age, but he was new to the department, and I could tell he was intimidated by Niko.

"Sorry, I um, sorry, Vivian, I didn't mean to stare."

"Have some fucking manners," Niko hissed.

Dylan barked out a laugh. "Oh yeah, because this is about manners."

Everly looked up and her gaze moved between me, Dylan, and Niko as if she were trying to figure out what that meant. I shot a look at Dylan who shrugged and then headed for the dining room.

Niko was right next to me, and his pinky finger grazed mine and sent chills up my arms. I sucked in a long breath and looked over to see Everly was still watching. Intently.

I quickly moved away. "We're going to eat in the dining room."

I don't know who I was announcing it to, but everyone laughed as I left the kitchen.

Ashlan, Charlotte, and Dylan were already sitting at the table, and Everly came up behind me as we joined them.

"What was that about?" she asked.

"What? Rook? I don't know, I barely know him. He's new."

"I don't think that's what she's talking about," Dylan the little shit stirrer said under her breath.

"Niko didn't seem happy about it. What's going on with you two?" Everly cut a piece of lasagna and popped it in her mouth.

"Same ole, same ole," I sang out, trying my best to play it off.

"Did you hear that Dad RSVP'd 'no' to Jansen's wedding invitation," Charlotte said, completely derailing the conversation, and I smiled at her in silent thanks. I didn't think she knew what was going on with me and Niko, but she'd always been the most observant of the group.

I didn't want them to know. Because the minute everyone knew—my father would know. It would change my dad and Niko's relationship and I knew that would kill Niko. He loved my father. And when this ended, which eventually it would because we couldn't just keep sleeping together with no future forever, right? Dad would think he hurt me and resent him. And it would all be too messy. I didn't want any of that. This time was just for us. For me and Niko. And I was the happiest I'd ever been.

Someone rang the doorbell and Dylan hurried to her feet to answer. When she walked back into the dining room, she had one eyebrow raised and her arms were folded over her chest.

"Um, Vivian...you have a visitor." She turned to look over her shoulder at Jansen who was standing in the doorway. My jaw dropped and I moved to my feet and grabbed my jacket, pushing him back outside. The last thing I needed was my dad and Niko getting involved.

I pulled the door closed behind me. "Jansen. What are you doing here?"

"I came home for Thanksgiving. I, um, wanted to see you."

"That's a little strange seeing as you didn't bother to call to tell me you were engaged, but I guess seeing as you kept the relationship a secret, why start telling the truth now?" I didn't hide the anger from my voice.

"I know. I don't know what I was thinking. Katie forbade me from calling or texting you, but my mom thought I should invite your family. I think Katie's just a little insecure about our past."

I rolled my eyes. "You cheated on me with her, and you're marrying her. I would think she would feel fairly secure."

"That's the thing, Vivi. It's eating me alive. I never got to properly apologize to you, and I hate that we can't be friends anymore."

"Friends don't betray one another, Jansen. Listen, we weren't happy, and I was more than aware of that. I was coming that night to end things. So, trust me when I tell you that I'm not upset that things ended. But the fact that you didn't have enough respect to just tell me that you were carrying on with her, I can't tell you that it didn't hurt. It did. So, I don't know how to be your friend right now."

"I know. I know that I fucked up." His hands flailed around. "But don't you miss me?" He moved closer, pushing my back against the door just as it flew open. Niko was there, and he caught my arms in his hands. I glanced over my shoulder and the look on his face was murderous.

Chapter 14

Niko

"What the fuck is going on out here? Are you okay?" I turned her in my arms and pulled her against my body. Her face was pale, and she hadn't said a word.

"Hey, Niko. Vivi and I were just talking," the dickhead said.

"Oh, yeah? It appears you were getting in her grill as you had her backed up against the door. Am I wrong?"

"It's fine. We were just talking," Vivi said, clearing her throat and turning back to face her ex-boyfriend. "It's good to see you, Jansen. I think you need to head back home."

"All right. I'll talk to you later," he said, and she sucked in a breath before nodding.

"Goodbye." She turned and pulled the door open. Her sisters all ran from the window where they were clearly spying, and Vivi glared at them.

"What? He's a douchebag and he said he saw your car in the driveway after trying to find you at your house. How can we not spy?" Dylan said as if her defense made perfect sense. I kind of agreed but I wasn't about to say that.

"And who ran and got Niko?" Vivian had her hands on her hips and turned to look at me before looking back at her sisters.

"Sorry, Vivi. He seemed like he was getting a little aggressive and I got worried." Ashlan tore off a piece of garlic bread and popped it in her mouth.

"Obviously, we were worried about you," Everly said, taking a sip of wine before setting her glass down. "What did he want?"

Ain't that the million-dollar fucking question.

Vivi rolled her eyes and let out a long breath. "He wanted to apologize."

My hands fisted at my sides, but I did everything in my power to remain unaffected. Why now? He'd had six months and he hadn't said a word. But now, a few weeks before his wedding, he wanted to make amends? I wasn't fucking buying it.

"That little fucker." Dylan's fists came down on the table and everyone gaped. "Too little, too late."

"I don't want to talk about this right now," Vivian hissed, and everyone startled because outbursts from Dylan were the norm, but Vivi never had them.

My chest squeezed. Did she actually miss that asshole? Was she wishing things were different? I mean, she was fucking around with me—someone who could never give her what she wanted. What the fuck was I even doing messing around with her?

Vivian moved to sit back down and started eating without another word about the asshole. I walked back outside, and most of the guys were on their second helping of food. I ate in silence as I tried to figure out what the hell to do. When we finished up, I cleared my plate and waved off the assholes I worked with.

"I'll see you tomorrow. Thanks for dinner, Jack."

Vivian and her sisters were just finishing too and making their way toward the kitchen.

"You working tomorrow, Niko?" Everly asked.

"Yep. Your dad has me coming in to do some training for a couple days."

"Ah…good to know. I'll see you tomorrow. Dad wants me to come work my magic over there." She waved her fingers like she was performing some voodoo.

"She's going to psychoanalyze all of you. Have fun with that," Dylan said, leaning into me and giving me a half hug.

"Great," I grumped.

"I'll see you on Thanksgiving," Ashlan said as she walked into my arms and hugged me tight.

"Yeah. I'll see you soon."

"Bye, Niko." Now it was Charlotte's turn to hug me. The Thomas girls were huggers and I'd just learned to accept it a long time ago.

Vivian studied me. "I'm heading out too. I'll walk with you."

She quickly said goodbye to everyone in the kitchen, and Rusty and Samson looked up at me and wriggled their brows. I flipped them the bird as I walked toward the door, and laughter erupted behind me.

When we got outside, I walked toward Vivi's car. She pulled her coat tight around her neck and leaned her back against the car.

"Are you coming over?" There was doubt in her voice. Damn, she knew me well. Knew what I was thinking. What I was feeling.

I ran a hand through my hair, pushing it away from my face. "Not tonight, Honey Bee."

"Because Jansen came over?"

"Because I don't know what the fuck I'm doing. And fuck yeah, your ex-boyfriend suddenly wants to make amends with you? Are you telling me that's not messing with your head? He'd probably call off this fucking wedding if you were willing to take him back. You're not having second thoughts after being with the dickhead for years?" Anger spewed and I didn't even know where it was coming from.

"No. I'm not having second thoughts. And do you know why, Niko?"

"Why?"

"Because I think I stayed in that relationship for years because it was convenient. Because it was the only relationship that allowed me to spend all my time with you because my boyfriend didn't live here. Because it's always been you."

"Can't be me, Honey Bee. You know that."

"I'm not asking you to marry me, Niko. I'm asking you to give us a chance. No more secrets. I want to give it a real try, because these past few weeks have been the happiest of my life," she said, and her words broke on a sob as a tear streamed down her cheek.

Here we go. This was what I feared. I'd ruined the best thing in my life.

"You're betting on the wrong horse, Vivi. Can't be what you want. What you need. What you fucking deserve."

"What are you so afraid of?" she shouted, startling us both.

"This. Hurting you. Failing you."

"So, you'd rather not try because it might not work? That's your logic?"

"If that's how you want to look at it. I am not who you fucking want. And I don't need you talking to my sister about what happened between me and my dad. She talked to me today about what you said to her. I don't want to fucking talk about that shit with Jada, and I don't need you trying to fix me. You can't change me. I am who I am."

Her mouth gaped open, and she squared her shoulders. "You're mad that I talked to your sister. You're mad that Jansen came by. Why not just say that? Instead, you're looking for any reason to run. You're a coward, Niko."

"You might be right. But either way, this ends now. I love you, Vivi, but not the way you need me to."

She whipped around and climbed into her car and slammed the door. I stepped back as she started the engine and took off down the road.

It was for the better. But I didn't expect my chest to feel like it was caving in. Fuck this. I did the right thing for her.

For both of us.

. . .

The next morning, I showed up at work and Rusty had just given poor Rook a monster wedgie and the kid was howling as I dropped my bag on my bed. The smell of bacon wafted through the firehouse, and I made my way downstairs to the kitchen, and everyone filed in and dropped to sit around the enormous table.

Rusty whistled. "So, Niko, I heard Vivi's ex was back last night. What are you going to do about that?"

My gaze moved from him to Jack who had a smirk on his face and raised a brow at me.

"Shut the fuck up. We're friends. I've always got her back. I'm not going to do anything about that."

"Dude. Are you the only one who buys that bullshit story?" Jace asked around a mouthful of pancake.

"You know what happens to the guy who sits on the sidelines, don't you?" Gramps said, and everyone looked up because the man never had much to say.

"What happens to the guy on the sidelines?" Hog asked and everyone laughed because he acted like Gramps was going to solve all of life's problems with this answer.

Gramps finished chewing and looked right at me. "He stays on the sidelines because he's afraid of the game."

The whole table erupted in laughter and Rook and Little Dicky looked between me and Gramps.

"Maybe some of us aren't into games."

"Perhaps. Or they're just afraid to play," Gramps said before biting off half a piece of bacon and eating ridiculously slow as we waited for him to finish his thought. "But life is boring on the sidelines."

What the fuck was this? Gramps suddenly thought he was Gandhi, and he was going to teach me all of life's lessons.

"I personally like the game," Hog said as he reached for his juice.

"I'm not even sure what the fuck we're talking about?" I said as I pushed to my feet and dropped my plate in the sink. I was in no mood for this shit. I'd hardly slept because now that I'd spent every night in Vivi's bed, I didn't like sleeping alone. This was exactly what I didn't want to happen. I hadn't heard from her since I'd left her father's house, and I knew she was pissed. I'd spend the next three days here and let her cool down.

"Hey, who am I talking to first?" Everly said as I tried to make a quick getaway from the kitchen.

"Niko. Since you're done eating, why don't you go first," Cap said, and when I turned to argue with him, he gave me that look.

There was no negotiating.

"Fine."

"Have fun," Tallboy said over his laughter.

I followed her into her father's office, and she closed the door and motioned for me to take the chair across from her. She sat in his seat and folded her hands, looking like she was ready to dive in.

"What is this, Ev? I thought you worked with athletes."

"I do. But I'm equipped to work with anyone. And while I wait for interviews, I need to keep myself sharp."

"But don't you basically deal with athletes that are having mental blocks? Struggling to get back in the game."

"Sure. But all people experience mental blocks. Different forms of trauma, right? Are you exempt from all of that? Life is just too perfect?"

That rubbed me wrong, and I barked out a sarcastic laugh. "Far from it. But I don't know what you talking to me is going to fix."

"Just because someone listens and empathizes with you doesn't mean they're trying to fix you. You seem to have a real hang-up with that. With people wanting to fix you, huh? Trauma is trauma, Niko."

"Trauma is part of life. Shit happens. I don't need to be fixed."

"So, let's talk about what's going on with you and my sister," she said, and leaned back in the chair like this wasn't the least bit uncomfortable.

"Nothing's going on with your sister." I cleared my throat because the topic made me uncomfortable.

"And why is that? Best friends who love each other. She's finally done with that jerk, Jansen. And you don't take your shot?"

"Jesus," I shouted and pushed to my feet, pacing around the

room as I ran my hands through my hair. Why was everyone riding me today? "There is no shot to take. Vivi can do much better. You know where I come from. I can't believe you're even suggesting it."

I surprised myself with my outburst. My anger. I was normally better at keeping it in check when I wanted to, but Everly didn't even flinch.

"I'm going to tell you something and I really want you to hear me, Niko. You are correct...trauma is a part of life. Shit does happen. We lost our mom far too soon, and to say that it affected all of our lives is a massive understatement. And yes, we keep moving forward, but it doesn't mean that it doesn't hurt. It doesn't mean that it doesn't affect the way that we handle relationships moving forward. But we talk about it. We talk about her all the time."

"What does that mean, Ev? You want me to tell you that my father's a piece of shit and my mother isn't much better? Does that make you feel better? Because it sure as shit doesn't make me feel better. Living. Fighting fires. Moving forward. That's what I do." I moved back to my chair and dropped to sit. It felt good to get it off my chest.

"I get that, but you'll never escape it, Niko. Burying yourself in work is not dealing with it. Facing it. Feeling it. Grieving. Crying. Sharing. It's a process. But I will tell you this. Trauma is the ultimate thief. It may have robbed your past, but only you can let it rob your future."

I nodded. Some of what she said made sense. Maybe I had been sitting on the sidelines, but I wasn't sure I minded. Never thought I'd wanted more than that until these past few weeks.

"Vivi's just so...good, you know? She deserves the best," I said, my voice strained and tired.

"I couldn't agree more. I guess the big question is, why don't you think you're that person? I don't know that I've ever seen two people who love each other more than the two of you do, not since I was young and saw the marriage my parents had."

"But if I fuck it up, I lose everything." I scrubbed a hand down my face.

"But if you don't try, you lose everything anyway, right? I mean, she's not going to stay single forever, Niko. And aside from Jansen, most guys are not going to be okay with the friendship you two have. You're forcing her hand because you're afraid."

"I'm not afraid," I hissed. I hated when people said that. It's the one thing I had. Never showing fear. "I'm trying to do the right thing."

"For who?"

"For her," I shouted before letting out a long breath of frustration.

"Then you don't know my sister as well as I thought you did."

The alarm sounded and I was on my feet and racing toward the door.

"We're not done, Niko!" she called out as I ran for my locker. I was in uniform and running outside in less than two minutes. The truck was pulling out and I jumped on.

"It's a bad one," Jack said as we hauled ass down the road. "The six-story office building on the edge of town is up in flames."

"Damn. That sits on the edge of the forest, doesn't it?" I asked.

"Yep. Get ready to attack, Niko."

I forced myself to get my head on straight.

Game time.

Chapter 15

Vivian

"How do you do all this? I can't believe how many Thanksgiving orders you got," Jada said as she boxed up another pie and popped it in the freezer.

"I'll stay late tonight and tomorrow night and finish up the rest of these orders. Jilly will be here all day tomorrow helping as well. What are you and Mabel doing for Thanksgiving?"

"Mom and I are going to cook, and Gram and Pops are coming over, I guess. I think Niko is going to double-dip again," she said over her laughter. "That boy sure can eat. He'll stop by our house and eat before heading to yours."

My chest squeezed at the mention of him. We hadn't spoken since I left the house last night, which was long for us. I wasn't going to reach out, the ball was in his court. I knew what I was getting into when we started this, and I couldn't be angry if he was done with it. But it didn't mean it didn't hurt.

"That sounds like a good plan."

"Yeah. Mabel is at a fun age for the holidays, so I'm looking forward to it."

Dylan came around the corner with a cookie in her hand and a chip the size of Honey Mountain on her shoulder. "You have a visitor. Again." She made no attempt to hide her irritation.

Jada peeked her head out of the kitchen. "Is that Jansen Clark? He's back in town?"

I groaned. He'd texted me a few times last night and I'd ignored him. Because the truth was—I was more upset about my conversation with Niko than my conversation with Jansen.

"Can you guys finish wrapping these pies and label them, please?" I asked.

"Of course," Jada said.

Dylan stopped in front of me. "Take no shit, Vivi."

"Thank you, oh wise one. I've got this."

I stopped at the sink to wash my hands and dried them off, untied my apron and dropped it on the counter before heading out to the front room. The rush was over, and we'd be closing soon.

"Hey, Vivi," he said, pushing to his feet where he sat at the table in the back.

"Hi, Jansen." I moved toward him, and we hugged. It was awkward and I just wanted to end things amicably. "What are you doing here?"

We both moved to sit in the chairs across from one another. "I wanted to come by to finish our conversation from last night. I shouldn't have come by your dad's house. I should have called first. I just, I don't know. I don't know what I'm doing, Vivian. And I feel like shit over the way things ended between us."

I nodded. "Listen, Jansen. I hate the way things ended between us too. Walking in on you and Katie was definitely not a pleasant experience. But you should know, I was coming there to end things. Our relationship had run its course. I think we both knew it. But I wish you'd have shown me the same decency by ending things before you jumped in bed with your co-worker. But…you're marrying her, so it must be something special, and for that, I'm happy for you." I wanted Jansen to be happy. Obviously, it stung that he was unfaithful, but we hadn't been happy for a long time, and we both knew it. And I'd moved on now.

"Thank you. I don't know why I did it. I love you, Vivi. I always will. But I always felt like you had one foot out the door when we were together." He put his hands in the air to stop me from interrupting him. "I'm not blaming you. I'm just being honest. I always resented Niko, you know? Because what you two shared was always so much deeper than what we had. But I should have talked to you about it. Instead, I tried to force your hand. Get you to move to San Francisco. And when things didn't go my way, I crossed the line with Katie."

I thought about his words, and he was right. We never did share a deep connection. We were always just sort of going through the motions. Jansen Clark had been safe. I had never realized that until now. He couldn't really hurt me because I wasn't all in. Never had been. Even when I'd found him in bed with another woman…it stung, but it didn't devastate me. I wasn't heartbroken over our relationship ending.

"Listen, Jansen, I've had time to reflect on this. You can let all that guilt go. The truth is, we weren't meant to be together long-term. You were a good boyfriend up until the end, and I really do want you to be happy," I said.

He smiled and reached for my hand. "I need you to know that you were the best thing that ever happened to me, Vivi. I just hope I didn't blow it by not fighting harder for us. I love Katie, I do. But I have a lot of regrets about the way things ended for us."

My chest squeezed because he was taking all the responsibility for why our relationship failed, and I owed him the truth. Yes, he'd cheated. But I hadn't been completely honest with him either.

"Listen, Jansen. This isn't all on you. I think I was in love with Niko for a long time, and my relationship with you was more of a safety net. And with you being long distance, it allowed me that freedom to spend as much time as I wanted with him. I never acted on it. I was never unfaithful to you. But my feelings for Niko are more than friendship, and you and I finally letting things go allowed me to explore that."

He leaned back in his chair. "Really? Wow. I always thought I was crazy paranoid about him. I guess I was onto something."

"I guess you were." I shrugged.

"So, you're okay, Vivi?"

"I am. I'm happy." My heart still hurt about Niko walking away from me, but none of that had anything to do with Jansen Clark.

"Okay. Well, I appreciate you talking to me. Coming home to where I spent so much time with you had me all nostalgic," he said, squeezing my hand once more before pulling it away. "So, you forgive me?"

"I do. I truly want you to be happy."

"That means the world to me. I'll always love you, Vivi." He pushed to his feet, and I did the same. He wrapped his arms around me for longer than usual. "Goodbye."

"Bye, Jansen. I hope the wedding is amazing."

He nodded before heading out the door.

Mrs. Winthrop, the owner of Sweet Blooms, walked in as he walked out, and they said a quick hello before the door closed.

"Oh my word, have you met his fiancée? Is that awkward for me to ask you that after you dated him all those years?" she asked, as I made my way to the other side of the counter.

"Not awkward at all. And no. I haven't met his fiancée."

She rolled her eyes dramatically. She was in her mid-sixties, and she was most definitely 'in the know' when it came to everyone living in Honey Mountain.

"Oh my. Let me tell you, Miss Vivi…he traded down. The girl is a real piece of work. She keeps sending me fabric swatches to match her florals perfectly. Endless screenshots of Pinterest photos, and she's all over the place. One minute she wants peonies, and the next she wants roses. She can't make a decision if her life depends on it."

"Ohhhh, are we talking about the future Mrs. Clark?" Dylan asked as she came around the corner and hopped up to sit on the counter. She'd always had a soft spot for Mrs. Winthrop.

"We sure are. She's a real…what do you kids call it these days…a *biotch*?"

Jada came around the corner and she and Dylan broke out in a fit of giggles. I did not join in because I hoped it was all gossip as I really wanted Jansen to find happiness.

"A biotch is exactly right," Jada said over her laughter.

"Well, good. I'm in a mood and Mr. Winthrop had a colonoscopy yesterday, so he wants all sorts of treats. Do you know what that is? They literally flush the shit right out of you. All of it. And let me tell you…Mr. Winthrop is full of shit."

Dylan fell back against the wall laughing and Jada did the same. I tried hard not to join in, but it was impossible. I covered my mouth to try to mask it.

"Oh, girls. This is no joke. He eats more hot dogs than any human should ever eat. I can only imagine what they cleared out of him. So…I'll take a dozen cookies, mix them up, a few of each. I'll take four cupcakes, four brownies, and three croissants."

"That's a lot of shit to reload," Dylan said, as she hopped down and grabbed a box and helped me package it all up.

Jada grabbed her coat. "I'll see you guys tomorrow."

We waved goodbye and I rang up Mrs. Winthrop. She collected her boxes and said goodbye, and Dylan locked the door behind her.

"Hey, you okay today? You seemed a little off. What happened when you and Niko left last night? I texted you a few times but never heard back, so I guessed you were having some fun." She wriggled her brows and chuckled.

"No. That ship has sailed." I moved to grab a rag and wiped down the counter.

"Because of Jansen stopping by? Did that freak him out?"

I shrugged. "I really don't know. I think he was looking for a reason to run. Jansen just provided one."

"I'm sorry, Vivi. Why didn't you pick up the phone last night? I would have come over."

"Because I knew this was inevitable. I don't want the girls or Dad to know anything, so it's best to just not make it a big deal."

"Everly was asking me all sorts of questions. She thought she picked up on something between you and Niko."

"You didn't tell her, did you?"

"No. Of course not. I am capable of keeping a secret."

I smiled. "Thanks, Dilly."

"Do you want me to stay and help you with the pies?"

"No. I've got this. I'll put some music on and get them all finished. I know you have to study for your test next week. You can take off."

"Hey, with Ev and Ash both home, why don't you spend

the night at Dad's? He's working tonight and tomorrow, but us girls can have an old-fashioned Thomas sleepover like old times. Popcorn, chick flicks, and maybe we can prank call some of my ex-boyfriends, do a couple shots of tequila?"

I laughed. "Okay. I'll come over when I'm done. Call me if you want me to pick up dinner on my way."

"I've got dinner covered. Love you." She kissed my cheek which was out of character for Dylan, and it meant that she knew I was hurting, and this was just our way of dealing with it.

"See you later."

I spent the next few hours making more than a dozen pies. The next two days would be crazy with pickups and deliveries. Ashlan and Charlotte were both going to come in tomorrow and make deliveries for me, as Charlotte was off school for break now. I needed the help and was thankful that my sisters were willing to step up.

I went straight to my dad's house after work. Music was playing when I stepped inside, and I kicked off my snow boots. The snow was ridiculous right now, even for Honey Mountain. An unusual amount of snow had been falling for the past few days with no reprieve.

Ashlan came bouncing down the stairs. "I'm so happy you're spending the night."

I hung my jacket on the coatrack and hugged her. "Me too. And I'll need to borrow everything because I came right from work."

"We've got you covered, girl. And Dylan made Everly go pick up Mexican food for dinner."

We were all around the same size, give or take a cup size when it came to our boobs. But we shared clothes and shoes and makeup. Always had.

"That girl sure can delegate, huh?" I laughed as I walked into the kitchen to see the center of the table filled with chips and salsa, rice, beans, a platter of tacos, and a few burritos sliced up.

"Hey, Vivi, I'm so excited you're sleeping over. I barely got to see you last night," Everly said as Charlotte and Dylan walked into the kitchen. We all dropped into our regular seats and started diving in.

"I know. I could use a girls' night."

"I heard Jansen came by the bakery?" Everly asked as she spooned some rice and beans onto her plate.

I glanced over at Dylan with a raised brow.

"What?" She shook her head. "Was that a secret?"

"No. It's just not even worth talking about. He just wanted some closure. We didn't end on great terms and he feels bad about it." I reached for a chicken taco and topped it with some cheese and salsa.

"Well, that's what happens when you're in a relationship and you decide to stick your dick in someone else," Dylan said over a mouthful of burrito. "But he'll have to live with his choices, because Mrs. Winthrop said Jansen's fiancée is a royal bitch."

Charlotte and Ashlan burst out in laughter and Everly rolled her eyes. "That woman does not hold back, does she?"

"Hey, I love a straight shooter." Dylan took a sip of her wine.

"Of course, you do," I said. "How was the firehouse?" I wanted to change the subject.

"You know, it was interesting. Firefighters aren't that different than athletes. They were a bit closed off at first, but several opened up to me. The biggest surprise was Niko."

I set my taco down and studied her. "You talked to him? About what?"

"Sorry, Vivi, I can't discuss that with anyone. It's private."

She smirked.

"You're not a damn MD. You've got a Ph.D. And what's he going to do? Sue you for telling his bestie that he's a tortured soul?" Dylan reached for a chip and dipped it in the salsa before taking an oversized bite.

"Listen, you're one notch away from owning the title of 'the town crier' in Honey Mountain, Dilly. As soon as Mrs. Winthrop and Busy Betty pass you the torch." She laughed. "But I'll tell you this much. It was good. He opened up a bit. I opened up a bit. And I gave him something to think about."

"Can you at least tell us what you were discussing?" I hissed. It was important to know if he mentioned me in his therapy session because then I knew that Everly knew, but more importantly, he cared enough to talk about me.

"Sure. The main topic was you. Seems you're very much on your best friend's mind, Vivi." She winked.

"I say we play suffocation and torture her," Dylan said, and everyone laughed.

"God, I hate that game. You guys almost killed me in high school." Charlotte shook her head with disbelief.

"So sensitive, Charlie. You need a little more fight in you. We were helping you," Dylan said.

"Do you remember when I locked myself in my room that one night Dad was on duty and Dilly wanted to kill me? I stayed in there all freaking night," Ashlan said.

"Dude. You put my cashmere sweater in the dryer. I freaking babysat the Bonsack boys for months to save up for that sweater. The little heathens were terrible, but I was determined to buy that three-hundred-dollar sweater, and you shrunk it to the size of a toddler's."

I covered my mouth with my hand to keep from laughing.

Ashlan had run for dear life, and Dylan took our game of suffocation a little further than the rest of us.

"Well, my favorite part was always suffocating Vivi anyway," Dylan said.

"She was terrifying." Charlotte shook her head at me, eyes dancing with amusement.

"You'd never guess our little Vivi had superhuman strength," Everly said, swiping at her tears from laughing so hard. "Remember when you chucked Dylan across the room, and she fell against the door."

We were all unable to control our hysterical laughter now. The game was ridiculous. We'd each take a turn lying down on the bed and the others would hold you down and put a pillow over your face and see how long you could go. Of course, Dylan invented the game of suffocation, and it killed her that I was always the quickest to break free.

I guess in a way I'd learned to survive at a very young age.

And I'd survive the hurt I felt over Niko jumping ship the minute things got real.

Happily ever after wasn't meant for everyone.

Chapter 16
Niko

"Man, little kids scare the crap out of me," Gramps said as we pulled the fire truck into the parking lot of Mabel's school.

"You have four children and a half dozen grandkids," Cap said, and everyone laughed.

"Yeah. Those people have to be nice to me. I'm Dad and Grandpa to them. But these kids, they don't know me from shit, and the way they fire off questions every year like they work for the goddamn CIA. And half the questions have nothing to do with fires. Last year that little girl asked me if I was married. What the hell does that have to do with fire?" he hissed as we stepped off the truck, and even I struggled not to laugh this time.

"Maybe she was asking for a friend," Rusty said over his laughter.

Six of us had made the trip over here while Jace and the rest of the guys held down the fort. Me, Cap, Gramps, Rusty, Tallboy, and Rook were taking on Mabel's pre-k class.

"Niko is leading this one since he agreed to do this," Cap said, and I rolled my eyes. What choice did I have when Miss Adams asked me to do it for the kids?

"It's fine. You're a bunch of pussies. They're four years old. How bad can it be?" I walked toward the entrance.

"I don't think you can say pussy at a school," Tallboy snarked.

"Sure, you can. Kids love pussycats." Rook held the door for everyone and followed us inside.

"Behave, boys. These kids look up to you," Cap said, making our way to the front office.

"Oh, they're here," Mrs. Beaver shouted to no one and jumped to her feet.

"Niko, Jack, thank you for agreeing to do this," she said, and I did not miss the way she watched Cap. I put my hand over my mouth and coughed to keep from chuckling at her shameless attempt at flirtation.

"Not a problem, Anita," he said. Hell, I hadn't even known the woman had a first name. She'd lived in Honey Mountain her entire life, and she was the school librarian at the public school I attended back in the day, and now she ran the front office at Mabel's school. Vivian was always terrified of her because she ran a tight ship in the library. If you whispered, she'd kick your ass out. I used to do whatever I could to mess with Vivi to make her laugh because she'd get so nervous, she'd break out in a fit of giggles and we'd both end up out in the hallway.

I missed my girl. We hadn't spoken in several days, since I told her that we needed to end things. I thought it would be better to take some space, but it was the longest I'd ever gone without speaking to her, and I wasn't okay with it. I hadn't been sleeping, hell, I barely had an appetite, which was most definitely not the norm. The distance was fucking killing me.

I missed her. I missed my friend. And lover.

I dreamed about her in the few hours I actually slept.

"Okay, I'll take you all down to the multipurpose room, and all the pre-k kids will be arriving soon," she said as she led us through the courtyard and over to a building that I hadn't been in before. "You stop by and say goodbye on your way out, you hear, Jack?"

He nodded and cleared his throat. "Will do, Anita."

When she left the room, Rusty slapped his legs and wailed out in laughter like the asshole he was. "Are you fucking kidding me, Cap? And is her name really Anita Beaver?"

"Yeah. What about it?" Cap hissed. "And watch the cussing. The kids will be in here soon."

"Say it slowly," Rusty said. "Aaaannniiitttaaa Beaver."

I rolled my eyes at the dickhead, but it was impossible not to laugh.

"I need a beaver too. Something fierce," Tallboy howled.

"All right, that's enough beaver talk," Gramps hissed.

The door opened and Miss Adams led her class in, followed by a bunch of other classes. Mabel's gaze locked with mine and her whole face lit up, but the little angel kept walking in line because the girl took pre-k very seriously.

"There must be a hundred of them," Gramps whispered to me, and Cap and I tried hard not to laugh.

"You, Rusty, and Tallboy will just stand in the back for the talk and be supportive," he said, not hiding his irritation that the man kept complaining about the kids. "Then we'll all give them a tour of the firetruck after. You think you can handle that?"

"I don't think I have a choice," Gramps said, with a wicked grin on his face.

"You could always go sit with Mrs. Beaver." Rusty smirked.

Janey Adams got her class settled and walked over to me with Mabel by her side. "Thanks again for doing this, Niko," she said, and her cheeks pinked when she looked at me. I scooped Mabel up in my arms and kissed her cheek.

"Anything for this little angel," I said. "We're happy to come talk to the kids about fire safety."

"Great. The last class just came in. So maybe you can just tell them the basics about what you do and fire safety, and then we'll take questions?" she said.

"Sure, that sounds good."

Gramps groaned and I shot him a look as I set Mabel back down on her feet, and she followed her teacher back to sit with her class on the floor.

Rook had set out our firefighter suits and gear on the table so we could talk to the kids about that as well.

I cleared my throat and moved to stand in the center of the room in front of all the kids. Cap stood beside me, and the rest of the guys remained behind us.

"Thanks for coming out today to hear us talk about fire safety."

"Thank you," the group yelled, startling me as I didn't expect a response.

I chuckled. "Of course. Happy to be here. I'm Mabel's uncle Niko, and I'm a firefighter, along with these guys." I motioned behind me. "This is our captain here, and he'll be taking questions as well when we're done."

I dove into the basics of what we do. I talked about the gear we wear and the different types of fires we see. I told them about the training, about the medical requirements of being a firefighter, and most importantly, about fire safety for kids. About having a fire plan with your family and a meeting place when exiting your home. About not being afraid of a firefighter if they came into your house to help you during a fire. I had Rook put on all the gear and crawl on the floor and demonstrate what it looked like when a fireman came to find you. They thought it was hysterical, and they laughed at the poor guy as he did his best to look serious. He did a demonstration of Stop, Drop, and Roll, which had them laughing harder. Not sure that's the response we were hoping for, but they were four years old, and it was a start.

"So, that's the basics of what we do, and we'll take some questions from you," I said, looking over at Cap and motioning for him to jump in with me.

I kid you not that every fucking hand went up, and Gramps coughed and gave me a knowing look. I ran a hand across the back of my neck because this was going to be a long day.

Cap pointed to a little dude in the front row. He pushed to his feet proudly, even though standing wasn't a requirement. "Does the captain fight the most fires?"

"Not necessarily," Cap said. "I've fought my fair share of fires, but so have these guys."

"That's cool," the boy said before dropping to sit down.

I pointed to the girl that waved her arm so frantically I thought it might fall off. "Hi, Mabel's uncle Niko. You're handsome. Are you married?"

I cleared my throat, Gramps barked out a laugh, and Rusty clapped his hands behind me like the fucker was thrilled she was putting me on the spot.

"I am not." I left it at that and quickly searched for the next question, pointing at a little guy in the back.

"Are you doctors? What if someone you save is sick?"

"That's a great question," Cap said. "We're all EMTs, which means we can help sick people too. Me and Niko are also paramedics, which allows us to help those that are really sick if needed."

I pointed to a girl waving her hand at me and nodded for her to go ahead.

"I like oranges a lot. Do you?"

I rubbed my hands together and chuckled. "I do. I'm a big fan of the orange."

Mabel giggled and her little hand went up in the air, and I nodded for her to go ahead.

"I love you, Neek, Neek." She placed her little chubby hands over her heart, and I thought my chest might explode.

"I love you too, little bug."

We proceeded to take questions for the next thirty minutes about everything from fires, to tacos, to our favorite flavor cupcake, before Miss Adams saved us all and called it done. We agreed to meet them out front for a tour of the firetruck, and by the time we finally pulled out of the parking lot I was exhausted. I dropped to sit in the middle seat next to Jack, and everyone was busy making small talk about a few of the crazy questions.

"So, it appears Miss Adams likes you," Jack teased.

"Nah. We're old friends. She's a nice lady."

"Is there a reason you don't want to date her?" He raised a brow, and I knew this man well enough to know he was hinting at something.

"Meaning?"

"Don't sit on your ass when you have a good thing right in front of you. Because it may not be there forever," he said, leaning in so only I could hear him.

I knew what he was talking about, but I was surprised because he and I had never discussed my relationship with Vivi. Hell, she'd been dating someone for as long as I'd been working at the firehouse up until the last six months. It had never been a possibility.

Was it a possibility?

I scrubbed a hand down my face. "Jansen came to see her, and I freaked out. She deserves better than I can give her."

"Sounds like an excuse to run if you ask me. He's no threat to you. Hell, I never thought he was even when they were together."

I narrowed my gaze, surprised by his words. "I wouldn't think you'd be okay with it, if I'm being honest. You know me, Jack. You really think I should pursue something that I'll probably fuck up?"

"Damn straight, I know you. You don't think it's odd that she dated a guy she didn't even seem that into for all those years? Come on, Niko. We all see it. We've been seeing it for years. And you've been pursuing my girl since the first time you climbed through her window."

My eyes widened and I looked away. "Clearly not as stealthy as I thought I was. I hope you know that nothing ever happened back then. I never touched her, and I respected her relationship with Jansen all those years. Hell, it's Vivi that I respect, and it's her that I'm trying to protect."

Why the fuck was I talking about this with her father?

"I know who you are. I've always known. I never worried about that at all. You've always had her back, no question there. And I don't think everyone needs protecting. My daughter is a strong woman, Niko. You know that. But I've never seen her happier than when you two are together. Hell, I've never seen *you* happier than when you two are together. I think it's time to shit or get off the pot, son."

"Ooohhh, does someone need to take a shit?" Rusty popped his head in between us and barked out a laugh. "I sure do. All that talk about oranges and tacos has my stomach on edge."

I used my thumb and flicked it at the back seat. "Sit your ass down."

We pulled into the firehouse and Jack clapped me on the shoulder. "If you're waiting for my approval, you already have it. I couldn't pick a better person than you for my daughter. The only one who doesn't know it is you."

I nodded, surprised by his words. I respected the hell out of this man, and I figured he'd have my ass for what went on between me and Vivi.

"Just not sure I'm that guy," I said, as I pushed to my feet and followed him off.

He turned around and laughed hard. "None of us are, Niko. All it takes is one good woman to become that man. At least that's how it was for me and Beth. Once I met her...I changed all my deviant ways."

He was still laughing as he slapped my back and walked away.

"Looks like you got the fatherly blessing. What are you waiting for, Dipshit?" Tallboy came up beside me and leaned in way too close to my ear.

"I agree. Green light, baby." Rusty slapped my ass and I barked out a laugh. Because these fuckers were always in my business.

I made my way upstairs and found Jace sitting on the couch by himself, holding his phone in his hand, anger radiating from him.

"You all right, brother?" I asked as I dropped to sit beside him.

"Karla's gone. Met some guy in a bar and left town. Left the girls." He ran a hand through his hair. "It's so fucked up and I'm so tired of trying to fix her."

I nodded. The girl was a mess. Always had been. "Listen, you stepped up and tried to do the right thing by her. I think it's time to let her go and start a new journey with the girls."

He shrugged. "I'm fine with letting her go. Hell, it's been awful for years. But I just hate that she left them, you know? I didn't want them to grow up this way."

I saw the pain there. Jace was one of the best dads I knew. He reminded me a lot of Cap with his girls. He loved them fiercely and that's all any kid really needed.

"Listen to me. You've been playing the role of mom and dad since they were born. Karla was never there. They are going to be just fine. Hell, it might be better than having her come and go all the time. I know who you are. You know who you are. You've got this, buddy."

He looked up and I saw the exhaustion there. He worked hard. This would be a lot for him at first, but he'd find his rhythm, because it's who Jace was.

"I think you're right. Now how about you take your own damn advice and stop second-guessing yourself."

"What the fuck does that mean?" I asked.

"It means you should stop fucking around when it comes to Vivi. I know who you are too, Niko. And I know how hard it is to find someone worth taking a risk for. And that girl is worth it. She won't be around forever, and I promise you, if you let her get away it'll be your biggest regret."

"When did you become a fucking therapist?" I barked out a laugh.

"When my fucking life imploded. Trust me. If you get a chance at happiness, you should fucking take it. And that girl is the real deal." He clapped me on the shoulder as he moved to his feet.

I thought about Vivian, and I wanted to run down to the bakery and tell her I was an idiot for ending things.

The siren sounded, and Jace and I were moving toward our lockers as fast as we could. I needed to put this fire out first, and then I'd be dealing with the growing fire building between me and Vivian.

Because it was the one that mattered most.

Chapter 17

Vivian

On Thanksgiving morning, Jilly and I delivered the final pies for our local orders. She and I had agreed to drop off the last twenty orders between the two of us, and to say I was relieved to be done when I got to my dad's house was a massive understatement.

When I pushed the front door open, it smelled like pumpkins and turkey. Everly was burning her favorite candles, and my dad had obviously gotten up early to get the giant bird in the oven.

Growing up, my mom and dad always made this meal together. We had everyone from the fire department over for Thanksgiving, and it had just become tradition for us. I had a stack of pies and two casseroles that I'd made, and I set them on the counter.

It was just Dad in the kitchen, and he was drying off a frying pan as he turned to look at me.

"Where are the girls?" I asked.

"You know, they're upstairs probably blowing a fuse or two while they get ready." He chuckled.

I moved to put the casseroles in the refrigerator. "I heard you guys were at the school yesterday? Jada said that Mabel was so excited."

I'd seen such a change in Jada since the day I'd had a bit of a meltdown on her. She was trying hard. Stepping up. I was proud of her.

I was dying to ask my dad if Niko was coming over today. I still hadn't talked to him, and it was killing me. But I would not make the first move. I wasn't the one who had ended things and pulled away. That was on him. And this would be the first Thanksgiving ever we didn't spend together if he didn't come.

"Yeah. Niko did a great job leading the talk. The kids were grilling him about his favorite fruit, asking if he was married, one little guy even asked what kind of car he drives." My dad laughed and shook his head.

My heart squeezed at the thought of my best friend standing in front of a group of kids talking about firefighting. He was so patient with kids, and it always surprised me. The way he took his time listening to Mabel and answering questions that she asked two or three times in a row.

"I'm sure they loved him. So, is everyone coming today?" I asked, glancing out on the patio to see the heaters already on and two long tables covered in white tablecloths. I moved to the cabinet and started pulling out the plates.

"As far as I know, everyone will be here. If not, we'll have enough food for a small army." He chuckled, and I moved out to the patio with the plates and started setting up.

"Hey, girl," Everly said as she joined me with a stack of linen napkins. "Dylan bought a ton of fall décor yesterday in those bags, and we figured you'd work your magic and make it all look good?"

I laughed. I loved being in charge of table décor for the holidays. "Of course."

"Did you get everything delivered? Are you done for the day now?"

"Yep. I am officially on vacation for the next forty-eight hours. The bakery is closed tomorrow."

"Good for you. And what about Niko? Have you talked to him yet?" Of course, I ended up spilling the beans to my sisters after we went through two bottles of wine on our sleepover the night before last. I'd never been great at keeping anything from them.

"Nope. I guess he's really done. But hopefully we can get our friendship back on track."

She set the napkins on the left side of the plates and paused to look at me.

"Really? That's it?"

"I mean, yeah. He was honest from the beginning. It is what it is. It was temporary." I shrugged, but a large lump formed in the back of my throat. I hadn't slept much the past few nights, as I kept checking my phone. The thought of him being just completely done with me terrified me.

Was I so easy to walk away from?

My eyes started to water and Everly moved toward me, dropping the rest of the napkins on the table.

"Vivi, no. come on. This isn't you." She pulled back to look at me. "You've got to fight for it if it's important to you."

I shook my head and swiped at my cheeks. "He doesn't want me. Not the way that I want him."

"Bullshit. We all see it. You were dating Jansen because he

was safe. You've been in love with Niko West for as long as I can remember. But you're still playing it safe," she said.

"No, I'm not. He knows how I feel. It's him who's afraid. After everything with his dad, I just don't think he'd allow himself to be truly happy." I shrugged.

"I don't buy it." She pulled out a chair and motioned for me to do the same.

"You don't buy what?"

"That you aren't afraid. I think you have a lot more to do with it not going anywhere than you want to admit."

My mouth fell open. "What? How?"

"Vivian, you're scared too. You lost Mom, and you kicked into gear while I ran off and chased my dreams."

"That has nothing to do with this," I said.

"Doesn't it?" She swiped at her cheek as a tear sprung free. "You're a caretaker. You want everyone else to be happy. And you and Niko have one thing in common," she said.

"What's that?" I whispered.

"You're both terrified of being happy. He doesn't think he deserves it, and you're afraid of loving someone so much that it would hurt like hell if you lost them. Because you've already experienced how much that hurts, right?"

I nodded as the tears fell. The holidays were always harder without my mom. "I miss her."

She wrapped her arms around me and hugged me tight. "Me too. But that doesn't mean you can't love that hard again. And whether you and Niko are dating or just best friends, it would hurt just as much to lose him. But you can't live your life in fear."

"I'm not," I said as I pulled back to look at her and shook my head.

"Aren't you? Dating a guy like Jansen for all those years.

That's safe, right? You didn't even cry when you found him in bed with another woman. But every time Niko gets called to a fire, I see the way you react. When we're on the phone, I can hear the fear in your voice. You love that man something fierce, so go after it, Vivi. Don't be afraid to love and to live. You're the best person I know, just don't tell Dilly, because she'll kick my ass."

I burst out in laughter as it mixed with sobs and tears, and I wrapped my arms around her again.

"Oh my gosh. What now? Why is everyone so emotional today? It's Thanks-freaking-giving, not a funeral, for God's sake," Dylan hissed from behind me, and I turned around to look at her.

Everly pushed to her feet first and then I did the same.

"We're just talking," Everly said and rolled her eyes.

"Well, Ash just had a meltdown because her straightening iron broke, and Charlie has a zit that no one can see without a magnifying glass and she's refusing to come downstairs at the moment. And now I find you two huddled in a pile of tears, and I just… I can't be the sunshine for everyone." Dylan threw her hands in the air, and my head fell back in laughter as Everly leaned forward to catch her breath from laughing so hard.

"You're the sunshine in this group?" my oldest sister said as she tried to pull herself together.

"Yes." Dylan crossed her arms over her chest. "It's just hidden behind a dark cloud."

I rushed my sister and hugged her tight. "I love you and your dark cloud, Dylan Thomas."

"What's happening here? You're both acting very sus—"

"She hasn't heard from Niko. I'm just telling her not to fold so easily. I think she should fight for what she wants."

Dylan pulled back and studied me. "Maybe it's time you stop

taking care of everyone else and take care of yourself."

"Hey. I do take care of myself. I wanted to open my own bakery, and I fought hard for that," I said, looking between them with a raised brow.

"Well, you did. But then you opened a business that allowed you to bake the best treats and bring them to everyone you love. It was a total Vivian Thomas move. Find a business that helps you care for everyone around you." Dylan pursed her lips and clapped her hands together once in an I-told-you-so way.

"I love what I do," I said defensively.

"We know you do." Everly wrapped her arms around me, her chest to my back as she kissed my cheek.

"But wouldn't it be so much better to make butter cookies knowing that Niko was waiting for you naked in your bed at home when you finished?" Dylan asked, wrapping her arms around me on the other side.

We all three laughed as the back door flew open.

"What in the world is going on?" Ashlan shouted as she hurried over and burrowed her way into the middle of the hug.

"Well, make room for me and my gigantic pimple, because this thing has taken on a life of its own." Charlotte made her way over and we opened our arms and welcomed her in.

Nothing beat a Thomas sister group hug.

"For God's sake, is this all about the pimple?" my father said when he stepped out on the back porch. "I can't even see the damn thing."

We all fell back in a fit of laughter.

"It's huge, Dad." Charlotte pointed at her face, and there was literally the tiniest pimple there.

"Come on, zitalicious, let's go cover that with some concealer," Dylan said as she led Charlotte back into the house.

"Let's get a move on, girls. Everly, get the stuffing going. Ashlan, you need to make the cranberries. Let's let Vivian work her magic out here." My dad winked and the girls followed him inside.

I finished placing the napkins out and set the bags full of décor on the table. There were cute little chalkboard name tags that sat on a little wood podium that would go at the top of each place setting. I pulled out the chalk marker and started writing out everyone's names.

My stomach dipped when I wrote Niko's name. I set his nametag right beside mine. It would be weird if we didn't sit together. We always sat next to one another, long before we ever crossed the line.

My phone vibrated and I glanced down to see a text from him. It was the first text in several days.

Niko: Happy Thanksgiving, Honey Bee.

I stared down at the screen and my stomach flipped a few times. My sisters were right. Niko wasn't just my best friend. I loved him.

And it was time to fight for him.

I was done being afraid.

Me: Happy Thanksgiving. I'll see you tonight.

I planned on laying all my chips on the table. If they were going to fall, it wouldn't be because I was too scared to try.

I was going after what I wanted.

And I wanted Niko West.

Chapter 18
Niko

My gram and pops sat at the table nagging me about getting more food. I knew I was heading over to the Thomas' after I left here, and I was ready to get there. I hadn't seen Vivi in days and I was done keeping my distance.

I'd thought about what Jack had said to me, and I finally understood why Vivian had been wasting so much time with that asshat Jansen. She was just as scared as I was. I thought about what Jace said, and he was right. If there was one person on the planet that I would be willing to take a risk on, it was Vivian Thomas.

She was it for me. Always had been. So why the fuck was I so afraid of telling her?

I am not my father.

And no, it didn't mean that I suddenly wanted all the things that she wanted. Marriage wasn't something I had ever thought about, but that wasn't the big deal killer for me. I knew that Vivi wanted kids. Lots of them. The thought gave me hives.

But I'd tell it to her straight and put the ball in her court. Hell, I didn't want anyone else. I don't think I ever had. I think Vivian was the reason I've never had a real relationship, well, outside of the fact that I had a fucked-up father and a shit ton of reasons for not putting my faith in anyone. But in hindsight, I think I'd been in love with this girl long before I even knew I was capable.

"I'm heading to another dinner, so I want to save room," I said.

"Oh, I see. How is Vivian doing? I went by her bakery last month, but I need to get back there," Gram said.

"She's doing well."

"It sure was nice of her to hire you," Gramps said to my sister.

"I love working there actually. And she's a great boss. She's passionate about her work and we have a lot of fun there."

I never thought I'd hear my sister say she liked work. The girl normally complained any time she had to do anything that didn't involve reality TV and ice cream. Maybe she was finally growing up. Working at Honey Bee's had been good for her.

"Neek, Neek, will you ask Miss Vivi if I can come out to the lake this weekend and build a snowman out there?" Mabel slipped off her chair and climbed onto my lap.

"Of course. I'm sure she'd love to have you make her a snowman, baby girl."

"The way you coo over that little girl makes me think you should have some of your own," Gram said, and I set Mabel down on the floor.

"And that's my cue. Thanks for dinner, I'm going to head over to the Thomas' now."

I hugged everyone goodbye, and my mom pushed to her feet

and walked me to the door.

"All right, I want you to think about going with me to pick up your dad next week. I know he'd like to see you."

"That's not happening. Happy Thanksgiving, Mom." I kissed her cheek and headed out to my truck.

Normally, the mention of my father's return would have me going sideways, but I had one thing on my mind at the moment, and it was Vivian Thomas.

I didn't want to talk about my father's return or the fact that she was allowing him to come home after all he'd done.

Tonight, I wanted to do something good for myself.

And Vivi had always been good for me. Even when everything around me was dark and twisted, she'd shined her light my way.

I pulled up in front of the Thomas' house and there were at least a dozen cars there. They had an open-door policy, and everyone knew it, but Thanksgiving was always an event over here.

And now that I was here, I couldn't wait to get inside and talk to her. I made my way up the front steps and pushed the door open. The place was bustling with chatter and laughter, and they hadn't sat down to eat yet.

"There he is," Rusty said, pulling me in for a hug. "Hey, what are your thoughts on me and Dylan Thomas? I'm picking up on some sort of vibe from her."

I barked out a laugh because Dylan would eat Rusty alive. The girl was too witty for her own good, and Rusty wouldn't know what hit him. "Good luck with that."

"Hey, Niko," Rook said. The kid always seemed so nervous around me, and I knew I wasn't the warmest guy to people I didn't know well, but tonight I was feeling nostalgic or hopeful—I didn't know what the fuck I was feeling, but it wasn't the norm.

I slapped him on the back. "Relax. You aren't at the firehouse. I'm not going to ride your ass."

"I don't think the firehouse is the reason he's afraid of you," Tallboy said before he chugged his beer. "I think someone has a little crush on Jada."

Rook's cheeks flushed a deep red and for a moment, I thought he was having some sort of allergic reaction. But then he sputtered his words nervously. "No. I mean. Yes. I know Jada. I wouldn't do anything without talking to you, Niko."

I looked up and my eyes locked with honey browns standing there watching me from across the room. The gaze that always soothed me. "You know what, I'm not going to respond to that right now, because I have something I need to do."

Rusty whistled and Tallboy grabbed Rook and put him in a headlock, and I beelined it toward Vivi. A few people tried to stop me as I made my way to her, but I was undeterred. Hell, I'd missed her so much, I wasn't going to wait one more minute to get to her.

She set down the dish towel in her hand and squared her shoulders like she was ready for an awkward encounter.

"Hey," she said. "I, um, I…"

I put my finger over her luscious lips and moved my face closer. "Do you really want to give this a try? You and me. No secrets?"

Her eyes searched mine. "Of course. Nothing's changed for me."

That was all I needed. My mouth came down over hers, right there in the middle of the Thomas' kitchen with everyone watching.

And I didn't give a shit.

My fingers tangled in her hair, and I kissed her hard.

"Someone call the fire department because this place is about to go up in flames," Dylan shouted, and I finally pulled away. Everyone laughed and whistled and cheered.

Jack snapped me on the back with a dish towel. "I gave you my blessing, but that did not mean that I wanted you to do that in the middle of the kitchen when I'm cooking a damn turkey."

More laughter.

Vivian's fingers interlaced with mine and her breaths were coming hard and fast as she led me out of the kitchen and down the hall toward her childhood bedroom.

She dropped to sit on her bed, and I sat beside her. I loved her room when I was young. She had neon stars on her ceiling and her bedding was gray with little pink flowers and everything just felt homey.

"So, that was a surprise," she said, turning to look at me.

"Well, I guess I'm full of surprises."

"What changed?" Her fingers traced the lines inside my palm.

"I missed you," I said, tipping her chin up to look at me. "I was just scared, Honey Bee. I don't want to hurt you or fuck this up."

"You won't. Nothing's really going to change, Niko. We already spend all our time together. We've been having sex and that has been," she paused and then laughed. "It's been amazing. Now we just don't have to keep it a secret."

"I like the sound of that. I just...fuck, Vivi, I want to give you everything you want, but I don't know that I can."

"Everything I want right now is right here. Don't get ahead of yourself. One day at a time, okay?"

"I love you so fucking much it hurts," I said, tipping her back on her bed and kissing her soft and slow.

"Um, I truly hate to break up this moment," Everly said from behind me, and I slowly lifted off of her sister. "But everyone is sitting down, and Rusty just pointed out to Dad that you two were missing, and I think he's about to come looking for you."

I pushed to my feet and pulled Vivian up with me. "We were just coming to dinner."

"Sure, you were," Everly said, and we all three hurried to the screened-in porch where everyone was sitting with their hands folded waiting for us. Candles lit up the outdoor space and orange and red flowers ran down the center of the table.

But it was awkward as shit the way they all stared at us, and I wasn't big on awkward moments.

"Oh god," Vivian whispered as her hand squeezed mine.

"Mr. West. Care to tell us where you two have been?" Rusty asked with a dumbass smirk on his face.

"I'm guessing the boy finally got off the bench. Let's eat," Gramps shouted, and everyone started talking at once and passing the platters around the table, and I'd never been so thankful for Gramps' lack of manners. Jace was holding Hadley in his arms as she'd just turned a year old a few weeks ago, and Paisley sat between Ashlan and Charlotte, and they took turns piling food on her plate. I was happy he'd decided to come, because he was going through a lot of personal shit and the dude usually shut everyone out when he was struggling. This was a good sign. He was moving forward.

Vivian passed me the stuffing and she bit down on her juicy bottom lip, and I nearly came undone right there at the table.

"Don't tease me, Honey Bee. It won't end well for either of us," I whispered in her ear, grazing my lips along her sensitive skin, and she shivered.

"So, Vivi, what do you think about Rook here asking Jada

out? Niko didn't have much to say about the matter, so we thought maybe you could help him out, seeing as she works for you," Tallboy said before biting into a dinner roll and winking at me.

The fucker.

Vivian glanced at me and smiled. "Why don't you come by the bakery on Saturday? She'll be working."

Rook nodded and looked over at me. I didn't give any indication if I was okay with it, but he was a nice guy, and it would probably be good for Jada to be around someone like him. He wasn't a huge drinker or partier. The dude did have a wild hair for digital games, but I didn't see anything wrong with that.

"Okay. Can we stop talking about it now, Tallboy?" Rook hissed under his breath, but we all heard him, and the table erupted in laughter.

"So, Dylan. How about you? You ever consider dating a firefighter? Especially a good-looking one like myself?" Rusty asked, and Vivian covered her face with both hands and groaned.

"Rusty, do you not remember that you dated my best friend in high school, and you cheated on her? I suggest you take your business elsewhere. This shop is closed for business. Are you picking up what I'm putting down?" Dylan said, one eyebrow raised, and he just laughed.

"Rusty, did you really just ask my daughter out at the dinner table at my house? For God's sake, I've got this one disappearing down the hall with one daughter," he flicked his thumb in my direction. "And then you come out of left field. Can I please just enjoy my dinner?"

"Sorry, Cap. Apparently, I need to learn to read the room better," Rusty said over a mouthful of potatoes.

Tallboy was doubled over laughing, and Big Al shook his

head and shrugged. And I was exactly where I wanted to be.

And for the first time in as long as I could remember, I was content.

Happy even.

My hand found Vivi's beneath the table and I held on like my life depended on it.

Because in a way...it did.

Chapter 19

Vivian

"I can't believe you made me leave my car there. We wouldn't have been apart for long. It's a two-minute drive." I laughed as we pulled into my driveway. Niko had insisted I ride with him. Now that he'd come to his damn senses, he didn't want to spend a minute apart unless we had to. He'd stayed by my side throughout dinner, and even when I'd left to help with the dishes, I'd found his eyes on me every time I looked up.

"It took me a while to get here, Honey Bee." He turned to look at me, and I moved closer, as his arms came around me.

"I'm glad you stopped running. Now hopefully you'll stay awhile," I said, and he barked out a laugh.

"That's the plan." He pushed his door open and pulled me into his arms, my legs coming around his waist and my boots clanking together behind him.

"You do know that I can walk, right?" I chuckled.

"I like carrying you. Like letting the world know that

you're mine."

My stomach dipped at his words. Nothing had really changed in my mind. Not my feelings for him or the way I knew he felt about me, but he'd finally accepted it and that meant we actually had a chance.

"I think I've always been yours, Niko West," I said, reaching for my key and shoving it in the door.

Once we were inside, he carried me to the couch and dropped me down and I bounced. He pulled off his coat and then reached for my boots.

I pushed to my feet and shoved him down, and his eyes widened with surprise.

"I like taking care of you too," I said, untying his snow boots and pulling them off one at a time.

"Do you, Honey Bee?"

"I do," I whispered as I climbed on his lap, straddling him as I unzipped my coat and let it fall to the floor.

"How do you want to take care of me, beautiful?" His hands rested on my waist as I leaned down to kiss him.

"Like this," I whispered against his mouth.

We sat there making out on the couch for what felt like forever. I was so worked up I'd never been so desperate for more. My hands found the hem of his sweater and slipped beneath. I loved the feel of his muscled stomach and chest beneath my fingertips. He raised his arms and I pulled back to tug his sweater over his head. His gray gaze locked with mine.

He reached for my sweater and slipped it easily over my head, as his hand came around my back in one swift move and unsnapped my bra. His mouth covered my breast and I arched closer, tangling my hands in his hair. His mouth moved to the other breast, and a moan escaped my lips before I could stop it.

He chuckled against my skin, and it only made me want to do the same thing to him that he was doing to me.

I lifted up enough to reach his waistband and I unbuttoned his jeans, and he continued his slow torture, kissing his way back and forth between my breasts. I maneuvered his pants down just enough that I could grip his erection and catch him by surprise. His head popped up and his eyes were wild.

"You taking control, Honey Bee?"

"Are you going to let me?"

"I'm yours. Have your way with me." His deep voice was smooth and silky.

"I'd like that. I'm calling the shots tonight," I whispered in his ear.

I hopped off of his lap and reached for his hand, and he let his jeans and boxers fall to the floor before I led him to the bedroom. I walked right to the nightstand and grabbed a condom, tearing off the top with my teeth, just like he'd done dozens of times when we'd been together. He dropped to sit on the bed as he watched me roll the latex over his erection.

I stepped back, his eyes never leaving mine. I pushed my jeans down my legs and kicked them off, before slowly sliding my lace panties off too. His hands were fisted on the bed as if it took all his restraint not to step in and do it himself.

I moved toward him, urging him to scoot back on the bed as I climbed on and straddled him. I positioned myself exactly where I knew he wanted me, before slowly sliding down, inch by inch.

His hands gripped my hips, but he let me set the pace. His gaze locked with mine as I leaned down to kiss him, as I took a minute and adjusted to his size once again. I started to move, and he groaned into my mouth. The sound was so erotic, I fought the urge to pick up the pace, but I stayed the course. I pulled away from his mouth and started to move quicker as he watched me intently. His hands moved to cup my breasts and we found our rhythm. His hand came down between us, touching me where I needed him most. My hands reached for his free hand, our fingers intertwining as I cried out his name. He moved once, twice, three more times before he went right over the edge with me. Our breaths and gasps and moans were the only audible sound as we both rode out our pleasure. I fell forward because I couldn't hold myself up any longer, and he wrapped his arms around me and rolled us both to our sides facing one another.

"You okay?" he asked, and the smirk on his face made me smile.

"I'm good. How about you?"

"That was something. You can take charge any time you want." He stroked my hair and just watched me as I waited for my breathing to calm down.

He pulled out of me and made his way to the bathroom to dispose of the condom. I was so sated and relaxed I couldn't move if I wanted to. He slipped back in bed beside me as if he could read my mind, and he pulled me against his chest and wrapped his arms around me, as his fingers ran up and down my back in the most soothing way.

"I'm so sleepy," I whispered.

"Sleep, Honey Bee."

• • •

The next day we'd both been off work, so we'd slept in before having morning sex in bed, followed by morning sex in the shower. Every time with Niko felt like the first time because it just kept getting better even after I thought nothing could ever compare.

I had just slipped on some leggings and a sweater and made my way out to the kitchen because something smelled good.

"What are you making?" I asked as I came around the counter and glanced around at the mess. He wore a pair of navy joggers slung low on his hips, his chest bare and his hair a wild mess. I licked my lips as I watched him, still trying to grasp the fact that he was mine.

"Pancakes."

"You know I have pancake mix, right? You made them from scratch?" I said over my laughter.

He flicked some flour at me that was sitting on the counter and then pulled a plate out of the oven with a pile of golden-brown pancakes and set them down on the little island that had two barstools on the other side. It was where I ate most of my meals.

"Sit, smart-ass. I was trying to impress my girl. She owns a bakery," he said as he moved around the island and motioned for me to sit on the stool beside him. There were two glasses of orange juice there, two plates and utensils.

"Wow. I've heard your girl is kind of a sure thing when it comes to you. I don't think you have to go to such trouble." I poured syrup all over the stack he put on my plate and cut a large bite and shoved it in my mouth. "Holy wowzers. These are damn good," I said over a mouthful of pancake.

He chuckled as he took an oversized bite himself and nodded.

He pointed toward the large windows looking out at the lake. It was my favorite feature of this house. The entire wall was windows, and the snow was falling so hard it looked like a white winter wonderland out there.

"So, you're off today, huh?" he asked.

"Yeah. Will you go with me to pick out a tree?" I went

every year the day after Thanksgiving, and I'd grown up with that tradition. Jansen had always been in town, so this wasn't something that Niko and I had shared, and he'd always been more distant during the holidays anyway.

He cleared his throat. "Sure."

"You've never been a fan of Christmas. I think it's time we change that." I forked another bite and wrapped my mouth around the delicious goodness.

"Not sure it's something I can change, but it doesn't mean I can't help you pick out a tree." He stared out the window.

"How do you feel about your dad coming home this week?"

"Honestly?" He dropped his fork on his plate and reached for his juice. After he set his glass back down, he turned to look at me. "I wish he wasn't coming back. It's been six years since he left, and I don't miss anything about that man."

I nodded. "Do you think he'll be different? I mean, he has to be clean, right? He's been in prison, so it's not like he can drink. And won't he have a probation officer keeping an eye on him once he's out?"

"I don't think someone as evil as he is, is capable of change. And today, Honey Bee, you can get anything you want in prison, so no, I don't think he's totally cleaned up." He paused then said, "He wanted me to take the fall for the accident. I don't think I ever told you that."

"What do you mean?" I reached for his hands. I loved Niko's hands. They were big and strong and rough, yet they comforted me every time I needed it.

"That night he fled the scene. I'd just come home from football practice, and he came running into the house. He was all battered and bleeding, and he grabbed me and said that when the police came to the house, I needed to say that I was driving that car. The police showed up less than a minute later and they arrested him. He was screaming that I had driven the car and I told the officers that I'd just come from practice. I wasn't going to lie for that asshole and ruin my life for him. My mother stayed silent which I'm sure didn't make him happy. Hell, I felt relieved the day they took him away. Even if it messed up my plans for college, it was one of the best days of my life."

"What kind of man asks his son to take the fall for him?" I whispered, hopping off the stool and moving to stand between his legs and wrapping my arms around his middle and hugging him tight.

"A monster, Honey Bee. That's exactly what he is."

We stood like that in the kitchen for a little while before he kissed the top of my head. "Okay, that's enough of that. Let's go get you a tree and I'll even help you decorate it. I shoveled your drive while you were getting ready so we should be able to get out okay."

I squealed, because nothing could put you in the mood for the holidays like playing Christmas music and decorating your tree.

"Okay. Let's stop by the bakery and pick up some cookies to decorate too. I made a ton and didn't have time to frost them."

He chuckled. "How about you decorate them, and I'll eat them."

"No way." I raised a brow and slipped my coat on and then reached for my boots. "You're decorating too. They taste better when you know how long they took to make."

"Ridiculous." He pulled a beanie over his head and zipped up his navy down jacket.

We made our way outside to head to his truck and I hurried around the side where he'd piled the snow and made a snowball and then ran to the front of the truck and hurled it at him—it landed against the side of his head.

I laughed so hard I nearly fell over, and then a blur out of my periphery had me gasping as he came at me fast and pulled me against him and dove toward the mound of snow and we both fell to the ground in a bed of white fluffy powder. He rubbed his nose against mine and I chuckled.

"Don't play dirty, Honey Bee."

"What? You can't take a little snowball to the head?"

"Oh, I can take it. But paybacks are coming your way. I'll be the one in charge tonight." He wriggled his brows, and I squeezed my thighs together because just the thought of what he had planned for me had my body reacting in all sorts of ways.

He barked out a laugh. "Come on. If we don't leave now, I'll have you naked in about thirty seconds. That wouldn't be very Christmassy of me, would it?"

"Nope." He stood and pulled me to my feet. "But it's not a horrible idea."

"Get in the truck." He opened the door and then lifted me in, and I didn't put up a fight. He leaned forward and kissed me hard as he buckled me in.

Kissed me breathless.

And all I wanted was more.

Chapter 20

Niko

I hauled the tree into her house, and I got all her decorations out of her attic for her while she set up the cookies that she wanted us to decorate. I'd started a fire in the small fireplace in her living room, because I was freezing my balls off. The snow was coming down hard and I was happy that we were done for the day with outings.

I got the tree up in the stand and she clapped. It didn't take much to make Vivi happy and I'd always appreciated how much she cared about the little things. Most people didn't give a shit. But Vivi had always been different.

She opened the boxes of ornaments and started hanging them, while I dropped onto her couch and watched. I sipped the hot chocolate that she'd made, and the fire roared in front of me as I watched her. It all felt very...normal.

I'd never had a lot of normalcy in my life, but times like these with Vivian made me wonder if I could have them. I'd spent so much of my life in survival mode that I didn't know how to just be in the moment.

But I was doing it right now, and it felt damn good.

"This was the one my mom got me when I got my braces off." She held up the ornament with a girl smiling wide with white teeth and it had her name and the date that her braces came off.

She'd had an ornament from her mother every year since she'd been born. There was a golf ornament and one with a little cheerleader on it for her brief stints in the sports. I'd always loved Vivian's mom. She was everything a mother should be. She loved her girls fiercely and their family had always reminded me of something you'd see in a movie.

"Are the holidays harder? I know she loved this time of year," I asked as I watched her hang the ornament and then step back to look at it.

She came to sit by me on the couch. "I think about her every day, but the holidays make my heart ache for her, because she loved them so much."

I reached for her and pulled her onto my lap. It pissed me off. Guys like my dad who had no business being a parent, living a reckless life, and he gets to live. He gets to get out of prison and come home. And Beth Thomas doesn't get to see her girls graduate college or get married.

How fucked up is that?

"I'm sorry. She left this world way too soon."

"Yeah, she did. The only saving grace is that we were at least able to prepare for it. Cancer just isn't fair though, is it?"

"No. It's not. Does it help having all of your sisters home right now?"

She pulled back and looked at me. "It does. But do you know what is helping the most?"

"What?"

"Being with you. It's honestly the happiest I've felt since my mom died, Niko. *This*." She reached for my hand and intertwined our fingers. "This makes me happy."

I pulled her back against me and hugged her tight.

"This makes me happy too."

Now I just had to figure out how to not fuck it all up.

• • •

The weekend had come and gone way too fast. We'd brought Mabel over to Vivian's house to see the tree and eat cookies, and we'd built a gigantic snowman in the backyard out by the lake.

I was on duty the next three days and after the weekend we'd had, I didn't want to spend a night away from Vivi. The girl was turning my world upside down, and I just wanted more.

"Niko, you've got a visitor." Big Al cleared his throat as I pulled a hoodie over my head and studied him.

"Who is it?"

"Your father. He's downstairs. Wasn't sure if you'd want me to invite him inside or send him away."

"You did the right thing. I'll handle it," I said, reaching for my beanie and heading down to the ground floor.

He sat on a chair beside the fire truck like he didn't have a care in the world. He looked the same, maybe a little older.

"What are you doing here?" I asked as I crossed my arms over my chest and looked down at him.

He pushed to his feet. We were the same size, and I probably had an inch on the guy now. He was no longer looking down at me. I wasn't the little kid he used to beat up on, and I squared my shoulders, happy to make sure he knew it.

"Your old man can't come by to let you know I'm home?"

"There's no need. I knew you were coming," I said, looking

for signs of alcohol and drugs, but I didn't see any. His hair was cut close to his head just like it used to be, but now it had gray hair mixed in with the brown.

"Yeah, that's what I heard. You don't think my own daughter and granddaughter should be living there with me and your mom? You calling the shots now, Niko?" He moved closer and I did not back up.

My hands fisted at my sides, and it took all the restraint I had not to knock him out. Not to beat the shit out of him for all the shit he'd done to me growing up.

"I'm just keeping them safe. I obviously have my reasons. Or did you forget all that while you were rotting in a cell?"

"I didn't forget shit. And I came by to make sure you know that I'll be calling the shots for my family moving forward," he hissed.

"Good luck with that." I nodded, my expression hard.

He moved closer, hands balled up and ready to fight, an attempt to intimidate me. *It wasn't working.*

"You stay out of my business."

"Careful, old man. I'm not the little boy I used to be. You won't be pounding your fists into someone who can't fight back. I will not hesitate to beat the living shit out of you. In fact, I'm begging you to throw the first punch."

He chuckled and turned to walk away.

"That's what I thought," I said. "Get the fuck out of here and don't come back."

"Niko," he called out and he turned around with a wicked grin spread across his face. "Don't worry about not helping your old man out when you could have saved my ass years ago. You clearly have no loyalty to your family, but I let that shit go."

A maniacal laugh escaped my mouth. "It's good to know that

prison didn't change the asshole that you are. I thought maybe you'd realize that asking your kid to take the fall for your crime was a piece of shit thing to do, but obviously, we aren't there yet."

"You think you can judge me because you're—what? A fucking fireman in this shit town? You're no better than me. And I'm back now. I'll be happy to remind you of what a piece of shit you are every day moving forward."

"You're trespassing," a voice said from behind me, and I turned to see Cap standing there with a few of the guys behind him. "I believe your son asked you to leave. I'm here to tell you that you aren't welcome back."

"Ah...good ole Jack Thomas. I hear my boy is dating your girl. Sweet thing that Vivian always was. She seemed a little afraid of me though if I'm remembering right. I'm sure she's looking fine now that she's all grown up, am I right?" I charged him, but I was yanked back before I got there. Rusty and Tallboy were each holding an arm and their faces were bright red with anger. They wanted to punch the fucker too, but they knew it would only get us into trouble.

"Don't even fucking say her name," I shouted, and Cap moved beside me.

"You ever mention my daughter again, and I will let these guys unleash your son on you. I wouldn't wish that on my worst enemy, but here we are."

My father held his hands up and smirked. "I meant no offense. Just pointing out the obvious. I'll see you boys around. Why don't you stop by the house sometime soon, Niko? I need someone to shovel the drive."

"Keep talking, old man. I think it might be time to pay a visit to your probation officer. Offer to help him keep an eye on you," I said, and that was the first time I saw him falter for just a moment before his face hardened again and he turned and walked away.

"Fuck," I said under my breath. "That asshole is bad news. Always was, always will be."

"Do you have a way to reach out to his probation officer?" Gramps asked, and I turned around to see him standing behind me.

"No."

"I'm on it. I've got a friend who works over there. I'll make a call." He walked away and Rusty and Tallboy dropped my arms.

"Sorry about that, buddy," they said at the same time.

I couldn't speak. I was too angry. I just nodded and Jack told everyone to get back to work. I walked the other direction, out toward the street to make sure he was gone. Jack followed me.

"He just said her name to get under your skin. He's not going to do anything. It would be a one-way ticket right back to prison," he said.

"Agreed. But I wouldn't put anything past him. I definitely want to talk to his probation officer, but I think I'll call Brady down at the station and ask him to keep an eye on the bakery and Vivi's house just as a precaution." I'd grown up with Brady Townsend and he was a police officer now, and he'd always been a good guy.

"That's a good idea." Jack clapped me on the shoulder. "He's not going to be out long, Niko. You just need to bide your time. The way he was just talking…that's a guy that's ready to be back behind bars."

I scrubbed a hand down the back of my neck. "That would be the best outcome. I can't believe he fucking came here. The guy is just looking for a fight."

He'd come to the right place.

If he wanted a fight, he'd get one.

•••

I couldn't wait to get to Vivian's when I left the firehouse. She said she had a surprise for me, and I hoped she was cooking dinner naked. When I got to her door, I groaned when I found the handle unlocked.

"Why is the fuck…" I stopped speaking when Mabel came charging toward me.

"Neek, Neek! I missed you."

I scooped her up and kissed her cheek. "What are you doing here, little bug?"

"Mama had a date with a fire guy like you. Miss Vivi picked me up from school and we're making you supper."

"Is that so?" I asked as I set her on her feet and made my way into the kitchen. Vivian was stirring something on the stove and turned to look at me. Her lips turned up in the corners and a heavy feeling hit my chest like it did every time I saw her lately.

"That door was unlocked," I said, moving closer as she dropped the spoon on the counter and looked up at me.

"Because we just went outside to get the mail and you called and said you were on your way." She raised a brow, daring me to challenge her. "I set the alarm last night, and I appreciate you having that set up for me even if I don't think it's necessary."

"It's necessary, Honey Bee." I wrapped my arms around her and breathed in all that goodness. "What's the little nugget doing here? I thought I'd have you naked by now."

She laughed and tipped her head back to look up at me. "Rook and Jada are going to swing by here after dinner to pick her up on their way home."

"Wow. The dude moved fast. I didn't think he'd have the nerve to ask her out."

"He did. He was really sweet too. She seemed nervous and he offered to pick her up and then said they could grab Mabel on the way back to her house."

"That was sweet of you." I leaned down and kissed her hard. "Damn, I missed you, baby."

"Yuck. No kissin' in the kitchen, Neek, Neek," Mabel shrieked from behind me.

I barked out a laugh. "Who made up that rule?"

"I don't think Miss Vivi likes kissing in the kitchen. We washed our hands before we made you some cookies. But we didn't do no kissin'."

Vivian chuckled. "She is right about that. Kissing has no place in the kitchen, Neek, Neek. Who's ready to eat?"

Mabel jumped up and down and nearly lost her balance and fell over before I hurried over to steady her on her feet.

I helped Vivian carry the pasta and garlic bread to the small table between the kitchen and the family room. The snow was still falling, and the fire roared in front of us.

I helped Mabel into her chair after I set the food down and I scooped some spaghetti onto her plate. Vivian came to sit across from me, and the heated gaze in her eyes had me anxious to get her alone.

Mabel took an enormous bite of noodles and decided to speak at the same time. "Don't you love Miss Vivi's tree? Mama needs to get us a tree," she said.

"Hey, weren't you just preaching about rules and no kissing? How about no talking with your mouth full, princess."

She started laughing which made Vivian laugh. I leaned over and wiped Mabel's mouth with her napkin.

"Princesses sometimes talk with their mouths full. 'Cause they got so excited."

"That's a true story," Vivi said, winking at me.

We finished eating and I came up behind her while she was doing the dishes. "I can't wait to get you alone."

"Oh yeah?" she asked, turning around in my arms while Mabel colored at the table. "What do you have in mind?"

"I'm going to bury my face between your legs, for starters. That's why I skipped dessert," I said, leaning close to her and nipping at her ear.

She pulled back, one hand on each side of my face, and smiled. "You ate four cookies. You hardly skipped dessert."

"I saved the best for last," I said as the doorbell rang, and I pulled back. "It's about damn time."

She swatted me with the towel, and I held my hands up. "I'm kidding."

I helped Mabel pack up all the art supplies that Vivi kept here for her. I had a feeling my niece was spending more time here than I knew.

Vivian pulled the door open, and Rook stood there nervously with my sister beside him. He held up a hand. "Hey, Niko."

"You haven't been drinking, have you?" I moved closer and sniffed in his vicinity. "You're not driving my niece if you have."

"Um, thank you?" Jada hissed because I wasn't showing her the same concern.

"You're a grown-up. You can make choices for yourself. She can't."

"I had a Dr. Pepper at dinner," Rook said with a chuckle.

I grabbed Mabel's blanket and shoved it in her backpack. "Great. See you later."

Jada narrowed her gaze and Vivian closed her eyes because apparently, I was embarrassing her.

"Love you too, brother dearest." Jada kissed my cheek and

Mabel gave me one last hug.

"Drive safe," I said, and Rook nodded before waving goodbye.

"I thought they'd never fucking leave," I hissed when she shut the door.

"Really? You basically blocked them from coming in. You made it very obvious," Vivian said over her laughter. "And it's freaking snowing out there."

"They're fine. Rook fights fires in the snow." I scooped her up and pressed her back to the door. "Missed you, Honey Bee."

"Missed you too," she said with a grin spread clear across her face.

"Now spread those pretty little legs for me and let me make you feel good." I dropped to my knees.

It was exactly where I wanted to be.

Worshipping the woman that I loved.

Chapter 21

Vivian

I was shoveling my walkway after work when Brady Townsend drove by and waved. For the third time this week. I reached for my cell phone from my back pocket, pulled off my mittens, and dialed him.

"Hey, Vivi," he said. We'd grown up together and we'd remained good friends.

"Did Niko tell you to drive by my house? I noticed you coming by the bakery more than usual lately too," I said, setting the shovel on the ground.

"Can't a guy come get some baked goods without getting called out for it?" He chuckled.

"Don't lie to me, Brady. Remember I'm the one who set you up with Victoria. You said you owed me one, right?" I knew he and Niko were close friends. Always had been.

"He's just worried, Vivi. Give the guy a break. You know what a monster his father is. He's stuck at the firehouse, and he's worried about you."

I sighed. I understood it to an extent. But he'd had an alarm system installed and I hadn't even seen Billy West since he'd gotten out of prison over a week ago. Niko was in touch with his probation officer, and he hadn't had to see him again since the day he'd come to the firehouse and made a scene.

"I've got the alarm and I'm totally fine. Thanks for checking in." We said our goodbyes and I immediately dialed Niko because the thought of him being that concerned bothered me.

"Hey, Honey Bee. Everything okay?"

"Yeah. I'm just shoveling the driveway and thinking of you. Wishing you were here."

"You have no idea how badly I wish I was sleeping next to you tonight instead of listening to Rusty's ass snore," he said.

"I can hear you, douchedick," Rusty shouted. "Sorry I don't spoon you as good as Vivian."

"Rusty, what is with you constantly bringing up my daughters?" My father's voice followed, and I couldn't help but laugh.

"Look what you started," I said.

He must have walked away because it got quieter. "I'll shovel the rest of your driveway in two days when I'm off. Get inside and lock up, okay?"

I shook my head but didn't let him know that I thought he was being ridiculous. "Okay. I promise I'm fine. I think Dylan and Charlie are going to come over and watch a movie tonight." Ashlan had left to go back to school this morning and Everly had flown to Chicago for a few days to interview with a hockey team there.

"Good. Just make sure the alarm is set when they leave."

"I will," I said. "Love you, Niko."

"Love you more, Honey Bee."

I ended the call and moved to the other side of the driveway where the snow was piling up. The snow had finally stopped falling so it was a perfect time to get out there and get the driveway cleaned up.

I was just piling the last scoop when I heard my name. The sun had gone down behind the mountains, but it was still light enough for me to see just fine. I turned around to see Billy West standing right on the edge of my driveway.

"It's Vivian, right?" he asked.

I'd grown up living just a few doors down from this man, yet I'd always avoided him. Even before Niko started telling me about the abuse that went on. He'd always given me a bad feeling, and that hadn't changed.

"Yes." I stood with the shovel in front of me, positioning my fingers around the handle in case I needed to pick it up and swing.

"You always were a scared little girl, weren't ya?" he said, and his voice had an edge to it. He was big and tall in stature like Niko, but his eyes were ice blue and there was no warmth there at all.

"I've never been scared, nor am I scared now. I'm just trying to figure out what you're doing here." I squared my shoulders and looked him right in the eyes.

"Can't a man walk to town without being accused of a crime?" He laughed, but there was no sincerity there. Shayla West had moved off of our street after Niko's father went to prison and sized down to a smaller home. The house sat on the other side of downtown from mine, so if he were walking to town, he wasn't coming from his house.

"Of course, he can. Have a good day." I backed away from him but didn't turn around because I wanted to keep my eye on him and make sure he kept moving along. I'd been raised by a firefighter who taught his daughters how to protect themselves since the day we took our first steps.

He laughed again. "Look at you. Keeping your eye on the big bad wolf. I'm not going to hurt you, Vivian. Maybe you should worry more about Niko. Out there fighting fires. You never know when one will take him away from you, right?"

I narrowed my gaze and fought back the urge to strike him with my shovel. "You need to leave, now. I can have the police here in about two minutes, and I doubt that would fare well for you with your probation officer."

He nodded and looked away for a minute before looking back at me. "Let's hope there aren't any fires tonight. How would my boy watch out for you if he was tending to a big, bad fire, huh?"

Was he threatening Niko? Me?

I pulled my phone from my pocket and pretended I was dialing, and he started moving along with a laugh. "See ya later, Vivian Thomas. You best get inside where it's safe."

I moved forward and watched as he disappeared down the street before I hurried into the house, leaving the shovel on the front porch. I locked the door and dialed my sisters.

Dylan and Charlotte were there in a matter of minutes. I filled them in on the conversation and they both hugged me tight.

"That guy has always been such a creep," Dylan said. "He's one taco short of a combination platter."

"Yeah. I've always gotten a bad feeling from him." Charlotte hugged me tighter. "I think we should call Dad and Niko."

"No. They'll both worry and Niko's on duty, so he'll freak out because he's not here. Billy didn't do anything. I think he just likes to mess with people."

"Fine. But when you see him next and he's off, you need to

give him a heads-up that the crazy-ass is talking smack," Dylan said as she moseyed over to my kitchen and reached for a cookie.

Charlotte chuckled. "Well, I'd word it a little differently, but I agree. So, let's order takeout and watch a movie."

"I'm in the mood for Italian. And Rocco's has that cute delivery guy, so let's order from there."

"The cute delivery guy is Byron Jones. He's so young. He just graduated from high school," Charlotte said as her mouth gaped open.

"He's a mature eighteen. The guy looks like he's twenty-five. And I didn't say I was robbing the cradle, I just said he was easy on the eyes. After the run-in with creepy jailbird, Billy West, I think we could all use a little Byron Jones."

"You are such a dirty bird," I said over my laughter. "And need I remind you that Byron's mom was your kindergarten teacher. I doubt she'd appreciate you drooling over her son. But, with that said, I'll take the lasagna."

"Why must you ruin everything for me? Damn. I forgot about sweet Mrs. Jones. Although she did send me home from school once for unjust reasons."

"You kicked Mike Harkins in the balls," Charlotte gasped before falling over in laughter. "The poor guy had shoved a bead up his nose and asked you for help."

"I was trying to help, which is why her actions were unjust. I remembered hearing that if something hurt, like say you got stung by a bee on your hand. If someone punched you in the shoulder, you would forget about the bee's sting. I thought if I kicked him in the balls, he would stop whining about the bead that was shoved up his nostril."

We were all three laughing hysterically as Dylan placed our order online.

"Did your theory work?" I asked when I finally pulled it together.

"It sure did. Little Mikey was holding his sea monster for dear life, crying about me kicking him where the sun don't shine. And I paid the ultimate price by being sent home."

"What happened to the bead?" I remembered hearing about it back then, but I couldn't remember what happened because my parents were furious with Dylan for kicking the poor boy.

"Well, once he stopped fussing about his balls being on fire, Mrs. Jones asked why he sounded so nasally, and I shouted about him shoving that bead up his nose. I mean if I was going down for the crime, he should at least be held accountable for his part." Dylan set her phone down and smirked.

"He ended up at the hospital and they removed the bead. Do you remember, Dilly? He brought it in that little jar for show-and-share the following day."

"Oh, I remember just fine. Mom had sent me to my room right after dinner that night. She never yelled. But she let it be known that she was disappointed in me, which was worse. I begged Dad to just spank me, but they both refused. They said violence was never the answer. And stinking Mikey Harkins was treated like a freaking celebrity the following day at school. For what? Shoving a bead up his nose and taking a knee to his Johnson?"

Laughter boomed around the room again. Everything was always better when my sisters were around.

"Hey, I think Mike Harkins is single. I guess he and Colette broke up a few months ago," Charlotte said.

"I could never go there. Not after he let me take the fall when I was just trying to help him. He turned me in so fast, my head spun."

We spent the next half hour arguing over what movie we

would watch and settled on a rom-com, which was exactly what I needed to take my mind off of things.

The doorbell rang, and Dylan leaned forward and flipped her blonde hair over her head before whipping her head up and patting her hair into place as Charlotte and I both rolled our eyes.

"What? Flirting is my second language." She made her way to the door.

"I thought it was sarcasm?" Charlotte yelled.

"Fine. I'm fluent in both." She pulled the door open, and Byron Jones stood there holding a bag full of goodness. I hadn't seen him in a while, and damn, if my sister wasn't right. He stood a little over six feet tall, blonde shaggy hair fell around his face, and he smiled wide.

"Dylan Thomas. Say it isn't so," he purred.

"Byron Jones...it is so. Thanks for delivering dinner."

He handed her the bag and Charlotte and I watched them shamelessly flirt like it was the movie we'd selected. They bantered back and forth, making ridiculous small talk while my sister batted her lashes and flipped her hair over her shoulder.

"All right. Here you go." She handed him some cash and winked. "Don't spend it all in one place."

"I won't. You call again real soon, okay?" he said before Dylan pushed the door closed.

"Isn't he so hot?" she asked when she turned to face us and set the bag on the table.

"Ummm, I need some lessons on upping my flirt game. I'm actually sweating from watching that go down." Charlotte moved toward the kitchen and grabbed three plates and set them on the table.

"Please. That was nothing. If he were a few years older, I'd be all over that."

I barked out a laugh. "All over that? Who talks like that? Anyway, in a few years, the age difference won't matter."

"Good point." Dylan forked her spaghetti, twirling it around until she popped it in her mouth. We started the movie and watched it while we ate.

"I'm so full, I can't eat another bite," Charlotte said when all three of our phones started vibrating at the same time.

That was never a good thing. Not when you were a fire family.

"Oh no. The warehouse on Jefferson is on fire," Dylan whispered.

My stomach dipped and I looked down to see a text from Niko.

Niko: Don't worry, Honey Bee. We'll be fine. I'll call you after I get back.

"Lottie just messaged that it's a bad one. She's heading down there," Charlotte whispered. That was serious if Big Al's wife thought it was dangerous.

"Get your coats. We're going too." I hurried to get my beanie and my gloves, and we were in Dylan's car in no time.

"It's going to be fine," Dylan said over and over as I stared out the window.

"You guys don't think Billy West could have started this fire, do you? It's weird that he said something, right?" I fidgeted with my hands, unable to slow the increasing anxiety that was building.

"Let's first make sure everyone's okay. We don't even know if it was electrical or something like that. Don't let your mind get ahead of you."

I looked up to see the red, orange, and yellow flames lighting up the black sky. Smoke billowed around it, but it was by far the biggest fire I'd ever laid eyes on. Tears broke free and rolled down my cheek as Dylan pulled in behind all the fire trucks. There were police cars and paramedics, as everyone had come out to help.

"I don't have a good feeling about this." I shoved the door open and hurried out.

We found Lottie first. "This fire is out of control, girls. They've called in backups, but it'll take a while before the crew from Westberg gets here."

I scanned the area just as Big Al and Jace came out with someone slumped against them. "We need a medic!" he shouted, and I felt my knees wobble beneath me.

"Oh my god. It's Rusty," Dylan said, as we tried to move closer, but the police had the area roped off so we couldn't go any farther.

My heart sank as I looked up at the building engulfed in flames.

And there was no sign of my father or Niko.

Chapter 22

Niko

I'd been in a lot of fires in my time, but none had ever been like this. We just couldn't seem to get control of it, and I was thankful that backup was on the way. Rusty had taken a bad fall as the floor beneath us had given out. Cap, Tallboy, and I moved together, putting out the fire on the west side of the building as best we could. The warehouse stood three stories high, and the only reason we continued to move through this hell was because we'd been told there were two guys working on the top floor that had been trapped in the fire. The four guys down below had already been safely evacuated.

"We need to get out of here," Tallboy shouted as the walls started to creak in an eerie way that only happened when fire breathed through an open space.

"Help," someone called out from what seemed to be a few feet up ahead. I wasn't sure I was hearing it right, because when fire blazed, the sounds it made could often be confused. The smoke surrounding us was growing unbearable.

"Did you hear that?" I asked.

"I did. Tallboy, you just use the line and do what you can to tone this down and Niko and I will try to get back there," Cap shouted.

Tallboy held the hose in his hands and started aiming it in the direction that we were moving.

"I'll lead," I said. I promised Vivi I'd always have her father's back when we were fighting fires, and I'd always honored my word. This man was like a father to me, and I'd never allow him to get hurt as long as I was by his side.

Regardless of what that meant.

Cap nodded and I forged ahead. The heat nearly took my breath away, but the voice calling out for help grew clearer. I motioned with my hand to keep going in that direction and I made my way to the door. Tallboy was behind us, aiming the line at the threatening flames as we moved in the direction of a door where the voice continued to beg for help.

"In here." I stood back as I watched him aim the hose and blast it as best he could.

I knew time was running out, and as I checked the door before kicking into it with a force, I pictured my girl in the back of my head. Thoughts of Vivi flooded me as I found two men huddled in the corner. Cap and Tallboy were behind me, and Cap was shouting to someone over the speaker system urging them to bring the ladder around to the west side of the building. We weren't going to be able to get them out the way we came in. We'd be exiting through the window and our only hope was that they could get the ladder up on this side, as most of the building was up in flames. We helped them to their feet, and I stepped over to the window and saw the ladder coming our way from down below. It was our only exit strategy, as the balconies on the stories below us were already on fire. Several lines were brought over as they sprayed at the flames that would be trying to halt us from coming down.

This wasn't my first time in this situation, but it never got easier. Not when other people's lives depended on you. Not when you finally had something important to live for.

Vivian.

"They've got the ladder. We need to move quickly," I shouted as we helped the first guy over to the ladder. Tallboy assisted him to step out. Flames blazed around him as I watched him descend.

"Fuck. I don't know if I can do that," the other man cried out as I glanced at the door to see the fire coming dangerously close.

"You don't have a fucking choice. Go." He and Cap moved quickly out the window, and Tallboy used the line to try to hold back the flames. The guys were doing all that they could from below as well, but I could hear the shouting and the concern, and I knew that they couldn't control this growing fire for much longer.

"Drop the line and go," I shouted at Tallboy.

He didn't fight me. He was out the window and the minute he was halfway down the ladder I practically dove through the window as flames engulfed the room that we were in. I caught up to Tallboy as I hurried down the rungs, being chased by flames that showed no grace to those who wavered. The guys down below were spraying the building, and everything blurred as I saw a few more fire trucks pull up at the scene.

Thank Christ.

The building sat too close to the forest behind it, and we couldn't risk this moving in that direction. Tallboy fell to the ground, and I jumped from about six feet up so they could take the ladder down.

It was chaos below and I looked back at the building completely overtaken by flames and wondered how the hell we made it out of there.

"How's Rusty?" I asked Cap as he came over to stand beside me.

"He's going to be fine. They have him in the ambulance. I think the fall just knocked the wind out of him."

"Jack, can you give us an update?" Ray said as he walked over. He was the captain from the Westberg fire department, one town over.

Cap and Ray stepped aside as I moved toward the truck and pulled off my mask as they moved in. I was happy for the reprieve as I reached for a bottle of water and chugged it.

"Niko," Vivian cried out and I turned around to see her running toward me.

"What are you doing here? You shouldn't be this close to the fire," I said, looking around to see that they had the area roped off, but that clearly didn't stop the Thomas girls from getting in. Dylan and Charlotte stood off waiting to speak to their father.

"It doesn't matter. Are you okay?"

"I'm fine." I pushed the hair out of her face and kissed the tip of her pink nose. It was cold as fuck out here, and she didn't need to be anywhere near this fire. "You need to head back home. It's going to be a late night."

"I need to tell you something," she said as she wrapped her arms around my middle and hugged me tight.

I held her there for a minute before reaching for her chin and tipping it up to look at me. "What is it?"

"I was shoveling the driveway earlier tonight and your dad walked by," she said. Her gaze searched mine and I saw the worry. The fear. It pissed me off that this man had come back and disrupted all of our lives.

"Did he say anything to you?" I tugged off my glove and cupped the side of her face. Needing to comfort her even though I was in several pounds of fireproof gear.

"He said it would be a shame for you to get hurt in a fire tonight," she said, her words frantic. "I didn't want to tell you until I saw you because I was afraid you'd be worried about me. But I never thought he'd actually start a fire. My god, Niko. What if he started this? I should have said something sooner."

"Baby, relax. First of all, don't worry about me. But from now on, when you see him, you tell me. Whether I'm working or not. We need to know what he's up to at all times because I don't trust him. Secondly, if he started this fire, he'll be on his way back to prison very soon. The arson investigator will know right away if this was arson, and my dad isn't smart enough to know how to start a fire without getting caught." I wrapped my arms around her and held her close to me as the wind whipped around us.

"Niko, we're going to double team this bitch," Tallboy said as he walked up. "Hey, Vivi. I need to steal your boy back, all right?"

She pulled back to look at me. "Please be safe. I love you."

"Love you, Honey Bee. Go home. Stay with your sisters tonight. I'll call you as soon as we're done." I kissed her hard before slipping my gloves and my mask back into place.

And headed toward the flames burning in front of me.

• • •

"What exactly is this?" I asked as I stirred the bowl of powder and liquid together as instructed by my girl.

"It's pottery. I thought it would be nice to do something

different tonight," she said as she stirred her bowl and smiled.

I chuckled and leaned over and swiped the gray substance from her cheek. "And why are we making pottery?"

"Because it's something fun and different to do. We make our pieces tonight and then we can paint them tomorrow. Do you know what you're going to make?"

"I'm making a honeybee. They're my favorite." I winked.

She tilted her head to the side and smiled. "I'm making a heart for you to keep at the firehouse."

"Oh, that won't get me a ton of shit from the guys." I barked out a laugh imagining them razzing me for bringing a heart-shaped piece of pottery to work with me.

"It'll sit on the little table beside your bed. It's a piece of me."

"Anything you make me will be perfect," I said.

"Are you still good to go Christmas shopping with me tomorrow?" she asked as she concentrated on shaping her dough into a heart. Of course, the girl was a master at this kind of thing, because she had been baking most of her life. My honeybee looked more like a blob than a bee. Vivian came over and her hands slipped over mine as she helped me form the body. "Just do one part at a time and then we can put it together."

"All right. And yeah, I need to do some shopping too." The gift I was most excited about was the one for Vivian. I had two things I'd already been working on.

"Me too. Have you heard anything back about the fire?" Her eyes pinched together, and I didn't miss the concern. She'd been beating herself up that she should have told me about my father before that fire had been started. She was wrong to blame herself for anything that bastard did. His evil ran deep, and most people couldn't wrap their heads around it.

I'd been raised with his evil. I'd had a front-row seat for just how dark that drunk bastard could get. I put nothing past him. Hell, a part of me hoped he'd started that fire and that it would send him away for even longer this time around. Even if she'd given me a heads-up, we wouldn't have known what he was up to until after he started it. But I still wasn't convinced he'd done it. I didn't think he was smart enough to pull off a fire of that size, and he'd never been good at covering his tracks.

"It was definitely arson and Chuck's got a few leads, but nothing concrete yet. But he's not a guy who quits until he gets to the bottom of it. Apparently, there are some teens who have been graffitiing a bunch of buildings and destroying property downtown. He thinks they may be upping their game. There was a group of kids seen fleeing the site that night. But I've met with my dad's probation officer and shared some of my concerns. He seems to be aware that the man has no boundaries. No remorse for his actions in the past. He hasn't come by again here or the bakery, right?"

"Nope. And Jada said she's only seen him once."

"I hope she's telling the truth. The man can be very manipulative when he wants to be, and he doesn't like that I made them move out of the house before he came back. As if that piece of trash has any business being around a little girl."

"I think she's telling the truth, but I do think she struggles with it. She and Rook are getting pretty serious though, which is a good thing. He stops by the bakery often."

I chuckled. "Yeah. The poor guy can't even look me in the eyes right now because he's so terrified that I'm going to be pissed. I think he's been good for her."

Her head fell back in laughter. "He's so sweet and shy."

I was on my feet pulling her from her chair and into my arms. "Is that what you like? Sweet and shy?"

"I don't think there's anything shy about you, but you're definitely sweet beneath all that…"

"All that, what? Muscle?" I laughed.

"I was going to say broodiness, but muscle works." She was laughing as I tickled her sides and tossed her on the couch.

"I love you, Honey Bee. It's you that's made me sweeter. And it's only for you."

Her hands moved up to each side of my face, caressing my cheeks. "It's always been you. You just weren't mine yet."

"You've always been mine, Vivi. It just took me a bit to claim you."

She nodded and smiled as her eyes welled with emotion.

"Claim me, Niko," she whispered.

My mouth came crashing over hers. Claiming and taking and needing this girl in a way I never thought possible. The more time we'd spent together, the more I wanted.

I never thought forever was a thing I'd give a shit about, but Vivian Thomas was my forever.

I scooped her up and carried her to the bedroom, dropping her on the bed and watching her hair fall around her. I yanked my shirt over my head as she watched me. My jeans fell to the floor next, and she scooched up on the bed and reached for the band of my boxer briefs, tugging them down as well. She held her hands in the air for me to lift the sweater over her head, and I did. And then she pushed to her feet and stood as I dropped to my knees. I tugged her jeans down and pressed my face between her legs, breathing in all that goodness. She groaned as I leaned back and pulled her panties down her legs as well, leaving all of our clothes in a heap on the floor. I pushed back to stand and walked forward as she moved backward until her legs hit the bed and she dropped to sit. I leaned over her, crowding her space.

"What do you want, Honey Bee?"

"You," she whispered, and I moved her back on the bed before reaching in the nightstand for a condom.

"I'm all yours, baby."

I rolled the latex over my throbbing cock and settled between her legs, teasing her entrance.

"Always mine?"

"Always," I said before I thrust forward, and her hands tangled in my hair. We'd found our rhythm together and nothing had ever been better.

She arched off the bed as I continued to move slowly, making us wait for the release we were both chasing.

"Please, Niko," she whispered, and my hand came down between us. Touching her just where I knew she needed me.

She dug her nails into my shoulders and moaned, as she cried out my name. I moved faster. Harder. Chasing something I never knew I could feel, yet I felt it every time I was with her.

I followed her right over the edge.

Just like I always would.

Chapter 23

Vivian

I sat beside Niko at Mabel's school play. Our fingers intertwined and hands resting on his big thigh as I glanced up at him as he watched her recite her lines, his lips moving along silently with her words.

"So, on this holiday, spread love and joy to your family and friends," Mabel said as she stood in front of the microphone, and then hurried back to her seat. Niko had been practicing with her every time she'd come over to the house lately, which had been often with Jada and Rook spending so much time together. He looked over at me and winked, and I noticed the welled emotion in his gray gaze. He swiped at his eyes with the back of his hand, and I nearly lost my breath. This big broody man had a heart of gold, and I was lucky enough to be the one he showed it to.

I leaned against his shoulder. "She did good."

The kids sang one more holiday song and we were all on our feet, clapping. Jada and Rook were on the other side of Niko, and all of my sisters sat beside me. Ashlan was home for winter break now, and they'd all made the effort to be here. Charlotte taught at this school as well, so her aide was covering her class while she attended the show. They loved Mabel, but I knew the real reason they were here was because they all loved Niko like a brother, and this little girl was so important to him. Jilly was holding down the bakery and I knew we needed to get back before the lunch rush bombarded her. I didn't see Shayla West, but I guessed she must have come in late and taken a seat in the back.

Mabel's teacher thanked us all for coming and she led the kids out of the gym. We moved from our seats and headed for the exit.

My sisters all said their goodbyes, and Dylan said she'd get back to the bakery to help Jilly. Charlotte hurried back to her class, and Everly and Ashlan were off to do last-minute Christmas shopping. Jada and Rook followed the kids back to the classroom and she told me she'd meet me back at the bakery soon.

I looked up and squeezed Niko's hand when I realized his mother was walking toward us with Billy West beside her. Her cheek was bruised and swollen and impossible to miss. Once closer, I could see that she had tried to cover it up with makeup. It made my chest hurt at the thought of him putting his hands on her.

"Mabel did great," she said as she stopped in front of us.

"Yeah. My grandbaby sure is talented, am I right, Niko?" Billy said, raising a brow at my boyfriend and I felt his shoulders stiffen beside me.

"What happened to your face?" Niko directed the question toward his mother, and it was impossible to miss the edge in his voice.

"She ran into the damn door. She always was a klutz." Billy shrugged.

"It's funny. I never noticed that in all the years that you were gone," Niko said, his gaze never leaving his mother.

"I tripped over the leg of the chair and hit the door." Shayla raised her chin.

"Nice to see you again, Vivian. Crazy thing about that fire the other night shortly after we spoke, huh?" Billy moved closer and the wicked smirk on his face sent chills down my spine.

Niko moved between us. His hand found my forearm behind him, and he kept me there. "You start that fire, old man? It wouldn't be such a bad thing. It would mean you'd be going back where you belong pretty soon."

"Nah. I plan on staying right where I'm at." He reached for Shayla's hand, and she took it easily. When I peered around Niko's shoulder, I didn't see any sign of distress from his mother. How was that possible?

Billy turned and led his wife out of the gym, and Niko placed his hand in mine as we made our way toward the exit.

When we got in the car, he remained completely quiet. I texted Dylan and asked if she, Jada, and Jilly could hold down the bakery today. I knew he needed me right now, even if he wouldn't admit it. Dylan said it was fairly slow and they'd be fine.

"I don't need to go back to work today. The girls have it covered."

He cleared his throat. "All right. I've got some errands to do. Do you want to come with me?"

"Sure," I said, his hand intertwined with mine.

We stopped by the firehouse so Niko could grab his jacket that he'd left there. We went to the drugstore to grab a few toiletries, and the entire time he remained silent. When we arrived back at my house, I noticed my grocery delivery order was sitting in big plastic tubs on my front porch. Niko helped me carry it all in and we put it away, but he still hadn't spoken more than one-word answers in response to my small talk. He went outside to shovel the driveway and said he had to run over to his apartment to grab a few things. I tried not to take it personally. I knew this man well. He was processing all that had happened today. I did some laundry, called to check on the bakery, and started dinner.

When Niko arrived at the house, he took off his coat and glanced at the table. "Thanks for cooking. I was going to offer to go pick something up."

"I don't mind. I just got all those groceries, so I'd rather eat in." I moved to the table and set the two plates down as we both took our seats. "Do you want to talk about today?"

"What is there to talk about?"

"Your father being at the school. The bruise on your mother's face? The fact that your father mentioned the fire? I'd say there's a lot to unpack there?" I cut a bite of chicken and popped it into my mouth.

"There's not much to say, Vivi. She'll never go against the man."

"She did that one time, when he tried to blame you for the accident," I said.

He wiped his mouth with his napkin. "She just kept her mouth closed, which is what she basically did my entire life. She welcomed that monster back into her home. She wasn't the one who insisted that Jada and Mabel move out, I was. She would have subjected that little girl to his darkness without a second thought." He pushed to his feet, startling me. "Listen, I don't want to talk about this. It's the same shit, different day. You don't need to hear it."

"What if I want to hear it?"

"I don't want to do this, Honey Bee."

"You need to talk to someone about all of this. A therapist, or even Everly. She's in a similar field. She could do that for you."

He leaned forward and kissed the top of my head. "That's not for me. I'm going to go take a shower."

I pushed to my feet and followed him to the bedroom door. "Do you want company?"

"How about later, okay? I'm in a shit mood. I thought about staying at my place tonight, but I don't like the idea of you being alone." He turned to face me from where he stood in the bathroom doorway.

His words stung. He didn't want to be here. He was only here because he didn't think I was safe.

"I'm fine by myself. Take your shower and if you want to leave after, I think you should." My words came out harsher than I meant. Or maybe I did mean them, I didn't even know anymore. I told this man everything, and I couldn't get him to open up about being angry about seeing his abusive father?

He nodded and pushed the door closed. It felt like a metaphor in a way. He was shutting me out literally and figuratively. I stormed to the kitchen and reached for the plates, still covered in food, and brought them to the sink.

The doorbell rang and I walked toward the door and glanced through the peephole.

Jansen Clark stood on the other side. He wore only a T-shirt, no jacket, and there was a car with bright lights shining on my door behind him.

"What are you doing here?" I asked as I pulled the door open.

"I need to talk to you, Vivi," he said, and his words slurred. His hair was disheveled, and he reeked of booze.

"I thought we already cleared things up. I'm not upset with

you. I'm okay with you getting married. I'm with Niko now, and you can't just come over every time you come to town and get drunk. Go home, Jansen."

"That's the thing. I don't exactly know where that is. I called off the wedding. Katie kicked me out and I came home. That's Bowers out in the car. He took me out so I could get sloshed tonight, and guess what we talked about, Vivi? *You.* I blew it. I should have fought harder for you."

I let out a long breath and shook my head. "You're romanticizing this, Jansen. We hadn't been happy for a long time. Hell, I don't even know if we ever were, which is the reason that I forgive you for cheating on me. But the truth is, you came along at a time when I was grieving the loss of my mother, and I just needed something to believe in. But we hardly even saw one another over the past five or six years. Why in the hell would you call off your wedding?"

"She's awful. I'm talking about a bridezilla on steroids," he said, reaching for my hand, and I tugged it away.

"I want you to be happy, Jansen, I really do. But you're not going to find what you need here. I'm with Niko now. He's my future," I said, and I glanced out at Stew Bowers who was watching us through the window.

"I knew you were always in love with that dude. But he can't give you what I can give you, Vivi. I've thought about this long and hard. I'll move back to Honey Mountain if it makes you happy. I shouldn't have drawn a line in the sand. I shouldn't have demanded you move to the Bay Area for me." He burped and then his head fell back in laughter. "Let me come in? It's cold out here."

"No, Jansen. I've been very clear with you that this is over. Hell, I hardly heard from you after we broke up. You're just feeling lonely because you ended things with Katie. You need to go home."

"Because you love Niko? Is that the fucking reason?" he said, startling me because Jansen rarely showed any emotion. But he was completely unhinged now.

"Yes. That's the fucking reason. Now please leave. And don't come back here drunk again."

"Is he here, Vivi? Come on. Let me in," he said, and he placed his hands on each of my shoulders and tried to push me back. I nearly tripped over my own feet because he'd caught me by surprise.

"No!" I shouted. "Go home."

"Make me," he said, and the anger in his eyes shocked me. I'd never seen Jansen angry. Even when I caught him in bed with Katie and he chased me out, he looked pathetic. Sad. Never angry. We never fought or argued in all the years we were together. How could I have dated this guy for that many years and not have really known who he was?

I saw Niko out of my peripheral as he charged up beside me and managed to gently move me out of the way before he was on Jansen. They were outside and I chased them out to the front yard as Niko took him down in the snow. He was on top of Jansen with his fist in the air.

"She asked you to fucking leave, motherfucker!" he shouted.

Jansen covered his face. I knew he wasn't a fighter, whereas Niko fought for sport. He'd never backed down from a fight.

"I'm sorry," Jansen whimpered.

"Niko, get off of him. Let him go home," I said, placing my hands on his shoulders. He stiffened beneath my touch and moved to his feet just as Bowers got out of the car.

"Get back in the fucking car, Stew." Niko pointed at him and yanked Jansen to his feet. "And take your asshole friend home and keep him there."

Jansen stumbled over to the car and Stew got back in the driver's seat and gave me an apologetic look before pulling out of the driveway in a screech.

I looked down to see Niko's feet in the snow and I gasped. "You don't have any shoes on, and your hair is wet."

He stormed past me and moved inside, grabbing his boots and slipping them on before going to the counter and reaching for his keys.

"What are you doing?" I shrieked.

"I need to go," he said, moving past me without a second glance and pulling the door closed behind him.

I stood there dumbfounded.

What in the hell had just happened?

And why did it feel like he wasn't coming back?

I dropped onto the couch and covered my face as the tears started to fall.

And I let them.

Chapter 24
Niko

I drove over to Jada's house, and I stormed up to the door and banged three times before my sister opened it with a panicked look in her eyes.

"What's wrong? Is Mom okay?"

I shook my head. "She's fine. Or as fine as she can be, considering she's living with a monster."

Mabel came charging around the corner and dove into my arms. I scooped her up and kissed her little cherub cheek.

"Mabel, can you go pick out your jammies and let me talk to Uncle Niko for a minute, please?"

"But he's my Neek, Neek," she pouted when I set her back down on her feet.

"I'll come in and see you when we're done, okay?" I asked.

"Yay," she sang out as she danced her way down the hall toward her bedroom.

"So, what's going on?" Jada asked, folding her arms across

her chest as I moved toward her dining room. I pulled out a chair and dropped to sit before scrubbing a hand down my face.

"Did you see the bruise on Mom's face?" I hissed.

Jada looked away before turning back to meet my gaze. "She said that she tripped and fell into the door."

"Come on, Jada. You don't really fucking believe that?"

"What do you want me to say, Niko? Mom loves him. He's our dad," she said, and I pushed to my feet.

"He's a fucking sperm donor." I threw my hands in the air. "Let me ask you something."

She dropped to sit on the couch and tears streamed down her face. We never talked about the things that we both knew happened. They may not have happened to Jada, but she had a front-row seat to the abuse that I endured.

"Okay," she said, and her voice shook.

I moved back to the couch and sat beside her, waiting for her to look up at me. "You knew the shit he did to me. How are you okay with that? How were you going to subject Mabel to that man? How are you okay with what he's done to our mother?"

She shook her head frantically. "I, I don't know, Niko. I just try not to think about it. And once he went away to prison, I think I tried to make him out to be someone he isn't. I don't want our father to be a bad guy. Hell, I already got knocked up at fifteen. Everyone instantly thinks I'm a fuck-up. So maybe I just like to pretend that I have a decent family."

Fuck.

I reached for her hand. "You're not a fuck-up. There's an amazing little girl in that room down the hall that proves as much. I've seen a huge change in you these past few months. You're a good mom, Jada. But I need to know that I'm not in this alone."

"You've never been alone, Niko."

"It's not like we have a mom who came to my aid, Jada. She turned the other cheek. She always fucking has his back, even after all he's done."

"I didn't mean Mom. And I didn't even mean me, because I know I haven't been there for you the way I should have been. But you've had something me and Mom have never had." She squeezed my hand, as tears continued to stream down her face.

"What?"

"You've had Vivian. She's always had your back. And now that you guys are together, I see a difference in you too."

"In what way?" I rolled my eyes.

"All of this is coming up not only because Dad is home, and you're right, Niko. I still have nightmares about the things that I heard behind my closed door. And I was too much a coward to come out and help you," she said over her sobs.

"I never wanted you to come out and help me. I want you to protect that little girl. I want you to know that he's a bad guy, Jada. He hasn't changed."

She nodded. "I wasn't done. I was saying it's not only because Dad's home, but it's because you're finally happy. You're in a relationship with someone you love, and that's got to be terrifying for someone like you," she said as she barked out a laugh over her sobs when I reared back at her words. "I don't mean it that way. I just mean, it's hard for you to trust, and you've found someone who would walk through fire for you. She's never going to hurt you, and you probably don't even know what to do about it."

"She wants me to see a therapist, and you know that shit isn't for me," I said, pulling my hand away and shoving the hair out of my face.

"I think we could both use a little therapy if I'm being honest. Dylan wants me to talk to Everly. I guess she's got all sorts of experience with fucked-up people." She shrugged.

I was happy my sister had grown close to Vivian and Dylan Thomas. They were exactly the kind of friends that she needed.

"That's not a bad idea. She's talking to the guys down at the firehouse. I guess she's getting in all the experience she can before she gets hired by one of those pro teams." I pushed to my feet.

"If you don't want to talk to a therapist, Niko, find someone you trust. If you keep it all bottled up, it's going to destroy you."

I rolled my eyes, but I knew she was right. It already was eating me alive. The anger seeping so deep in my veins I feared it would take over.

"I'll think about it."

"I'm not letting him meet Mabel. I didn't allow them to come into her classroom, and I informed the school that Mom isn't allowed to pick her up anymore. I don't trust her, Niko. For whatever reason, she chooses him every time."

I nodded as I heard little Mabel shouting my name from down the hall.

"Neek, Neek," she called out.

"I need to go say goodbye to her." I made my way down to her room and the door was cracked just enough that I could see twinkle lights coming from her room. I pushed the door open, and a small white tree sat in the corner of Mabel's princess bedroom which Vivian had painted and decorated for her. There were little white lights covering every branch on the tree. I moved closer as she stood beside it.

"Look at what I gots," she said, holding her little arms out to the sides.

"I like it. How'd you get this many pink ornaments?" I laughed.

"Miss Vivi got this for me yesterday. She told Mama she had a surprise for me, and she dropped it off when I got out of school. And me and her and Mama decorated it. She said she went to four stores to gets all the pink ornaments she could find."

My chest squeezed.

Honey Bee.

"It's real nice," I said, bending down to study the ornaments.

"This one's my favorite. It's a pink pig. Do you know pink pigs are my favorite, Neek, Neek?"

"I do. You sleep with that filthy pink pig every night," I said with a laugh.

"His name is Oink, Oink. He keeps me real safe."

I scooped her up and walked back out to where Jada still sat on the couch swiping away the last of her tears. I kissed Mabel's cheek and set her on her mama's lap.

"I've got to go."

"Love you," Jada said. "Think about what I said."

"I will." I already knew the one person I trusted most in the world. That's the person I would talk to. The only one I'd ever fully trusted. "I'll see you later."

I drove straight to Vivian's house and knocked on the door. It was cold as hell out here, my hair still damp, and I hoped she wasn't so pissed that she wouldn't let me in, because if that was the case, I'd be sleeping on her front porch.

I'd overreacted about Jansen showing up here, because I was looking to pick a fight. I was not threatened by Jansen Clark. I trusted Vivian with my life. I just came with a shit ton of baggage that was fucking with my head.

The door opened and she stood there looking like I felt. Her eyes were puffy, her cheeks red, but the empathy in that dark gaze was there just like it always was.

"Hey," she said. "Glad you came back."

I moved forward and tipped my head down, resting my forehead against hers. "I'll always come back, Honey Bee. I'm sorry."

Her hand came up to caress my cheek as she rubbed her nose against mine. "What are you sorry for?"

I scooped her up and her legs wrapped around my waist, as I kicked the door shut behind me. I walked to the couch and dropped to sit, and her legs remained on each side, so she was straddling me.

I pulled my face back and studied her before letting out a long breath. "I'm sorry for running out of here after that dipshit Clark came by."

She let out an incredulous laugh. "Are you sorry for tackling the poor drunk guy in the snow? You're twice his size."

"I'm not sorry for that." I shrugged. "You want me to be honest, right?"

"I do."

"He's lucky I didn't do more. I saw his hands on you, and you asked him to leave more than once. That's when I stepped in."

"Fair enough. So why the dramatic departure?" She raised a brow and smirked.

"Fuck. I can't talk to a therapist, Vivi, and I don't want to talk to your sister. But I can talk to you. You're the only one I want to talk to."

Her gaze softened and she smiled, as she stroked the hair away from my face. "I'm good with that. Tell me why you left?"

"Because seeing my dad fucks with my head. Seeing my mom with a big bruise on her face—it brings up things. It reminds me of a past I don't want to remember. And it pisses me off because I worry about her, even though she never worried about me." A lump formed in my throat which also pissed me off, and I slipped Vivian off my lap and set her on the couch before I moved to my feet and started pacing. "I don't like talking about this shit."

She was on her feet and wrapping her arms around my middle, her chest to my back. "I know, but I promise you it helps. Tell me why you think your mom never worried about you."

"Because she was scared, but she knew what he was doing, and she hid in her room. I can forgive her for that because I understand being afraid, because I was afraid for a long time, Honey Bee. I used to fear the man when I was young. But she's welcomed him back from prison with open arms, and I can't forgive that. I want to be angry and not worry about her, because she chooses him over and over."

I turned to face her and looked down to see tears streaming down her face and I swiped them away with my thumbs. I hated that my shit made her cry.

"But you can't, can you? You feel bad for her because you're a good man, Niko."

"I don't want to tell you this shit and make you cry," I hissed and started to pull away, but she held on to my hands.

"I'm crying because I love you. You don't need to run from me. I'm not going anywhere. But yes, it hurts to know what he did to you. That's love. That's not a reason to pull away. Tell me about your relationship with him. I mean, I know what he did when we were young, but you stopped telling me about it in high school. When you stopped coming through my window," she said, and her lips turned up in the corners.

"That's because I knew I couldn't be trusted in a bed with you at that point. And then you started dating Jansen the cocksucker and I didn't want to cause you any trouble."

"I don't think that's the reason, Niko. I think the older you got, the more guarded you got. Even from me, when it came to your father. You never told me he tried to blame the accident on you, and we talked all day every day. Always did. So, tell me what happened during those years. I guess I'd just convinced myself that he'd stopped putting his hands on you, but I knew in my gut that he didn't."

She led me back to the couch and once I dropped down, she climbed back in my lap, resting her head on my chest and stroking my forearm with her gentle touch.

"Tell me, Niko."

I cleared my throat. "It happened less often as I got bigger. But he'd catch me off guard. Come home drunk when I was sleeping. I started locking my door when I was old enough to figure out that most of the beatings happened during the nights he was wasted, which was pretty much all the time. One time, I was maybe fifteen or sixteen, and he kicked the door open, startled me from my sleep. He hit me so hard in the head with a pan that he knocked me out. I stayed home from school for a few days after that because I'm fairly certain I had a concussion."

She pulled back to look at me. Her gaze searching mine. "I remember that. I brought over soup and brownies because you said you were sick."

I nodded. "I was sick in a way. And the thing that burns is that he never mentioned it the next day. There were no apologies. He just called me a pussy for staying home."

"And what did your mom do?"

"She'd play along with me saying that I was sick, even though I remember seeing her in the doorway just as the pan hit my head. I'm guessing she ran off to her room to hide. Yet there she was the next morning making that asshole breakfast and acting like everything was fine. I hate thinking about that home. I was so happy when she sold the place, even though it meant moving farther from you. I hate that fucking house."

"I get that," she said, her fingers tracing my jawline. "Did it happen often after that?"

"No. He'd get drunk and pass out on the couch. After that, I never slept the same. I'd wake up constantly wondering if he was going to come in and beat the shit out of me with no warning. I think he just got weaker and drunker as the years went on. Our senior year, not long before the accident, he came into my room one night. The door never locked again after he'd kicked it in."

"What happened?" she whispered.

"I was ready for him. I sat up and punched him so hard in the face that I knocked a few teeth out. He just laid there on the ground yelping and hollering for my mom. We never spoke of it, and it was the last time he ever tried to lay his hands on me. I wish I'd done it sooner, but I hadn't been certain I could take the son of a bitch before then. He's a big dude. And he's angry."

"He's a monster. I hate him."

I leaned forward and kissed the tip of her nose. "I don't need you hating anyone for me."

"Well, I do. And that's not going to change. Do you sleep good now?"

"I do. Ever since I moved into my own place. I never spent the night with a woman before you, because I didn't trust having anyone in my bed or that someone wouldn't come in while we slept. I slept alone in my apartment, or I spent the night here with you even before we were together, and I slept well."

She smiled. "That makes me happy. You're safe with me, Niko."

I chuckled. "Oh yeah? You going to keep me safe, Vivi?"

"Always."

I kissed her, tangling my fingers in her long hair. Because I knew she was right. When I was with her, everything was better. Always had been.

Chapter 25

Vivian

I woke up with my body wrapped around Niko's. We always slept tangled up in one another and I loved it. I loved listening to his heartbeat as my head rested on his chest. I loved the warmth of his body. I ran my fingers over his forearms, fighting back the emotion I felt when I looked at those cigarette burns. He'd opened up to me last night, and that had been a breakthrough, because Niko didn't like talking about his father.

We'd stayed up late, and I'd prompted him to keep sharing with me. He'd told me more about the nightmare that was his childhood and a piece of my heart shattered into a million pieces as I listened. Niko was big and strong and there was a fierceness there. Vulnerability was not something he ever showed, but he'd given me a glimpse.

A glimpse of the pain and the heartache and the sadness that came with the abuse that he experienced.

I wanted to beat his father with my own fists, and I'd never longed to hit another human being before.

I wanted to shake some sense into his mother. I understood her being afraid of him, but she'd never once called the police, according to Niko. She hadn't filed for divorce when he went to prison, and she'd welcomed him home when he got out. Yet he empathized with his mother. Shayla West wasn't an evil woman. She was a broken woman. Anyone could see that.

"What are you thinking about, beautiful?" Niko asked as he stretched his arms above his head and looked down at me.

"Just how strong you are."

He chuckled and pushed to sit up against the headboard, pulling me along with him to keep me resting against his chest. "Oh yeah? You checking me out?"

"Always." I smiled up at him. "Have you heard anything more about that warehouse fire?"

"Nothing more than the fact that Chuck Martin thinks it was definitely arson. No doubt about it. I know he brought in a bunch of those teens for questioning, but I haven't heard anything more. I think my father talks a big game, but I don't even know if he has the wherewithal to set a fire like that."

"Do you really think your dad would go that far while he was out on parole?"

"I don't think my father thinks rational thoughts. He never has. He's already drinking again because Tanner shot me a text to let me know that asshole has been to Beer Mountain several times since he got out."

"He's already drinking? That's not good."

"I don't think he ever fully stopped using even in prison. I think the drugs were rampant in there because he seems more fucked up than he was before. But his probation officer, Wayne, seems to be aware of the situation. He's been messaging me often with updates, and he even let on to the fact that he didn't think my father would be out for long. I got the feeling he's dealt with men like my dad many times. He's an older dude, but he seems to be sharp as a tack. But catching my father in the act is always tough because the man is a pathological liar."

I shivered, and Niko pulled the blanket up over my shoulders. "I hope they catch him doing something soon."

"Yeah. So, we've talked plenty about the asshole, right?"

"Meaning?"

"Meaning, I'm trying to show you that I'm, I don't know, growing or maturing," he said as he barked out a laugh. "But I don't want to talk about him anymore. And it's Christmas in a few days."

"That's fair. You're very mature, although Jansen might not think so," I said over my laughter.

"Do you ever regret ending things with him? I heard him say that he'd move back here for you. He could give you the fairy tale, Honey Bee. That dude is definitely the white picket fence kind of guy, even if he's boring as hell."

"I'm partial to the sexy firefighter with the broody disposition. And the body and the face on him..." I fanned myself dramatically. "Don't even get me started."

He had me flipped on my back before I could process what was happening. He tickled my sides and smiled down at me. "Oh yeah? You like what you see, huh?"

"I really do."

"Me too." He kissed me, and my fingers tangled in his long hair. "I love you, Vivian Thomas." He pulled away and his gaze studied mine. "I really love you. Do you know that? More than I ever thought possible."

My breath caught in my throat. "I love you too."

"Even if I can't give you everything?"

"What is it that you think I need that you haven't given me? Do you think I want to get married today? Is that what you're afraid of?"

"No. I think you want to get married someday, and to be honest, I'm not opposed to it. Never thought it was something I'd want, but I know that you're my forever, and I don't mind saying that to the world."

My heart raced at his words. My gaze searched his. "But?"

"I know you want a big family. I don't think I can give you that. The thought of me being responsible for another life, it scares the shit out of me. I don't want to fuck anyone up the way my father fucked me up."

I pushed him back, before sitting up on my knees in front of him so I could face him and be eye level. "Niko, you aren't fucked up. You survived something terrible, and you're still standing. You are the best uncle to Mabel and the best boyfriend to me. My sisters love you. Everyone at the firehouse loves you. You're the most amazing man I know." I sniffed as the tears started to fall. It had been an emotional last twenty-four hours for us, and I was feeling it.

Feeling all the things for this man.

"What does that mean? You'll take me as I am?"

"Always. I'm not in a hurry, because I'm happy for the first time in a very long time. You make me happy."

"You make me happy too, Honey Bee."

With those words, I leaned forward and kissed him. I kissed him like it was forever.

Because I knew that it was.

• • •

The bakery was hopping busy, and I was thankful that the last of the rush had just left. Everly sat on the counter as I restocked the pastries in the display case.

"I thought you'd be happy about this? They're a pro hockey team, and it's in the Bay Area so you'll just be a few hours away by car. It doesn't get any better," Dylan said. It was just the three of us sisters here now, as Jilly and Jada had already left for the day.

"What part about Hawk Madden being on that team do you not understand? And they haven't offered me a job, they've offered me an interview. We have a long way to go. I feel like I have so many people interested, but no one wants to pull the trigger."

"That's not true. It's just a big job. I mean, so many teams are finally coming to terms with hiring a sports psychologist for their athletes, and it's a competitive field. Everyone wants to work with the pros," I said as I handed her and Dylan each a snowman cookie covered in white glitter.

"Look at you being all philosophical." Dylan barked out a laugh as she bit the head off her snowman and chewed. "I think Hawk put in the good word for you, because they reached out to you, right? You never applied there, so it had to come from him." Dylan wriggled her brows, knowing that she was annoying Everly. Hawk and my sister had dated all through high school, and to say that us Thomas girls had loved him would be a massive understatement. He was part of the family until their relationship ended, and obviously when forced to take sides, we'd always have Everly's back.

"Whatever. He and I haven't spoken in a long time. Not that he comes back to Honey Mountain much now that he's a well-known hockey player," Everly hissed, before taking another bite of her cookie.

Dylan and I both laughed. Everly did everything she could to avoid Hawk when he was home. He'd come by the bakery and ask about her, but she preferred to stay away from him. I knew it was because she still cared, but she'd never admit that.

"Um, well-known? Your ex-boyfriend is the Tom Brady of the ice, girl. He was on the cover of *Sports Illustrated* last month and graced the cover of *Hockey Puck Magazine* this month, as the IT boy of the sport." Dylan shrugged as she jumped off the counter and brushed her hands together to rid herself of any crumbs, which meant I had to sweep again.

"Since when are you checking out hockey magazines, you traitor. He and I don't speak, so you certainly can't be swooning over him." Everly raised a brow and her gaze hardened. He'd been the only guy I'd ever seen her affected by. She never talked about why they broke up, and though she'd dated plenty of guys since, she never seemed happy with any of them the way she'd been with Hawk.

"Listen. I have no shame in my game. Your ex-boyfriend is a freaking hot-ass legend. He fights and scraps on the ice, yet we know he's a teddy bear off the ice. Mmm, mmm, he's sexy as sin. And I didn't seek those magazines out. I saw the latest one at the grocery store when I stopped for gum and tampons this morning. Do you want to see it? I bought you a copy." Dylan burst out in a fit of laughter and ran toward the back room where her purse was.

"I cannot with her." Everly threw her hands in the air, and I just smiled. My oldest sister put on a good front, but I knew she was dying to see that magazine. She'd called me after the *Sports Illustrated* issue was released and asked if I thought he looked happy. But then she'd quickly changed the subject and said she didn't want to talk about him anymore.

Dylan came around the corner and handed it to Everly, just as the door swung open and Charlotte walked in holding a bag.

"Hey, what are you doing here?" I asked.

"Well, I just spent the day catching up on my Christmas shopping now that school's out, and I had a deep craving for a gingerbread cookie. But I stopped at the store to grab tampons, and look what I found," Charlotte said as she pulled a magazine out of the bag and handed it to Everly. We all burst out laughing that they'd both bought it.

"Damn. You and I are always on the same cycle. So beware, ladies, I feel a bad mood coming on," Dylan said as she went to the display case and handed Charlotte a gingerbread cookie.

"Yeah. You two are a pair. Sweet twin and Spicy twin," Everly said as she stared down at the magazine in her hand. "He looks good. I mean, he should. He has more money than God, right? I'm sure he gets a lot of work done." She tossed both magazines on the counter.

"Oh, please. That is not work, my friend. He's got a scar on his cheek and a black eye. That is just sheer good looks and sexiness. Don't try to blame it on the cash." Dylan smirked. "And I don't appreciate that you all think I'm the spicy twin. I can be sweet too."

"Of course you can," Charlotte said.

"Says the sweet twin," I teased, and we all laughed some more.

"So, you're coming for Christmas Eve dinner tomorrow night, right?" Everly asked me. "And what about Christmas morning? Will you and Niko still come over early so we can open gifts?"

"Yes. And I invited Jada and Mabel to Christmas Eve dinner because she doesn't want to go to her mom's house now that her father is home, and I don't blame her."

"Oh, that man," Dylan groaned. "Billy West gives me the heebies. I saw him the other day in town, and he was asking all about you, Vivi. I just ignored him, of course. I channeled my inner bitch rather well, if I do say so myself."

"What was he asking?" I prodded.

"Just how you were doing? If you and Niko were still together. I gave him the death stare and he took the hint."

"He gives me the creeps, too," Charlotte agreed. "I've never liked that man. I feel bad that Niko and Jada had to grow up with him until he went to prison."

"Yeah, I feel the same. He's just bad news. Always has been. But he has two amazing kids," Everly said. "How are things going with Niko? I can't believe how easily he adapted to being in a relationship. Never thought I'd see the day."

"It's because he was always in love with Vivi," Charlotte said, resting her head on my shoulder.

"It's going really well. Although he was being all cryptic today and he wouldn't tell me what he was up to on his day off. Kept saying it was a surprise."

"What if it's an engagement ring?" Dylan shrieked and clapped her hands together. "I'd be so good with that. I'd just hope he'd do it at the house so we could all be there."

"Spicy twin has a sentimental side after all," Everly teased. "Do you think that's it?"

"No. We've talked about it. I think it'll happen someday, but it's still new for us, you know? But he does surprise me with how romantic he is most days. He's always getting me flowers and cooking me dinner when he's not at the firehouse."

"Look at her face when she talks about him." Charlotte beamed up at me. "I need to find me a boyfriend that makes me feel that way."

"That would require you to actually go out now and then. You're acting like you're eighty years old now that we're out of college." Dylan chuckled and Charlotte rolled her eyes.

"You try spending your day with sixty kindergarteners, half in the morning and half in the afternoon. It's exhausting. And if my prince is out there, he'll find me," Charlotte said as she scooped up her purse. "All right, I need to go. I have a few more gifts to get."

"I'm coming with you," Everly and Dylan both said at the same time, and we all laughed.

"All right. I'll see you tomorrow. Love you." I hugged them each goodbye and sent them on their way with a box of holiday cookies. "Save some for Dad."

"If he's lucky," Everly called out and waved as they headed out into the late snowy afternoon.

I finished sweeping and cleaned things up as I was going to be packed tomorrow afternoon, and closed on Christmas Day and the following day, so I was looking forward to some time off.

I flipped the lights off and grabbed my keys and heard someone knocking on the front door. I peeked around the corner and saw Billy West through the glass. I moved away quickly so he wouldn't see me, and I slipped out the back door and locked it behind me before I hurried to my car and drove away.

I had no idea why he'd be stopping by after hours.

And I sure as hell did not want to find out.

Chapter 26

Niko

I was late getting to Vivi's house, and I didn't quite know how I was going to give her the surprise. I had gotten her quite a few things for Christmas that I'd take to her dad's house Christmas morning, but this one was just for her. I'd thought about doing it for a long time, and it turned out even better than I'd imagined.

I knocked on the door and she pulled it open, looking like a fucking vision. She wore a white sweater that hung off one shoulder and some faded blue jeans that hugged her slight curves in all the right places. Her long hair tumbled around her shoulders and the corners of her lips turned up when her gaze locked with mine.

"Where have you been, handsome?" she purred.

I rushed her, kicking the door shut behind me. But I winced when I pulled her into my arms and her chest crashed into mine. She pulled back and studied me.

"I'm fine. I guess I better give you your surprise first," I said, and she clapped her hands together and wiggled her brows.

"Sounds good to me. You don't want to wait for Christmas?"

"I've got other plans for Christmas. This one is just for you and me." I guided her to the couch and then I tugged my coat and hoodie over my head because it was colder than ice-balls out there tonight.

She moved to her feet and gasped when she saw the large bandage covering my chest. "Oh my gosh. What happened?"

"It's okay, baby. I did something to show you how much I love you." I peeled back the gauze on the left side of my chest and showed her the honeybee that now resided there. It stood out in great contrast to the angry ink covering the rest of my body, just the way this girl stood out in great contrast in my life.

She was the light that shined through all of the darkness.

"Niko," she said, and her word broke on a sob. "What is this?"

"It's my honeybee and my heart. They're one and the same. I wanted to show you that you're my forever in every way."

"I love it," she said as tears streamed down her beautiful face, and she traced her finger gently around the black and yellow bee still shining in fresh ink. I loved the way Vivian felt everything. So genuine and real and vulnerable. A way that I'd fought hard not to be, yet I longed for that kind of honesty in my life. "I don't want to hurt you," she whispered.

"You won't hurt me." I raised her hand and kissed the back of it. "You've only saved me."

"Niko," she whispered as I shoved the bandage back into place and pulled her against me, wrapping my arms around her.

"It's the truth."

"You saved me too," she said, tipping her head back to look up at me.

I leaned down and kissed her. I wanted her to know just how much she meant to me. I'd never cared much about showing people that side of myself, but with Vivian, I cared.

I needed her to know.

She pulled away and swiped at her cheeks. "I have something for you too. I don't want to give this to you in front of anyone. This is just for you."

I followed her toward the kitchen, and she reached for the little white box sitting on the counter and she handed it to me. I tugged off the black bow and opened it to see a shiny silver key inside.

"What's this?"

She sucked in a long breath and her dark eyes darted away as she worked up her nerve to speak. I knew her well. I knew her tells. Knew when she was nervous. And she was definitely nervous.

I gently placed my thumb and my finger on each side of her chin and lifted, forcing her to meet my gaze.

"Is this a key to your house?"

She nodded. "I don't know if you're ready for that, but you're here every day that you aren't working, and you're paying rent for your apartment and Jada's place, so I thought…"

"Are you doing it to save me money or because you want me here?" I asked. I already knew the answer, but I wanted to hear her say it.

"Because I want you here. And I know that might be a lot for you, and it might freak you out," she said, but I put a finger over her lips.

"I want you, Honey Bee. I want to be with you every second that I can. But the only way I move in here is if I pay half of your mortgage." She started to shake her head, but I kept my finger there. "That's the only way this works."

"Well, that's not much of a Christmas gift then." She laughed. "It's just a key."

"It's the key to this." I took her hand and placed it over her heart. "I gave you mine and you gave me yours. It doesn't get any better than that, does it?"

"It doesn't," she whispered. "You really want to move in with me?"

"Abso-fucking-lutely. The more time I get with you, the better. But let me just speak to your dad before I pack my bags and we do this. Make sure he's all right with it."

"Niko West. Who knew you were so chivalrous?"

"Only for you," I said, leaning down and claiming that sweet mouth.

Just like I planned to do for the rest of my life.

...

Christmas at the Thomas' was madness, just as I'd expected. I'd been happy that Jada and Mabel had joined us for Christmas Eve dinner as my sister was not taking Mabel over to my mother's house as long as my father was there. Apparently, our talk had meant something to her because she'd pulled me to the side and told me that moving forward, she would have my back the way I'd always had hers.

I wasn't looking for fucking sympathy. I just couldn't wrap my head around the fact that my mother or sister would be willing to be around the man. Not after all they'd seen, heard, and for my mother, lived through.

She had her chance at a clean break. He'd gone to prison for six years. She could have filed for divorce. Could have refused to let him come back home. But she did neither. And she'd brought him to Mabel's school, opening that up to him. It pissed me the hell off, and I hadn't spoken to her since.

We all sat around the tree as we went around the group opening one gift at a time. I'd never experienced a Christmas where anyone gave a damn what the other got. I didn't grow up in a house full of Christmas spirit and love. But this house had it in spades. It's probably why I'd always been so drawn to it. It's what every kid wanted.

"Okay, we all get to open our Niko gifts now," Dylan teased, shaking the package that Vivi had wrapped for me. She tore open the present and smirked. "Oh my gosh, is this the ice scraper that you have that I've been coveting?"

"It sure is. Not the most exciting gift, but I remembered you trying to clear off your window with your mittens." I chuckled. Aside from the honey bee tattoo, I was more of a practical gift giver.

"I love it," she said as she pushed to her feet and leaned down to hug me.

Everly opened her book that Vivi helped me pick out for her sister. It documented the best sports psychologists for NFL teams and their journeys. Charlotte opened her gift, which was a survival guide for kindergarten teachers, and I gave Ashlan a Starbucks gift card because the girl always had the infamous white and green cup in her hand when she was home.

They all gave me gifts as well, just like we'd always done, although I'd never spent Christmas morning here because Jansen had always been in town. Dylan got me a pocketknife and said it was to use if the dipshit Jansen stopped by the house again. *Her words, not mine.*

Mine would be worse. But I didn't need a blade to fight off Vivian's ex-boyfriend. I'd be happy to use my fists if necessary. I had a hunch he wouldn't be coming around for a while.

Everly got me a gift card to my favorite restaurant, Ashlan wrote me a sweet poem about being a firefighter, and Charlotte got me two pounds of my favorite chocolate.

"Vivi, open your gift," Ashlan said as she handed her the package from me.

She looked over her shoulder and smiled as she sat between my legs on the floor. She gasped when she took out the gold necklace with the tiny honeybee hanging from it.

"This is so pretty," she said. "I love it." I helped her clasp it behind her neck and then she handed me a package as well.

When I tore it open, there was a photo album inside the box. On the cover was a photo of me and Vivian in first or second grade standing in front of the school. She was smiling, I was frowning. It was very fitting. I flipped the pages and couldn't help but smile at the photos decorating page after page.

"It's our journey to here. The last pages are blank, and we can fill them in as we go," she said.

It was the most sentimental gift I'd ever been given, and it fucking meant the world to me. She'd already gifted me a down jacket and some leather gloves, and I'd given her some boots I knew she'd wanted with the help of Everly, and a new pastry gun that Dylan told me she wanted.

But this was the best gift I'd ever received.

"I love it. Thank you." I wrapped my arms around her and hugged her tight, as the girls continued to tear into their packages.

When we were finished, they were piling their presents in laundry baskets to take to their bedrooms, and Vivian made a pile of our gifts near the front door. I followed Jack into the kitchen and glanced over my shoulder to make sure we were alone.

"You got a minute?" I asked, clearing my throat as I pulled out a chair at the kitchen table.

"Sure. What's up?"

"Well, Vivi and I were talking about living together. I wanted to make sure that was okay with you." I cleared my throat.

He studied me for a long minute and clasped his hands together. "I see. So, you want to shack up with my little girl, huh?"

Jack Thomas had one of the best poker faces I'd ever seen. I couldn't tell if he was pissed or just giving me shit.

"I plan on proposing to her at some point, I'm just struggling with all of it." I ran a hand down the back of my neck.

His gaze softened. "What are you struggling with? Do you love her?"

"Of course. More than anything. I just don't know if I'm cut out for the whole white picket fence bullshit. I don't know if that's me. But I know I want to spend my life with her." It felt good to say it to him. He'd been more like a father to me than anyone. I respected him. Hell, he was one of the most decent people I'd ever known.

Jack glanced over his shoulder. "Did you know that my dad was an alcoholic? Have I ever told you that?"

"No. I've never heard you talk about him."

"Exactly. He was a mean drunk. Abusive. Toxic." He took a sip of his coffee. "He never went to jail for his crimes like your father did, but I'd say we grew up pretty similar if I were a betting man."

I leaned back in my chair and let out a breath. I'd never have guessed that. "I'm sorry to hear that."

"Don't be. We're all on a journey, Niko. He was part of mine. He is the reason that I don't drink. He taught me everything I didn't want to be, so I could go out there and be what I wanted.

A good husband. A good father. And a damn good firefighter, if I do say so myself." He chuckled.

I was stunned speechless as I shook my head with surprise.

"Think about that, son. You aren't your father. He robbed you of your childhood. Don't give him your future too. Go be all the things that you want to be." He took another sip of his coffee and set down his mug. "I've seen you with Vivian, and I have no doubt that you make her happy. That's all I care about. If you want to live together first, I'll give you my blessing, as long as you make me a promise."

"What's that?" I asked.

"You don't let fear hold you back from making my girl happy too, all right?"

"I can do that."

"I know you can. That's the only reason I'm on board with this." He raised a brow.

"Thank you, Jack."

"Don't thank me. Just do right by my girl."

And that's exactly what I planned to do.

Chapter 27

Vivian

The next few weeks had flown by, and some of the snow out front of the bakery was starting to melt. Everly had gone to San Francisco to interview with the Lions, and she'd flown out to Chicago to interview with their hockey team as well. She was going to have options.

I turned on my KitchenAid and added the flour slowly as I whipped up another batch of my famous Honey Bee butter cookies.

"Hey, I'm going to head out. I've got a paper due tomorrow so it's going to be a late night for me," Dylan said, biting into a brownie. "I'm going to miss working here next year." Her schedule was going to change drastically, so she'd need to focus on school and there would be no time for working.

I laughed. "I'll keep you well stocked. Get out of here. I've got a few more batches to make before I call it a night."

"I saw Jada leave with Rook. Those two are getting serious,

huh?" She laughed.

"They are. I think they're really good for one another."

"Damn. You're all finding love and I'm going to die a lonely spinster."

I barked out a laugh. "You went on a date last night."

"With the world's most arrogant dude on the planet. I'm sorry, but if you refer to yourself in third person, don't even talk to me. You aren't that important, buddy. It sounded like a college résumé the way he sang his own damn praises. I nearly fell asleep at the table from boredom."

"Well, you've always been picky when it comes to the opposite sex, so I'm not surprised you hate everyone you go out with."

"They make it all too easy." She winked. "I'll see you tomorrow. Love you."

"Love you, Dilly."

She went out the back door and I got back to work. Niko was working at the firehouse tonight and I always used those days to work later so I could get off early on the nights he'd be home. Living together had proved to be better than expected. I loved shacking up with Niko West. He'd been the missing piece all along. I always thought maybe the empty spot in my heart had belonged to my mother. I'd never felt complete during my years with Jansen, and I'd written it off to the fact that I was grieving. But everything had changed since Niko and I had admitted our feelings for one another. That hole had gotten smaller. The loneliness that I'd often felt had gone away.

I was the happiest I'd ever been, and happier than I'd ever thought possible.

A knock on the door pulled me from my thoughts. I wiped my hands on my apron and walked to the front to see Shayla

West peering through the window. I hadn't seen her since Mabel's school show. Niko had drawn a line in the sand for his mother, and as long as she was living with Billy, he had cut off all communication unless she was willing to leave the man, which he doubted would ever happen.

I hurried to the door and unlocked it, letting her inside. "Shayla, hi."

"Hi, Vivian. I know you're closed, I just wondered if we could speak for a minute?"

"Of course. Come in. Can I get you a cookie or a cupcake?"

She sat at the front table. "Sure. I love your treats. Surprise me."

I grabbed two bottles of water, two of my favorite maple bars and a couple napkins. I settled in the chair across from her. "Is everything all right?"

I studied her face, looking for signs of bruises, but I didn't see anything. I'd learned from Niko, who'd shared all of the horror stories from his childhood with me over the last few weeks. The beatings. The verbal abuse. The drunken, unpredictable behavior that he'd been exposed to most of his life. And the lack of safety that he felt.

Anger filled me as I looked across the table at the woman who should have protected him. I wanted to hate her, but all I felt was empathy. Because Shayla West was a victim too. Yes, she was an adult, but she was a broken woman. One who'd been through more than any one person ever should be. And even though I didn't agree with the way she'd neglected her son, I still had compassion for her.

"Yes. I haven't spoken to Niko in quite some time. He doesn't take my calls—he just sends me short texts in response. Tells me to let him know if I need anything. I feel like it's an ultimatum in a way," she said, as she picked off a little piece of her maple bar and popped it into her mouth. Her eyes were puffy, and she looked like she'd aged quite a few years since I'd seen her last.

"I guess, in a way, it probably is. I'm sure you can understand why he can't have a relationship with you under these circumstances, right?" I took a sip of my water.

"Was I supposed to turn Billy away? Is that what this is about?"

Was she serious?

"Yes. You were."

"He's my husband," she said, and her eyes welled with emotion.

I reached across the table and covered her hand with mine. "He hurt your child, Shayla. Hundreds of times. That's not okay."

She nodded. "He doesn't mean it. He's got a drinking problem. When he's not drunk, he's not a bad guy."

"Is he ever a good guy?" I asked because I wanted to hear it from her. "I know he's hurt you too. Do you really want to live that way?"

She looked away and we sat in silence. "He was a good man once."

I shrugged. "That's not good enough. He hasn't been that man for as long as I've known him. Your son has the scars to prove it. And from what I've seen, he hasn't changed at all. Niko suffered," I said, and my words broke on a sob. "Do you understand that? He took the brunt of it. And you stood by and allowed it. Yet your son was still there for you. He'd still be there for you. But you let this man back into your home, and honestly, it was a slap in the face to your son. And that's the truth."

A sob escaped and she swiped at her falling tears. "If I left him, he'd hurt Niko and Jada. He's made that clear."

I sat forward. "You could go to the police."

"Vivian, you don't know this man. He's my husband. I made the choice to marry him many years ago, and it's one that I've honored. Even with all he's done. But he will go after them if I leave, and the police can't do anything to stop him. I went to them once, the first time he put his hands on Niko, and guess what happened."

"What?" I whispered.

"Nothing. They came to the house and gave him a warning. So, the bruises stopped appearing on my face, and they were left for my body. He made a promise to me that if I ever opened my mouth again, he wouldn't come after me. He'd come after my children."

"That is no way to live." I squeezed her hand as tears streamed down my face.

"It's the only way I know."

"You need to talk to Niko. Maybe you could both go to the police. Tell them everything."

"He's a smart man. He goes out drinking almost every night, yet his parole officer hasn't been able to catch him at it. Or he intimidates him and others as well. I don't know. But I came here today to see if you could speak to Niko. I'd still like to have a relationship with my son. It hurt me deeply not seeing him on Christmas." I knew that Jada had invited her mother over to see Mabel on Christmas Day as long as she came without her father.

"I think all of this has hurt him deeply as well. But Niko will not be around Billy, Shayla. Nor should he be asked to," I said.

My words came out harsher than I meant for them to. "Can I ask you something?"

"Yes. Of course." She nodded.

"When Billy tried to blame Niko for the accident, you didn't back him up? Why not? You just always seem to be loyal to him, but not that one time?"

She fidgeted with her napkin before looking up at me. "I knew one of them was going to jail, so if Billy went, he couldn't hurt Niko. I was okay with that. But don't think I didn't pay the price for that all these years later."

"Shayla, there are shelters. There are people who can help you. Hell, you could stay with me and Niko if you need to until this gets settled. You do have options."

She shook her head frantically. "I don't want to do that. He's my husband. This is my cross to bear."

"Why?"

"Because not everyone gets to have a happily ever after, Vivian. But I'm glad that my kids seem to be chasing it."

"You can too," I said.

There was a knock at the door, and I nearly jumped out of my chair when I saw Billy West standing there through the glass. He didn't look happy.

"Can you grab me a box of cookies, please?" She slid twenty dollars toward me on the table, her hand shaking badly. "I said I needed to grab some pastries for the house." I pushed it back toward her.

I held my finger up to him, because I'd made a promise to Niko that I wouldn't allow his father to step foot in Honey Bee's. And I didn't break my promises.

"Your money is no good here. But he isn't welcome. Let me grab you those cookies, but please think about what I said." I hurried to my feet and put some pastries in a box and wrote my phone number on the back of my business card. "My number is on the card. Stick this in your purse. You always have a choice, Shayla."

"Thank you," she whispered as I walked her to the door. Her husband stood there, red in the face, as he glared at me through the window.

I unlocked the door and made sure my body was blocking his way inside. "Come again soon, Shayla."

"What? I'm not welcome at the town bakery? Seems like that might be against the law to be refusing ex-convicts."

I refused to give him any reaction and I closed the door and locked it.

He knocked again and when I looked up, he shouted. "Our boy is working tonight at the firehouse, right? I hope nothing bad happens."

Chills ran down my spine and Shayla yanked on his arm before they walked away. I locked up and walked straight to the firehouse.

"What? No cookies," Rusty said as he sat at the table when I made my way up the stairs to the kitchen.

"Oh. I'm so sorry. I had a box and I forgot it. Is Niko here?" My chest was racing, and I felt sick to my stomach. I knew my dad wasn't working today, but Niko was.

Rusty moved to his feet. "Yeah. You okay? You look a little pale."

I waved my hand and tried to take away the concern I saw etched on his face. "Oh yeah. Just a long day."

"All right. He's up in the room cleaning up. He got called out to a few medical calls this afternoon, so he's been busy."

I nodded as I made my way up another flight of stairs to the bedroom where Niko slept when he was here.

"Niko?" I called out because I didn't see anyone in the room, and panic from my meeting with Shayla and my run-in with Billy was coursing through my veins.

He came running out of the bathroom and his gaze locked with mine as I hurried toward him. "What's wrong, Honey Bee? You okay?"

I shook my head and pulled back trying to catch my breath, because now that I was here, the reality of what I had to tell him was setting in.

"Your mom came by to see me and we talked for a bit. But then your dad showed up."

His eyes hardened. "Did he come into the bakery?"

"No. We were already closed. I opened the door for your mom to leave and he shouted something through the door that scared me."

"What did he say?" Niko stroked my cheek with the pad of his thumb. His long hair fell all around his shoulders as he watched me intently.

"He said that he knew you were working tonight and that he hoped nothing bad happened to you," I said, my voice trembling as the words left my mouth.

He pulled me close again and wrapped his arms around me. "He's just messing with you. He's a sick fucker. Nothing's going to happen to me."

"We still don't know if he started that fire at the warehouse. Have we heard anything more about it?"

"Your dad spoke to Chuck yesterday, and they are working on several leads. Don't worry about this, baby. He can start all the fires he wants, and we'll just keep putting them out until there's enough proof to put his ass back behind bars where he belongs."

I nodded. "I don't know why he's doing this. Why wouldn't he just come out of prison and start living his life again?"

"Because he's a miserable fuck. He's mad that I moved my sister and Mabel out of the house. Mad that I'm not a scared little kid anymore." He bent his knees, so he was eye level with me and kissed the tip of my nose. "What did my mom want?"

I took his hand and led him over to his bed and he dropped to sit, and I climbed onto his lap. "She wants me to talk to you. She misses you."

He let out a long breath. "She made her choice. She chose him. She always does."

"I don't think it's that simple, Niko." I ran my fingers through his thick hair, tucking one side behind his ear. "She told me that he's always threatened to hurt you if she goes to the police. You and Jada. She said the one time she tried to do something about it, she and you both took a bad beating for it and the police didn't do anything about it."

He sighed. "She tried once? That was it? Hell, he hurt me anyway, so how did that help? And she could have divorced him while he was in prison. I think she actually loves that piece of shit. I can't have her in my life as long as he's around. He's toxic, Honey Bee."

I nodded. "I know he is."

"So, if he comes by the bakery when you're open, you just dial Brady. I've already talked to him. He'll have a car there to escort him out right away. It's private property and you can refuse him service."

"I know. Jada, Dylan, and Jilly are all aware to call Brady if he comes in. Your sister seems to hate him as much as you do now."

"Yep. I think she pulled her head out of the sand and realized that having him around Mabel was a bad idea. But I know it's hard for her not seeing my mom often now. They've always been close."

"And who are you close to, Niko West?"

"You, Honey Bee. Always you."

Chapter 28
Niko

Jace went with me to Honey Mountain Café, which sat on Honey Mountain Lake, to meet my father's probation officer, Wayne. The dude had been pretty receptive to talking to me so far, and I appreciated it. I didn't like the fear I saw in Vivian's eyes last night, and I needed to make sure this guy was doing his job.

"Well, well, well…if it isn't my two favorite firefighters," Delilah Joybill said with a wink.

"I'll bet you say that to all the guys from the firehouse," Jace teased. I really appreciated my best friend being with me. He knew the whole story of my miserable family—oh fuck, who am I kidding? The whole fucking town knew.

"Nonsense." Delilah chuckled. "I'm guessing you're meeting this gentleman over here. He said he was waiting for you, Niko."

"Yep. Thanks, Dee." I nodded.

Delilah and her husband, Dean, owned this place, and it had been in Dean's family for generations. They'd renovated it about a year ago, and it was the most popular restaurant in town, not that there were many to choose from. But it sure as hell beat out Rodney's Café, which smelled like onions and sauerkraut.

I reached over and shook Wayne's hand and introduced Jace. We placed our orders as I had shit to do after this and wanted to make it quick.

We sat at a four-top table, and I was seated directly across from Wayne.

"So, what's going on? Has he made any more threats?" Wayne asked as he sipped his coffee.

"He's a smart fucker," I said, nodding my thanks at Delilah when she set two coffees in front of me and Jace. "Nothing concrete, but he scared the shit out of my girlfriend last night. Just making his noncommittal threats about hoping I don't get hurt in a fire."

"Last time he said that there was a big one started out at the old warehouse, right? Anything happen last night?"

"Nothing big. Have you caught him boozing at Beer Mountain?"

"Nope. I've checked with the bartender over there and he says he orders a Coke and plays pool. But he also says that your dad seems sloppy by the time he leaves, so he could be bringing his own booze in with him and hiding it."

"He is. The dude is slick as fuck." I scrubbed a hand down my face. "What about my mom? Did you go by the house and check on her?"

"I did. She told me the same story that she told you. She tripped and hit her face on a door."

Delilah set our plates down and we started eating.

"You don't buy that shit, do you, Wayne?" Jace asked as he sipped his coffee.

"No. But I also can't say something happened without her admitting it. I'm just watching and taking notes for now. It's the best I can do. If you hear anything from that arson investigator, give him my number. Your father would have had no reason to be out at that warehouse, so if you find proof he was there, that would be enough to at least take him in for breaking the rules of his probation."

"We need something bigger. Something that actually keeps him there."

Wayne forked his pancakes and took a bite as he thought about my words. "Listen, Niko. My job is to help your father find his footing back in society. I know you have a history with the man, and if you find me something concrete, I give you my word I'll haul his ass back. But the goal is for him to be reformed and find his new place out of prison."

"He'll never be reformed. He was damaged long before he went into prison. That hasn't changed."

"Well, if he started that fucking fire, I'll personally be happy to teach that asshole a lesson. Any man who beats up on women deserves to be behind bars, and if he's starting fires and putting people's lives in jeopardy, that's even more of a reason," Jace said.

Wayne nodded and we continued eating before we finished up and I paid the bill and thanked him for his time.

"Thanks for breakfast," Jace said, clapping me on the shoulder. "Listen, Niko, we've been friends a long time. You never talked much about your dad, but with what I'm hearing now, the way he's put his hands on your mom," he said, stopping in front of his car and rubbing a hand down the back of his neck. "Did he hurt you as a kid? I didn't know you back then."

"Because you're old as fuck?" I said as I barked out a laugh.

Jace was six years older than me, so we hadn't been in high school together.

"Hardly. You wish you looked this good." He smirked before crossing his arms over his chest and waiting for me to answer his question.

"It's water under the bridge. I survived it. We'll leave it at that."

There was empathy in his gaze when I looked up. "Okay, brother. You know I'm always here if you need an ear."

I rolled my eyes. "Don't be going soft on me. That which doesn't kill us makes us stronger, right?"

His lips turned up in the corners. "Yeah, but you shouldn't have to learn that lesson as a kid. Damn, I think of the girls and what they're going through with their mama leaving the way she did, and it kills me."

I clapped him on the shoulder. "They've got you, man. They're going to be just fine."

"Thanks. All right, I need to go relieve the babysitter." He saluted me as he walked to his car.

"I'll see you later." I held up my hand and started in the direction of Laley's. It was the nicest jewelry store in town.

"You've sure been on a mission to get somewhere this morning. What are you up to, West?" he called out after me.

"I'll fill you in later," I shouted and kept walking as he slipped into his car and honked when he drove past me.

Everly stood outside the jewelry store, looking down at her phone. Her coat was zipped up to her neck and she wore a hat and gloves.

"Hey, Ev," I said as I walked up.

"Hi." She dropped her phone in her pocket and hugged me. "Jeez, trying to go somewhere without Dylan giving you the third degree is a challenge."

I barked out a laugh as I held the door open for her. "The girl doesn't miss a beat, does she?"

"She does not. And I don't want her to slip and tell Vivi you're looking at rings," she said, bumping my shoulder as we stood in front of the glass-encased counter. I'd thought about inviting Dylan and Charlotte to join us, but with Ashlan out of town, I didn't want to risk hurting her feelings. So, I just called on Vivi's oldest sister to come and meet me.

"Hey there. This is a nice surprise," Mrs. Laley said as she came out from the back room. She and her husband were older than dirt, but they acted like they were young and spry.

Everly and I both greeted her, and I walked around looking down at all the rings. "I'm looking for an engagement ring for Vivian," I said, and I couldn't wipe the ridiculous smile from my face. I never thought I'd be shopping for rings, but once we moved in together, I knew this was something that I needed to do. I kept thinking about what Jack Thomas had shared with me about his own father. And the dude was the best dad I'd ever known, so maybe there was some truth to it. I wasn't sure where I stood with all of it, but I wasn't as adamantly opposed to the idea of a family as I'd always been.

Mrs. Laley clapped her hands together and gasped. "Niko West, I never thought I'd see the day. My oh my. Well, our Vivian is quite a special lady, isn't she?"

"She is," I said as I stared down at a ring that caught my eye. "I like this one."

Everly came to stand beside me, and she chuckled. "It's very Vivian. Vintage. Stylish. Elegant. It probably costs a fortune."

"I'm not worried about that. I only plan on getting the one, so I don't have a problem with splurging on it."

"Good point," Everly said, and her eyes widened as Mrs. Laley took it out of the case.

"It's a perfect round diamond with little diamonds all around the outside and along the band. It's a very regal ring."

"I love it," Everly said, holding it up and studying every angle.

"I'll take it," I said after I glanced down at the price tag. I handed her my card. I hadn't decided how I'd ask Vivian yet, but I wanted to do it right. The right time would present itself when it was time.

She wrapped it up and handed me the bag before coming around the counter and hugging each of us. "I'm happy for you, Niko. You got yourself a good one. She's one in a million."

I nodded. "She is."

When we stepped outside, Everly started laughing hysterically.

"What?" I asked, coming to a stop.

"You brought me with you, and you found your ring in two minutes. How'd you know that was the one? You didn't look at anything else."

"I've never shopped for jewelry before. I didn't know if I'd know which ring to get her. But when I saw it, it reminded me of her. The big diamond in the middle, with all the little ones surrounding it." What I didn't say was that it made me think of Honey Bee spreading all her sweetness to those around her. I sounded like a corny asshat, but it's the reason I chose the ring.

"Who knew you were such a romantic?"

"Only with Vivi. Let's keep that between us." I smirked. "Thanks for going with me."

"I'm really happy for both of you. I think I always knew you'd end up together."

"Yeah?" I scrubbed a hand down my jaw. "Well, you've

always been smarter than me."

"Amen to that," she said with a devious smile. "When are you going to do it?"

"I'm not sure. Waiting for the right moment."

"All right. I'll keep my lips sealed, lover boy. I'll wait for you to work your magic."

"Thanks, Ev. How are the interviews going?"

"Pretty good. I've got a second interview with the Lions in San Francisco, and the hockey team in Chicago is interested, so we'll see if either of those pan out."

I nodded. "Did you see Hawk when you interviewed with the team?"

She groaned. "Thankfully, no. But I'm guessing if I get hired, I'll have to deal with him."

I'd always liked the dude. We didn't get to see him much now that he was a rock star hockey player.

"Hawk's a good guy. He's the poster child for hockey now, so he seems to be doing good for himself."

She rolled her eyes. "I'll cross that bridge when I get there. Hockey teams are new to hiring sports psychologists so it might not even happen. So, for now, I'll just spend my days psychoanalyzing firemen. I noticed you skipped your last session," she said with a chuckle. She had an open-door policy at the firehouse, and she stopped by a few times a week.

"Well, I noticed Rusty and Tallboy sure like to sign up to talk to you. I have a hunch it's more about spending time with you than opening up."

She rolled her eyes. "Yeah. Rusty acts like we're on a date and asks me about my interests. But trust me, I'm used to professional athletes, I can handle a few cocky firemen. I grew up with one, remember?"

I nodded. "You sure did. Hey, have you met with Little Dicky yet?"

She thought about it. "Nope. He hasn't signed up for a meeting yet. Why? You have some concerns? My dad asked me the same thing, but then he got sidetracked when Dylan came in with a box of pastries."

"Yeah. He's a good guy. But he's definitely struggling with fear, so it might be good to talk to him a little," I said, not wanting to say much because I didn't want to betray the dude, but I knew he needed some help with his choice of profession.

"What's he afraid of, Dr. West?" she teased.

"Fire." It's all I needed to say, and her gaze softened with understanding.

"I'll make sure I see him this week. Thanks for the heads-up."

"Yep. I'll see you later." I waved and started walking toward the bakery to see my girl. I slipped the ring in my coat pocket as I thought about Little Dicky. It would surprise people to know how often this shit happened. Where someone chose to be a firefighter, yet they were terrified of fire. Sometimes they got over it. Sometimes they became an engineer and drove the truck like Gramps. And sometimes they quit when the fear overtook them. My hope was that Everly could help him find where he fit. Because heading into a fire with a guy who was afraid of the flames was not safe for anyone.

...

"Whose idea was this anyway?" I grumped. We were going on a double date with Jada and Rook, and I wasn't big on double dates, especially when they involved my sister and Rook. Why would I want to see some dude gushing all over my sister? I didn't.

46ol

"Stop being a baby. I love double dating with my sisters. Jada really wanted to do this, and it's just dinner," Vivian said, looking at me with that sweet smile of hers.

"What if I wanted you all to myself?" I said, burying my face in her neck and wrapping my arms around her as we paused in front of Honey Mountain BBQ. They had the best ribs in town. Hell, they had the best ribs in the state of California as far as I was concerned.

"I'm all yours in a few hours," she whispered. Her words were breathy and filled with the need I felt just being this close to her.

I tugged the door open, and Vivian led us inside. Jada and Rook waved from a table in the back, and we made our way toward them. Vivian hugged them like we didn't see them every day, and I rolled my eyes. Rook extended a hand, and I could tell he was nervous as hell. I didn't know him as well, as we didn't always work the same shifts and he was still new. But I'd be lying if I didn't say I liked the dude. He was a good guy, no doubt about it. And I'd seen a change in my sister since they'd started dating. She wasn't whining about not getting to go out anymore, that's for sure.

"Who's with Mabel?" I asked, suddenly feeling panic move through my veins as we all dropped to sit around the table.

"She's with Dylan and Charlotte tonight," Jada said with a brow raised. She'd respected my wishes about keeping that little girl away from our father and I appreciated it.

"I can't picture Dylan babysitting," I said, glancing over at Vivi.

"Dylan is providing the food and the entertainment. Charlotte is providing the caregiver responsibility. Those are Dylan's words, not mine. She's actually great with kids, she just likes to pretend she's not." Vivi smirked.

"Mabel was so excited to go over to your dad's house with them. It's such a treat for her."

The Thomases had always been good to my niece, and it meant a lot to me.

The server came over and we placed our order, and I found Vivi's hand beneath the table. I didn't know when I became such a sap, but I didn't mind it. Not when it came to her.

The girls filled Rook and me in on their day.

"Have you told him about Busy Betty yet?" Jada asked over a fit of laughter. I studied my sister. She was different. Maybe it was working at the bakery and taking on added responsibility. Maybe it was dating Rook. Maybe it was just growing older and wiser. But there was a confidence there now that had never been there before.

Vivian looked over her shoulder. "So, Valentine's Day is coming up and Busy Betty wanted us to make a cake that she could jump out of for her hubby, Butch. You know...she'd wear something sexy and jump out of the big cake and surprise her husband."

I rubbed my temples. "That is not an image I ever want to picture. The woman has been like a second mom to me over the years. Rusty would shit his pants if he knew what his mother was up to. What did you tell her?"

"Well, I told her those aren't real cakes normally. That's more of a prop. So, we settled on red velvet cupcakes with white icing and a heart in the middle, and I'm going to leave the sexy time plans to Betty." Vivian's cheeks pinked and she covered her mouth as she laughed along with Jada.

"Ahhh...this might be good ammunition to use against Rusty the next time he decides to freeze my boxer briefs or put shaving cream in the palm of my hand when I'm sleeping."

I barked out a laugh. "Now you're thinking like a firefighter."

I had a good time hanging out with my sister and Rook...her boyfriend. But I was still anxious to get my girl home.

I always was.

Chapter 29

Vivian

Tomorrow was the anniversary of my mother's passing. It was also the day before Valentine's Day, so I was swamped at work. Niko would be on duty the next few days, and I'd come straight from work to my dad's house because Ashlan had just gotten home. We were always together, no matter where we were on this day. Everly had always flown home to be with us from no matter where she was, and everyone had followed suit. Dad always took this entire week off from the firehouse, as I think it was just a time of grieving for him. We couldn't bring Mom back, so I wasn't sure why we always rallied to be together this time of year, but it helped soothe the hurt that still lived inside me. Jansen had never understood it. He said that grieving wouldn't bring her back and he never quite grasped why I fell into a dark place every year when this date rolled around. He said that I always brought a dark cloud to Valentine's Day, but I never felt the nostalgia most people felt for that day. Hopefully it didn't show in my baking, which is where I usually poured all my energy into this time of year. Niko had always understood it. Maybe we just had a gift for recognizing one another's pain. But he'd call me more than usual, check in more, and help me out of the funk that usually followed.

I pushed the door open, and the smell of garlic and butter had my mouth watering.

"Hey," I called out, and Ashlan came flying down the stairs and into my arms. Our baby sister's heart was so big. She felt things deeply and truly believed that hugs could fix everything, and sometimes she was right.

"Hey," she said as she leaned back and smiled. "Please tell me you brought some of those oatmeal chocolate chip cookies?"

I handed her the box in my hand and chuckled. "Of course. Cookies and hugs can fix everything, right? How's Dad?"

"He seems fine. But you know him, he doesn't talk about it. We're going to all go to the cemetery in the morning, right?"

"That's the plan," I said, following her into the kitchen.

"Hey, sweetheart. How was work?" my father called over his shoulder as he set a large bowl of spaghetti with his famous homemade sauce in the center of the table.

"Good. And it smells delicious," I said, as Everly set a basket of garlic bread down and Charlotte placed a wood bowl filled with her favorite Caesar salad beside it.

"Where's Dilly?" I asked. She hadn't worked today as she had a big test coming up and she always dealt with her grief by retreating.

"I'm here," Dylan shouted as she bounded down the stairs and came into the kitchen making an entrance per usual.

We went around the table sharing some of our favorite stories about Mom. But I was lost in the memory of that final time I saw her. It had never left me. Everly had been crazed with her junior year of high school and consumed with where she'd go to college. In a way, I think it had been a coping mechanism not to deal with the fact that our mother was dying right before our eyes.

The twins were in middle school and busy with activities, and Ashlan buried herself in books as the girl always loved to read. I spent that last year educating myself about what stage four pancreatic cancer actually meant. Mom and Dad liked to tell us that she would fight it, but I learned early in the battle that she was just buying time. Putting her body through hell to try to stick around longer than it was willing to. I missed a ton of school those last few months. For whatever reason, I took on the role of caretaker and I liked it. Niko brought me my schoolwork at the end of the day, and he'd sit by Mom's bed and tell her all about his dreams of playing college football. Toward the end, the visits from friends and family lessened, as people were too sad to see her dwindling away the way she did. My sisters checked out emotionally because it was all too much. Mom didn't want to go into a hospice facility, she wanted to spend her final days in home hospice. Dad had to keep working, as his insurance was paying Mom's medical bills and his paychecks were keeping us all afloat. And I sat bedside with her those last few weeks. Niko came by every day, no matter what shape Mom was in. He never flinched when he saw her or acted affected by it. And I didn't feel so alone when he was there.

"You need to drink, Mom," I said, bringing the cup to her cracked and dry lips. The home nurse that came by once a day told me staying hydrated would help her, so I did my best.

"My sweet Vivi. You should be in school." Her words were weak. Fragile. A true reflection of her physical state.

"I'm exactly where I want to be. Don't you worry. Everyone

is fine, Mom. The twins have a soccer game today, and Everly is going to go cheer them on after school. Dad's at the firehouse and he keeps calling to see how you're feeling. And Ashlan is staying after school to do homework in the library."

Mom squeezed my hand. "You shouldn't be here, baby girl. I'm sorry I wanted to come home. I need to feel you all around me. But I shouldn't be doing this to you."

Her words broke on a strained sob and my chest ached. I wasn't sure if there was a medical term for what I felt. A constant ache in the center of my chest. As if I were present to watch my heart slowly break a little more each day. A painful, drawn-out, torturous pain that was unlike anything I'd ever felt.

We'd worked out a system. On the days Dad wasn't at the firehouse, he stayed with her all day. On the days that he had to be at work, I stayed home from school. Of course, Honey Mountain High School had been supportive. My mother attended there in her day, and she'd grown up with my principal, Mr. Stark. I kept up just fine, as she slept often, and I did my homework beside her. Everyone in town was heartbroken over the situation, as my mother was loved by all who knew her.

Her bed was set up in the living room, which looked more like a hospital room than our front room these days. There was a wheelchair and machines that beeped around the clock.

I relied on those sounds and sometimes felt like they mimicked the beat of my own heart. It had been three weeks since Mom had moved from bad to worse and been placed in hospice. Everly, Dylan, Charlotte, Ashlan, and I took turns sleeping on the couch every night when Dad wasn't here. And when he was here, he slept beside Mom, and I often woke up and wandered down the stairs to check on her, and I'd see his hand wrapped around hers and bags beneath his eyes the morning after. Watching the love of his life deteriorate right in front of him was more than any man should have to live through.

I turned up the volume on the TV for her after she took the smallest sip of water. "So, this is that home renovation show you love. I know you can't keep your eyes open, but I can tell you that you would love this one. They are renovating an old farmhouse like ours," I said as I climbed into bed beside her.

"I remember the day we bought this house," she whispered. "I was pregnant with the twins, and you and Everly were running wild through the place." Her voice sounded so weak.

"I remember that day too."

"I love you with my whole heart, baby girl," she whispered so softly I nearly missed it. I knew she was dozing off. Her exhaustion was contagious as I often fell asleep right beside her on days like these.

Watching someone you love suffer was an unfathomable thing to experience. There was no cure for Mom's cancer, and there was no cure for the ones she loved watching her slip away either.

I moved closer, needing to hear her heartbeat, as my falling tears landed on the back of my hand and the lump in my throat threatened to take my last breath. The sound of Mom's shallow breaths relaxed me, and I dozed off beside her.

The doorbell startled me, and I pushed up. Dazed. How long had I been asleep? I glanced at my phone and realized it hadn't been that long. Less than an hour. But my sleep had become so irregular that when I was able to doze off for short times, it almost felt painful when I woke up.

"It must be Niko with my classwork," I whispered as I stroked the hair out of her face and looked down at her.

Her chest wasn't moving.

Her lips weren't moving.

Panic gripped me like a vise.

"Mom?" I whispered, but the word broke on a sob. I leaned my ear down to her mouth and there was nothing. I placed my cheek on her chest, desperate to find a heartbeat, but there was nothing.

A sound that I'd never heard before escaped my mouth as I leaned down and covered her mouth with mine and breathed. I'd taken CPR classes before I started babysitting, but I'd never expected to be doing it on my own mother.

I pumped her chest as the tears fell from my eyes, dropping on her like rain from the skies.

"Mom!" I screamed. "Mom! Come back!"

I heard Niko's voice in the distance. Maybe he was calling for help. Maybe he was talking to me. I didn't know. I didn't know when he burst through the door.

I continued breathing and pumping on her chest.

I believed I could bring her back.

But the tears were blurring my vision and Mom just lay there lifeless. But I pumped harder. Breathed deeper. Hoped harder.

I could will her back to life if I just kept trying.

Warm arms came around me. Familiar and strong even as a teenager.

"Honey Bee, she's gone."

"No," I said, and my voice was hoarse and tired. I puffed again.

Breathe, Mama.

Sirens sounded in the distance and the whole scene played out in slow motion. Three men stormed in and moved me out of the way. Niko stood there with his arms wrapped around me, and when I crumpled to the floor, he dropped down with me and pulled me onto his lap.

Tears landed on my forearm, and I looked behind me to see them falling from his gray eyes. I'd never seen Niko cry. Not when he'd been kicked so hard by his father that he'd vomited blood. Not when he got his first or his fiftieth cigarette burn. Not when he'd been punched or beaten or broken.

But today he cried.

My father came charging through the door and my gaze locked with his.

Pain.

Despair.

Sadness.

He dropped to his knees and cried out her name. I buried my face in Niko's chest because I couldn't take another minute. He kept me there as Mom was wheeled out of the house, and he stayed with me that night and for weeks after when I cried for her.

Because she was gone.

And she took a piece of my heart with her.

"Earth to Vivi," Dylan said. "Dad just asked if you're sleeping here tonight?"

"No. I'm going to head home after dinner." I wanted to be alone tonight. This house was a reminder of those last moments. It was a brutal reality. The best and worst memories of my life lived here. But with tomorrow's darkness looming over me, I wanted to sleep at my house. I wanted to cry without fear of upsetting my sisters.

"You want me to stay with you?" Everly asked.

"No. I'm fine, guys. I'll be back in the morning to head over to the cemetery."

Everly studied me. I knew that she had always felt a lot of guilt that I'd been the one who'd been with our mother when she passed away. My dad had pushed me to speak to someone about it, but I never felt the need. The truth was, I'd been exactly where I wanted to be. I'd do it all over again, just to spend that time with her. As sad as it was, my mother got to feel my heartbeat when she took her last breath. She wasn't alone.

"So, Ev heard back from the Lions," Dylan said with a mischievous smirk as she wriggled her brows. "Apparently, Mr. Badass hottie Hawk needs the good doctor's help."

"A. I'm not a doctor. B. This isn't really the time to discuss this. Read the room, Dilly." Everly threw her arms in the air.

"I think it's a perfect time to talk about it," Dad said, surprising everyone. "Mom would be really proud of you."

Everly nodded and dabbed beneath her eyes to stop the tears that threatened to fall.

"Well, apparently he has a knee injury, but his coach thinks there's a lot more going on. They want me to come back out and meet with him. I haven't seen the guy in years, so I just don't know if I want to do it. It probably won't go anywhere. And I got another interview with a football team in Texas, and they're flying me out next week."

The conversation continued as we finished up dinner. I couldn't wait to head home. I felt a heaviness that found its way to my shoulders every year at this time. I hugged my sisters goodbye and kissed my dad on the cheek before heading out to my car.

I pulled into my driveway and turned off the car when the emotions overtook me. The lump in my throat so thick it made it challenging to swallow. I gripped the steering wheel as the tears started to fall. A sob escaped my throat, and I didn't try to stop it.

A slight tapping on my car window startled me and I jumped. *Niko.*

I turned off the car and pushed the door open.

"What are you doing here?" I croaked as the tears continued to fall.

"Where else would I be, Honey Bee?" He pulled me into his arms and my legs wrapped around his waist as he carried me into the house. I buried my face in his neck as the tears continued to fall. He set me on the kitchen counter and stood between my legs.

"I thought you had to work?" My voice trembled as he pushed the hair out of my face.

"I thought you might need me tonight and tomorrow, so I got Tallboy to cover."

I nodded. He was here.

He'd always been here when I needed him most.

Chapter 30

Niko

"Tell me what you need, baby," I said as I searched her dark gaze. The house was dim, with only the light from the moon shining through the windows. But I could see the sadness. The despair. Her eyes were puffy, her cheeks red, and her voice trembled every time she spoke.

"I don't want to think about it, Niko. Make me stop thinking," she whispered, and she tugged my mouth down to hers.

I knew exactly what she needed. She didn't want to think. She just wanted to feel something other than sadness.

Vivian didn't live in darkness like I often did. It was an unfamiliar feeling for her, and I wanted to take it away.

I kissed her hard. My tongue dipping in, teasing and tasting all of that darkness away for her.

"Please. Make it go away," she said against my lips.

I leaned her back on the counter, never losing contact with her mouth. My hands found the hem of her skirt and pushed it up, while my lips moved down her neck, licking and kissing as her breaths came hard and fast. I lifted her sweater and she pushed up just enough for me to lift it over her head.

I tugged at her bra, pulling the straps down her shoulder and exposing her perfect tits. My mouth came down over her hard peak and she arched in response as she moaned. I moved to the other, taking turns with each one, as my fingers moved beneath her panties.

"You're soaked," I said as I flicked her nipple with my tongue.

Her hands tangled in my hair as I stroked her, before slipping two fingers inside, as she gasped and moved against my hand.

"I want you. I need you," she whispered as I kissed my way down her stomach before shoving her skirt further up and pulling her panties down her legs so I could bury my face between her thighs.

Exactly where she needed me. My tongue took the place of my fingers as desperate moans and hot breaths filled the space around us.

"Niko," she cried out her release as she went over the edge. I continued to move until she rode out every last bit of pleasure against my mouth, and I'd never been so turned on in my life. The way she reacted to my touch did something to me and I fucking loved it.

Craved it.

She pushed up on her elbows and I pulled my head up to look at her.

"Better?" I asked.

She nodded and smiled. "How do you always know what I need?"

"Because I know you, Vivian Thomas."

"Better than anyone. You always have," she said.

I pulled her into my arms, legs wrapping around my waist once again, and carried her to the couch. My erection throbbed against her ass, and she chuckled when I dropped to sit.

"You think that's funny, do you?" I teased, brushing her hair away from her face.

She started grinding up against me, the only thing between us was the layer of denim from my jeans. My hands found her hips and I watched her. The moonlight was shining on her as she straddled me, eyes closed, wild hair falling all around her shoulders as she continued to move.

"I need more," she whispered as she reached down for my jeans and unbuttoned them. I lifted enough to shove them down, as my overexcited cock sprang free.

"I'm all yours, Honey Bee. Always have been, always will be."

"I'm on the pill. I want to feel you. All of you." She lifted up, positioning her entrance at the tip of my erection, and slowly slid down.

"Fuck," I said. She felt so fucking good.

Her fingers intertwined with mine as she rode me into oblivion.

Vivian Thomas was the sexiest woman I'd ever laid eyes on.

We both went over the edge at the same time. She fell forward and I wrapped my arms around her and held her tight.

Because tonight, this was what she needed.

• • •

I woke up to the smell of coffee and stretched my arms above my head. Vivian wasn't in bed, and I didn't know how she'd feel today. Grief was a motherfucker. It just took and took and took.

Every year I'd gone with the Thomases to the cemetery, and

I still remembered the day that Beth passed away like it was yesterday. The sound of Vivi's cries. The paramedics pronouncing her dead. Holding my best friend in my arms as she sobbed.

I'd been through some shit in my life, no doubt about it. But seeing Vivian hurt the way she did that day—it would stay with me forever. She'd put on a brave face for her family because it's who she was. She was strong and fierce and protective. But she hurt like the rest of us. And if I could be here to take some of that away, I'd do it over and over again.

"Hey," she said, walking over to me with two mugs in her hands. She handed me one and set the other on the nightstand beside her, before climbing into bed and looking at me. She wore my navy Honey Mountain Fire Department tee, and it fit her more like a dress, but she managed to look sexy as hell.

I took a sip of coffee and moaned, before setting the mug on the nightstand beside me and pulling her onto my lap. I wrapped my arms around her and nuzzled her neck.

"How are you feeling?"

"Better today, actually. Thanks for taking off work. I thought being with my family would help, but I don't know. Being there last night just made me think about things, you know? I just wanted to leave."

She found my hand and intertwined her fingers with mine.

"I'm glad I could be here. I'd been working on it for a few days, but we're short-staffed, so finding someone to cover right now isn't easy. Once Rook and Little Dicky aren't newbies, it'll be easier to take time off."

"I'll have to bring Tallboy some cookies to thank him next week," she said, as her cheek rested against my chest.

"You don't need to do that. I've covered his ass plenty of times. Let's just focus on today. What time are we meeting everyone? How did the girls seem? How about your dad?"

"They were all okay. You know Dad always gets quieter this time of year, but it's expected. We should probably get dressed and head over to the house."

We headed to the bathroom, and she pulled her hair into a long ponytail and we both got dressed. The sun was actually shining today, and it was nice not to be covered in so many layers.

Once we got to the house, everyone piled in my truck and Jack's car, and we made our way to the cemetery. We all stood around Beth's grave and each of the girls shared their favorite memory. Jack cleared his throat before speaking.

"You'd be proud of our girls, baby. They're amazing, just like their mama. We miss you." He kissed his hand before blowing on it and then he set a large bouquet of flowers on the ground.

"Well, grieving makes me hungry," Dylan said, breaking up the silence, and everyone laughed. The girl was like a bull in a china shop. "I wish you were here to make your famous mac 'n' cheese, Mama."

"I have the recipe," Charlotte snipped at her twin sister.

"Yeah, it's not the same, girl. You're so stingy with the cheese. It's mac and freaking cheese. Don't be so stingy with it."

"You are maybe the most annoying person on the planet right now," Charlotte said, crossing her arms over her chest. "Some of us are trying to cut back our dairy."

"Then don't make mac 'n' cheese and call it Mom's recipe." Dylan shrugged.

We were walking toward the parking lot, and I was trying not to laugh at the ridiculous conversation.

"Well, now I want mac 'n' cheese. Let's go to Honey Mountain Café," Everly said.

"I could eat," Ashlan piped in.

Jack barked out a laugh. "You girls make me crazy. You were crying this morning about Mom. Now you're arguing about noodles and cheese. Niko, I'd start praying for a house full of boys."

Dylan gasped and the rest of the girls burst out in laughter. We all knew he was kidding because the man loved these girls more than I'd ever seen a father love his kids.

"Don't let that freak you out," Vivian said when we got in the car. "I'm not thinking about babies."

The weird thing—I was imagining a house full of little Vivis. And it didn't freak me out at all.

And that alone completely freaked me out.

I reached for her hand as we followed her father's car to the diner. "I'm fine. How are you feeling?"

"I feel good." She squeezed my hand. "I wish my mom could see my sisters all grown up. How amazing they're doing. The woman was giddy if one of us got a good grade on a paper or made a sports team. But Everly's about to be a sports psychologist for a professional team. Dylan's going to law school. Charlotte's changing lives every day in the classroom. And Ashlan is out there conquering college like a rock star. I wish she was here to see it."

My chest squeezed at her words. She loved her sisters so fiercely, and I wished she could see herself through my eyes.

"And what about you, Honey Bee?" I pulled up in front of Honey Mountain Café, and we watched as Jack led his daughters inside. I turned to face her as she unbuckled and looked at me.

"What do you mean?" She tilted her head and smiled.

"Sticking around here and getting your degree nearby so you could keep an eye on your sisters. Saving every penny to buy the bakery and turning it into something everyone in this town loves. Buying your first home before the age of twenty-four. Employing your sisters when they need it. And rocking my fucking world every day by just breathing." I sounded like a sappy pussy, but I didn't care.

Vivian climbed onto my lap and put a hand on my cheek. "Rocking your world, huh?"

"You heard me."

"I love you, Niko West. Yesterday and today wouldn't have been tolerable if you weren't here by my side. Thank you."

I nipped at her bottom lip, and she chuckled.

"You're lucky we're in the truck and your dad's just sitting on the other side of that wall, or I'd have that skirt up over your head and be sliding into you right now."

Her breathing hitched. "Who's rocking whose world now?"

"Baby, I plan to rock your world until you take your last fucking breath," I said, shoving the door open and pushing out of the truck with Vivi in my arms. I set her down on her feet and adjusted myself because the last thing I needed was for Jack to notice the raging boner currently pressing against my jeans.

"How about we do that in an hour after pancakes? And I'll help you out with that, er, situation going on down south." She wriggled her brows and her cheeks pinked.

This girl.

I fucking loved her.

"Done. And quit staring at my dick. It gets him excited."

"Wow. Cemeteries and mac 'n' cheese and erections. Not quite where I saw the day going, but I'll take it." Vivian laughed as she linked her fingers with mine and we walked into the café.

"Never a dull moment with the Thomas girls," I said as we made our way to the table. Delilah Joybill pulled Vivi into her arms and hugged her tight. There wasn't a soul in Honey Mountain who didn't love Beth Thomas, and she was still greatly missed.

We took our seats at the large table in the back and placed our order because Dylan had the patience of a small flea. Once we ordered, Charlotte looked up at me.

"It's your birthday next week, right?"

I cleared my throat. I'd never been big on birthdays, but Vivian always made it a big deal. She'd made me a cake every year since fifth grade. Always trying new recipes and making it special. This year would be different because we were together, and I couldn't think of a better gift.

"Yeah, yeah, yeah. Don't make it a thing." I sipped my coffee and winked at Vivian.

"I need to find me a man who looks at me the way you just looked at Vivi," Dylan said.

Jack grunted. "Do you mind not talking about that crap when I'm here, please?"

"You just told Niko to wish for sons, you are in no position to bargain right now," Dylan said over her laughter.

"I think a bunch of boys would make for a quieter breakfast," Jack said with a smirk.

"I've been to the firehouse plenty and there's nothing quiet over there," Everly said, raising a brow in challenge.

"And all the burping and farting that goes on. It's disgusting." Charlotte rubbed her hands together when Delilah set a plate of pancakes in front of her.

"I agree," Ashlan said over a mouthful of scrambled eggs. "We're chatty, but we aren't pigs."

"Speak for yourself. I won the burping contest in fifth grade." Dylan bit off the top of a piece of bacon.

Charlotte's head fell back in laughter. "Craig Caldwell cried for an hour after you beat him and remember Derek tried to ban girls from joining in."

"*Haters gonna hate!*" Dylan barked out a laugh.

"I swear you've been competitive since birth," Everly said, and Vivian leaned into me and chuckled.

"You're a sports shrink, Ev. Here's what I think." Dylan sipped her coffee.

"Here we go." Jack rolled his eyes.

"We don't use the word shrink, oh competitive one." Everly leaned back in her chair and crossed her arms, waiting for whatever madness Dylan was going to spew.

"I think that losers always call winners *competitive*. It's a coping mechanism. They hate us cause they ain't us."

The table erupted in laughter.

"I think she's on to something," Vivian said over her laughter.

This was exactly what she needed.

But I couldn't wait to get her home and follow up on that earlier plan of having my way with her.

Chapter 31

Vivian

I put the final layer on top of the cake and spread a thin layer of buttercream before crumbling the topping together in a bowl which consisted of cake and rainbow sprinkles. I knew Niko would love it and I wanted to have it ready for tomorrow night so I could leave early to get home to make him dinner.

"That is gorgeous, girl," Jada said as she studied the cake. "Man, I want to learn to bake like you."

"You're getting there. Those cupcakes you made yesterday were delicious. It just takes time and practice. I started at a young age."

"Your mom was a great baker, right?"

"Yep. She was so talented. I remember I used to watch her when I was young and I wanted to be that good, you know?" I chuckled. "That's what made me want to have my own bakery."

"That's so amazing," Jada said, and the door chimed out front. "I got it."

Jada and Rook walked back into the kitchen. The guys at the firehouse had ordered a specialty cake to celebrate Niko's birthday today because he'd be off tomorrow.

"Hey, Vivian. Gramps sent me to come grab that cake."

I put down my spatula and wiped my hands on a towel. "I can't believe you guys made me make a 3D fire hydrant for him." I laughed as I moved into the walk-in refrigerator and brought the box out. I opened the lid to show it to him and his head fell back in laughter.

"That's absolutely perfect. It was Rusty's idea," Rook said as he chuckled some more.

"Are you working today?" I asked.

"Nope. I'm off. Going to go by and drop off the cake and sing to him now," he said before turning to face Jada. "You want to grab dinner tonight?"

Jada's cheeks pinked and I looked away. They were really adorable together. "I've got Mabel, so maybe we could just get takeout and eat at my place."

He shoved his hands in his pockets and smiled. "Sure. That sounds great."

"Hey, I've got an idea. Why don't you two drop Mabel off with me? We can make some cards for Niko for his birthday tomorrow. I would love to do that with her. And he's working tonight, so that would be fun to spend some time with her and you two can go grab dinner."

"Really? Are you sure you don't mind? I know she'd love that, and I never have any crafty stuff at home."

"I have a whole bunch upstairs in the office. Scrapbook paper and glitter and glue. All the works. We'll make some fun stuff, but I can't guarantee she'll come home clean." I chuckled.

"Thank you so much. That sounds great."

I handed Rook the cake. "Make sure you take a picture of him with it and send it to me."

"Will do." He smiled and Jada let him out the back door.

She wiped down the tables and went home to get ready for her date. I finished up a few things at the bakery and locked up before heading home. My dad and Rook both sent me a bunch of photos of Niko next to the fire hydrant cake. His long hair tied back in an elastic, and he was trying to hide his smile, but I could tell by the way the corners of his mouth turned up that he was having a good time.

I made my way home and Jada came by to drop off Mabel.

"You look gorgeous," I said after I kissed the little cherub on the cheek and took in her pretty mama. Jada wore dark skinny jeans and a white sweater and some cute heel booties.

"Thank you so much for doing this," she said before hugging Mabel goodbye.

"Do I look gorgeous too, Miss Vivi?"

"You sure do," I said. "I made us some spaghetti for dinner, and I forgot all the crafts to make Uncle Niko's cards, so after we eat, we'll just run over to the bakery and pick those up."

She clapped her little hands together. "Can I get a cupcake at Honey Bee's, too?"

The way she said the name of the bakery melted my heart. She had the slightest little lisp and it sounded more like Honey Beeth.

"Of course, as long as it's okay with your mama," I said, hugging Jada goodbye. "Now go have fun."

"Absolutely, my little sugar bug. Thanks again," she called out and I shut and locked the door behind her.

I scooped up some pasta on each plate and Mabel and I sat

down to eat together.

"I'm gonna make Neek, Neek the best cards in the whole world," she said over a mouthful of noodles which made me laugh.

"That sounds like a good plan," I said. "We've got glitter and glue and paint we can use."

"You gots any buttons? He likes buttons, I think 'cause he always says I gots a button nose."

I laughed and wiped my mouth. "We'll have to check the office. Charlotte brings a lot of supplies from school and stores them up there because she doesn't have room in her classroom."

"I sure hope there's buttons up there. I've never been in your office. But I hope it's by the cupcakes?"

I nodded and we continued to chat while we ate, before cleaning up and getting ready to go. I zipped up her coat as my phone rang and we made our way out to the car.

"Hey, Dilly. Mabel and I are running to the bakery to grab some stuff to make birthday cards for Niko."

"Ohhh, nice. Grab us a few brownies, please. Me and Everly are coming by in an hour. We have a pile of gifts for Niko from the four of us, and we figured you'd want to be alone tomorrow night, so we'd just drop them at the house."

"That was sweet of you. You got it. I'll be back in twenty," I said as I attached Mabel's car seat in the back of my car and buckled her in. Niko kept one at the house for her.

"Miss Vivi, can I play a game on your phone?" Mabel asked.

"Damn, she's so stinking cute. Give the girl the phone. I'll see you in a little bit."

"All right. Love you." I ended the call and pulled up Angry Birds on my phone because I knew it was her favorite and handed it to her. We drove the short way to the bakery, and I parked in front of Honey Bee's and got Mabel out of the car.

We unlocked the door, but I kept the lights off, because locals were relentless and if they thought we were open, they'd be banging on the door.

"Are we playing hide-and-seek and keeping the lights off?" she asked as I took her little hand in mine and locked the door.

"Kind of. We can turn the lights on upstairs, but if we flip the lights on down here, we'll never get out of here because people will want some treats." I stopped at the glass case and asked her what kind of cupcake she wanted. She chose a red velvet and I put it in her little hands and then filled a bag with five brownies for my sister and my dad before leading her upstairs and flipping on the lights.

Mabel gasped as she took in the shelves filled with supplies. "This is like a real school class, right, Miss Vivi?"

I chuckled. "I think so, yes. So, what do you think? You want to do some paints and glitter? And let's look through these tubs for buttons."

She had icing all over her face and we set the other half of her cupcake on the table while I went to the small sink and wet a paper towel to clean her up.

"You've gots a kitchen up here, Miss Vivi? And a kitchen downstairs?" she asked. The girl was so inquisitive.

"Well, I've got a sink up here, and that's about it. But it's nice because I can wash my hands if I need to when I'm up here organizing things."

"It's very nice," she said as she pulled out a couple rolls of ribbon that I used for packages. "Can we use these pretty bows?"

"Sure." I had a bag, and we were dropping supplies inside.

A noise sounded from downstairs, and I pushed to my feet and left her to play in the pile of crafts. Maybe it was the wind? I moved to the doorway leading down to the kitchen and saw smoke filling the entire downstairs. My heart raced and I stepped down a few steps and realized the entire kitchen was on fire. The flames were moving toward the stairs, our only exit. There wasn't enough time to grab Mabel and get out.

Holy shit.

I quickly closed the door as panic set in.

Calm down.

Think.

I reached in my pocket for the phone before remembering I never got it back from her, as a smoke detector went off and Mabel jumped.

"Miss Vivi, what's that?"

"It's okay, sweetheart. Do you have my phone?" I tried to keep my voice calm as I didn't want to terrify her.

She started to cry and covered her ears. "It's in the car, Miss Vivi."

This was not good.

"Okay. We're okay. The fire station is close, baby girl. They're probably already on their way. Get in this corner, Mabel." I led her to the furthest corner from the door and hurried to the sink. I soaked several kitchen towels that I kept upstairs, and I put them down to cover the crack between the floor and the door. I used one to cover the vent on the floor and I was thankful for the old building having vents on the floor and not on the ceiling.

Mabel was crying in the corner, and I moved toward her and tied a wet towel around her nose and mouth. "Keep this on here."

She nodded as tears poured from her sweet gray eyes.

Niko.

My heart was racing so fast it was difficult to think clearly. He didn't know we were here. Did anyone?

Dylan knew.

Jada knew.

They'd realize the bakery was on fire and call him.

My eyes were burning from the smoke that had already seeped in.

My dad had embedded all the things to do during a fire, and they spun around in my head. I moved to the window and tried to open it. It was our only way out at this point. But the paint was old and dried to the window frame, and it wouldn't budge. I pushed as hard as I could as I looked over and saw Mabel watching me with terror in her gaze.

I handed her another towel and told her to cover her eyes. I was coughing now as smoke continued to make its way into the room even with the door crack and the vent covered. It was moving too fast.

I grabbed the chair from behind the table and hit it against the window as hard as I could. The glass shattered and Mabel cried out.

"We're going to be okay, honey," I shouted. My voice strained as the smoke entered my lungs. I knew I should get a towel and tie it around my face as well, but right now, I needed to let them know we were up here.

I heard a siren in the distance, and I used a towel to wrap around my hand and I punched out the rest of the glass so that I could look out.

The whole freaking building was on fire now. I screamed out for help, and I thought I saw people running toward the building, but it was hard to see through the smoke.

"Help!" I screamed, hoping and praying they would know we were up here. The fire was heading toward the roof, so there would be no way for us to go out this way either. I remembered my father telling me to never climb out on a roof unless there were no other options. Help was on the way. I had to hold on to that.

I grabbed another towel and hung it in the window with some duct tape, so they'd know we were up here, before crouching down to check on Mabel.

She was sobbing in the corner, and I pulled her onto my lap. "It's okay, Mabel. They're coming for us."

Smoke was coming through the window now and I wondered if I'd made a mistake by breaking the glass. I secured the towel around her nose and mouth, and she buried her face in my chest as I wrapped my arms around her tighter.

The sirens were getting closer. I lifted my sweater and pulled it over my nose and mouth, but my coughing was out of control. Smoke was coming in through the window and from beneath the door.

We weren't going to get out of here in time. The fire was moving too fast.

"Don't move," I said to Mabel as I placed her back in the corner, as far from the window as she could get, and I moved back to look outside.

Two fire trucks were there. I didn't know if they could get these flames out before we were swallowed up. Tears streamed down my face, and I coughed so hard I dry heaved.

The hoses were out and aiming up at the window.

They saw me.

I hurried back to Mabel and pulled her into my arms. Her

little whimpers broke my heart, but I held her tight.

"They're coming for us. I promise, they're coming for us."

It was our only chance of getting out of here alive.

Chapter 32
Niko

"Why isn't she picking up the fucking phone?" I hissed, as Gramps pulled up to the bakery and I jumped out of the truck. I'd called Vivian the minute we heard it was Honey Bee's on fire.

"Niko! Dad!" Dylan and Everly were sprinting toward us with Charlotte not far behind.

"You're too close. Get behind the truck," Jack shouted.

"Vivi's in there with Mabel. They're upstairs," Dylan shrieked over her tears.

Every bone in my body went numb.

This wasn't possible.

I didn't respond. I started sprinting toward the building as Jack shouted out orders to get the line. The hose was aiming up at a window and I knew we couldn't get the flames out quick enough to get up there with a ladder.

"Jace!" I shouted. "Get both hoses aimed at the kitchen and one at the side of the building, I'm going up. Vivian and Mabel are up there."

He nodded, but I didn't miss the terror in his eyes. This fire was already out of control.

"You can't go in there, Niko," Tallboy said as he ran toward me with the line.

"Try to fucking stop me." I secured my mask as Tallboy and Jace aimed at the back door which was up in flames. We were inside in seconds, and they had the line full force aiming at the stairs and the kitchen. Big Al and Jack were beside me.

"We need more water," Jack shouted.

I couldn't wait. There was no life for me without Vivian. Without Mabel. I bowed my head and motioned for Jace and Tallboy to follow. They blasted the flames, making just enough of an opening for me to run through.

I'd been in hundreds of fires. But my heart had never raced like this. Because everything I loved was behind that door. Jack was hollering for another line, and I kicked the door open as smoke billowed around me.

"Vivian," I shouted, searching the room through the smoke to find her.

"Niko." I heard a faint squeak, and I saw my two girls crouched in the corner, the room a haze of gray. Honey Bee was sitting on the floor with Mabel, whose face was completely covered with a towel, wrapped in her arms.

"Neek, Neek," Mabel's voice called out to me.

I hurried to the window to check the situation. The flames were too close. Our best exit was back the way I came in.

"Niko," I heard Jack shout from below.

"They're in here," I shouted, looking out the door where I saw both Jace and Tallboy aiming the hose in every direction trying to keep the stairs clear. Jack was halfway up, and I ran to

Vivian. I scooped Mabel up and told Vivian to follow. I made it to the doorway and didn't think. I tossed my niece through the air toward Jack Thomas who held his arms open and caught her. I turned around to reach for Vivian's hand, but she wasn't behind me. She was in a ball on the floor coughing. I pulled my mask off and secured it around her face.

"Baby, we've got to get up." I scooped her into my arms and ran for the door. Jace was shouting that he couldn't hold it off any longer, and Tallboy was screaming for me to get out.

I don't know if I ran down the stairs or jumped as the flames blazed beneath my feet, because adrenaline took over and I flew through the doorway with Vivian in my arms. I stumbled outside into the air as she continued to cough aggressively in my arms. Two more trucks had arrived, and they were surrounding the building doing what they could to get it under control before it caught on to neighboring structures.

But all I cared about were Vivian and Mabel.

Jack was there, assessing his daughter as she lay limp in my arms, the only sign of life was her insistent cough.

"Vivi!" Everly screamed and Dylan and Charlotte were behind her, tears streaming down their faces.

"Niko," Jada cried out as she frantically ran toward me.

"Ambulance," Jack said to Jada, and he pointed. "She's okay. She was talking. Her face was covered."

Vivian had made sure of it. But she hadn't covered her own damn face. "Take the mask off her and let her breathe," I said.

She coughed hard, and her eyes were closed as two paramedics, Josh and Gruby, who I knew well, rushed me with a gurney in tow and tried to take her from me.

"I've got her," I hissed. "Don't you fucking touch her."

I laid her down and stroked her face as they pushed me back

and secured oxygen over her mouth and nose. Her skin was pale and bluish and her breaths shallow.

Jack held on to my arm as her sisters wailed in fear beside me.

"Come on, Honey Bee. Breathe. You're okay, baby," I shouted over their shoulders, and my voice was unrecognizable.

Fear.

Terror.

It was all there.

I couldn't see through my tear-streaked vision. Jack put his arms on my shoulders. "Let them assess her, Niko."

I nodded and swiped at my face as I watched. Everly reached for my hand and squeezed it, and Charlotte hugged her father as we all stood there watching the scene before us. Dylan paced and cried beside me.

"We're taking her in," Gruby said, looking over at me and Jack. "I think she needs to be intubated."

"Fuck," I shouted and Everly jumped at the sound.

I wasn't stupid. I'd been a firefighter for several years and I knew that more than half the deaths in fires were a result of smoke inhalation. This was bad.

"Hey, we're going to take Mabel to the hospital but she's breathing fine on her own, and she's going to be okay," Josh said, and I glanced up to my sister leaning against the truck with Mabel in her arms.

"I'm riding with you," I said, turning my attention back to Gruby. He nodded.

"I'll drive the girls," Jack said, his voice shaky. He knew the same thing that I did, and the next few hours would be crucial to see how she responded.

I climbed in the back of the ambulance and took her hand. Her eyes were blinking open and closed, and I stroked her cheek.

"I'm right here, Honey Bee. Mabel's going to be fine. You just need to worry about you right now, okay?"

It didn't surprise me that Vivi had made sure that Mabel would be okay. It's who she was. But fuck if I wasn't pissed that she hadn't taken care of herself. She'd done everything else right. Hung a towel in the window so we'd know they were up there, covered the vents and door with wet towels, and protected Mabel's face from the smoke the best she could.

The ride to the hospital was quick and everything blurred once we arrived. There were several people waiting for her when we arrived as the guys had called ahead. Vivian was whisked away without a word, and I stood there in the doorway staring with disbelief. How the fuck did this happen?

"She's a fighter. She's going to be okay," Jack said, clapping me on the shoulder and clearing his throat. But I didn't miss the fear in his eyes.

I nodded, and he led Everly and Charlotte into the hospital to the waiting room as Everly spoke to Ashlan on the phone. She must have been on her way here as Everly kept telling her to drive safely through her tears.

"How bad is it?" Dylan asked me, making sure no one else could hear us.

I ran a hand through my hair. "They'll get her oxygen up and she'll be okay. She inhaled a lot of smoke."

"Don't bullshit me, Niko. I need to know how bad it is," Dylan's words broke on a sob, and she lost it. I wrapped my arms around her and hugged her, because I'd never seen the girl cry before, aside from the one time at her mother's funeral.

"Listen to me, Dilly. She's going to be fine." I kissed the top of her head. "Let's get inside and wait to see what the doctor says."

She nodded and we both walked toward the waiting room.

The next few hours were the worst of my life. The waiting was agony. Dr. Prichard finally came out to speak to us. We all knew him well as he'd lived in Honey Mountain his entire life.

"She's doing okay for now. She's breathing better. We did insert a breathing tube as a precaution because she inhaled a whole lot of smoke. We've run blood tests and they look as we expected, and we're waiting on results of her chest x-ray. We had to stitch up her hand a bit as she must have cut it on the glass pretty good. We'll keep her here for a day or two and monitor her. But you both know how this goes…she'll need to take it easy for a while once she goes home. This can come back and bite you if you don't."

He was referring to the fact that victims of fires who inhaled a lot of smoke often appeared okay, only to have lethal reactions later.

"We'll watch her closely. I give you my word," I said, and Jack nodded.

"Is she awake?" Dylan asked as a sob left her throat. The girl had opened the floodgates because she hadn't stopped crying since the moment we arrived.

"Can we see her?" Everly asked.

"She's coming in and out, and she can't speak with the tube, but you can let her know you're here and tell her you love her, but then let's allow her to get some rest. We should be able to take the tube out tomorrow, and hopefully she'll be feeling better. Right now, she needs rest."

I let out a long sigh of relief. I knew we weren't completely out of the woods, but this was as good as it gets. Mabel had already been released to my sister and we'd all fawned all over her as she told us how Miss Vivi took real good care of her. She said that

Vivian had tied a towel around her face and broken the window to call for help. I kissed her cheek before Jada took her home to allow her to get some sleep. My sister made me promise to call her with updates on Vivian.

Jace, Big Al, Rusty, Tallboy, Rook, Gramps, Samson, Little Dicky...all the guys had come straight from the fire to wait for news on Vivian. Because that's what family did. I realized as I looked around the hospital room and thought about everyone who'd gathered in the waiting room, that my family was here. Jack and his daughters, my sister and Mabel, and the guys from the firehouse. But the most important one was hooked up to tubes and lying in a bed after surviving a brutal fire.

"Let's go," Dylan said to me, her father, Everly, and Charlotte, as we all followed the nurse down to her room.

The girls each took a turn holding her hand as she looked up at them. Her eyes were bloodshot, and her skin had color in it again. I waited as I stood against the door. Trying to keep it together.

Jack moved in next. "You're going to be all right, Vivi. You just take all the time you need, sweetheart."

I saw the corners of her lips turn up and it didn't surprise me that she'd be smiling at the sight of her family.

I waited. I needed to get it together.

"Okay, Dr. Prichard wants her to get some rest. You need to say your goodbyes," Holly Robins, the nurse on duty, said. I'd gone to school with her, and I'd helped her get her drunk brother home a couple times from Beer Mountain when she couldn't manage him.

Dylan, Everly, and Charlotte each kissed my cheek as they walked to the door. Jack clapped me on the shoulder.

"We'll be back first thing in the morning with Ashlan. Call

me if anything changes," he said, leaning in close so only I could hear him.

He knew me. I wasn't going anywhere.

I nodded and moved to the bed, taking her small hand in mine. I dropped to sit in the chair beside her and Holly finished scribbling in her chart when she looked up to meet my gaze.

"You know I'm not going, right?"

She blew out a breath. "You can stay, Niko. Just let her rest, okay?"

I jutted my chin out in agreement. She left the room and Vivi's eyes were heavy, but they met my gaze, and I squeezed her hand.

Before I could stop myself, a sob escaped my throat, and I broke down. Her dark eyes looked pained, and a few tears ran down her cheeks as she watched me. I bowed my head, resting it against the back of her hand.

"I love you, Honey Bee."

She nodded and her eyes closed.

I spent the rest of the night watching her sleep and thanking God that she was okay. Because I couldn't exist in a world that Vivian Thomas wasn't in.

I knew it.

She knew it.

And apparently God knew it because we'd gotten her out of there in time.

And everything would be okay as long as she was okay.

Chapter 33

Vivian

The past few days had gone by slowly, as I'd spent three days in the hospital before Dr. Prichard allowed me to go home even though I felt okay two days ago.

Yes, I still had a cough. But I'd rather recover back at home with Niko than in a hospital bed.

What I didn't expect was for everyone to drive me crazy in the days that followed. Niko had taken a week off from the fire department to take care of me. And for a broody, tough guy like him...I had not expected a hovering nurse. He watched my every move. He followed me to the restroom. Sat beside the tub when I bathed. Ordered takeout and had it delivered because he wouldn't leave me alone for even a minute.

My sisters and my father thought it was hilarious. Dylan made endless fun of him and called him all sorts of ridiculous names. Ashlan had come home to be with me in the hospital and I'd insisted she get back to school.

Jada and Mabel had visited every day as well, and we'd finally gotten through a visit where Jada and I weren't bawling big tears. Mabel kept asking why we were crying since we were fine.

And she was right.

The girl was resilient. She had no effects as of yet from the fire, and we were all so grateful.

The doorbell rang and Niko left me on the couch to answer the door. He'd been acting strange all day, getting the canoe ready to take me out as I'd insisted I needed fresh air. He came back to join me as I sat on the couch and set a package down on the table as he opened the top of the box. He handed me a gigantic fire safety kit and set the empty box down on the floor.

"I want you to keep this at the bakery from now on. There're masks, and a flashlight and other supplies in here."

"I don't have a bakery." I shrugged, reminding him of the reality that my business had been burned to the ground. Oddly, my first set of tears was over the fact that for the first time Niko wouldn't have a birthday cake from me. It had perished in the flames, along with my entire business. Niko thought it was hilarious that my first concern was his birthday cake.

I'd already started looking online for a new space, and my sisters were helping by touring the few that I found downtown today. Once I was up and moving, I'd get things going.

The incident had been ruled arson and my father was meeting with Chuck Martin, the arson investigator, to go over the findings today. The fact that someone would have intentionally burned down my bakery was a hard pill to swallow. Chuck had been investigating the group of teens who had been vandalizing buildings downtown, but I just couldn't fathom a bunch of kids would take things that far. I loved this town and the people in it, and I couldn't fathom it when Niko had told me that it was definitely arson. He hadn't said much, which wasn't like him, and it made me think he had an idea about what happened, but he didn't want to share it.

I hadn't pushed. Emotionally, it had been a lot. The scare from the fire, the bakery being burned to the ground, Mabel being stuck up there with me, and then the truth that it had all been done intentionally.

It was almost too much.

"You'll have one soon, baby."

I nodded. "The first thing I'm making is a birthday cake for you. I feel bad that we still haven't gotten to celebrate your birthday yet. How about we stop moping around and acting like I'm dying, and we go out for dinner tonight?"

His gaze narrowed and he moved to his feet. "I ordered us sandwiches and I've got a whole picnic packed up for us to eat out on the canoe. The sun's shining and it's a perfect day to go out on the water. That's the way I'd like to spend my birthday."

I smiled and stroked his cheek. "Okay then. Let's do this."

I pushed to my feet and grabbed my jacket. I couldn't wait to get out on the water. To breathe fresh air and stop thinking about all that had happened over the past few days.

I sucked in a long breath when I stepped outside and made my way down to the dock. He held the canoe as I climbed in and smiled at the fact that he had blankets and a picnic basket already waiting for us.

He climbed aboard and pushed off the dock as we started to move out on the water. It was a calm day. The crisp air smelled of fresh pine and sage. The clouds above swirled and I stared up at the sky as we glided across the water. I wrapped the blanket around my shoulders as he paddled us out to the middle of the lake.

"This is my favorite place in the world," I said, gazing around at the surrounding trees.

"Me too."

"I'm sorry you spent your birthday in the hospital. I'm going to make it up to you," I said, wriggling my brows.

Dr. Prichard said nothing about not having sex, but Niko was treating me like I was made of porcelain since we came home from the hospital.

"You already made it up to me by being okay. There was only one thing I had planned for my birthday that I'd still like to do."

I sat forward and rubbed my hands together because the man never wanted to celebrate his birthday, so this was a pleasant surprise.

"Sex on a canoe?" I teased.

He barked out a laugh. "That's not a bad idea, but I had something else in mind."

"Oooh, I can't wait to hear."

Niko's tongue swiped out to wet his bottom lip and he pushed the hair away from his face. "Since we decided to give this a try, I've realized a lot of things, Vivi."

"Yeah? What things?"

"Well, us being together has made me look at everything differently. My life. My future. What I thought I wanted. Needed."

My heart squeezed at his words. "What do you want and need, Niko?" My voice was all tease.

He reached into his jacket pocket and pulled out a little black velvet box. My breath caught in my throat. "Only you, Honey Bee. I think you were mine the first time I met you. I think you've always been mine."

"And you've always been mine," I whispered as tears streamed down my face.

"I want to spend my life with you. And I never thought I'd say this, I had a whole speech planned for my birthday when I asked you to be my wife. I was going to tell you that we'd figure the kid thing out. That maybe down the road I'd feel differently."

"Okay," I said. I knew we'd figure it out. I never worried about it the way that he did. I wanted to spend my life with Niko, and I knew we'd find our way as long as we were together.

"But after that fire. I sat in that hospital room watching you sleep that night and I realized what a pussy I'd been. I'd been scared about having a family and failing, but I realized that night, that I'm not my father. I am capable of loving deeply and I know it because I swear to Christ if you hadn't survived that fire, I wouldn't have survived either, Honey Bee. I would have died in those flames right along with you if I had to. I want you to be my wife. I want to put as many babies in you as you're willing to have. And I want to start our future now. You and me, and a bunch of little Vivians running around."

"I like the sound of that." My voice wobbled.

He opened the box and took out the gorgeous ring. "Will you be my wife, Honey Bee?"

"You don't even need to ask." The words broke on a sob. "Yes, of course. I've loved you my whole life, Niko. And I plan on doing it until I take my last breath."

He took my hand and slipped the ring on my finger, and I stared down in amazement. It was the most beautiful ring I'd ever seen.

"It's gorgeous," I said as I looked back up at him and shook my head with surprise. "So, you were going to propose before the fire?"

"Yeah. I wanted to do it on my birthday because I realized that the best gift I'll ever receive is you. No fucking doubt about it." He leaned forward and his mouth crashed into mine. I tangled my hands in his hair and held him close as he kissed me hard. Claiming and consuming in every way.

We sat out on the water talking and laughing and making out. We ate and drank and pondered the future. It was hard to believe that even after all that had happened over the past few days, I could be the happiest I'd ever been.

Tragedy had a way of reminding you how precious life was.

Reminding you about what mattered most.

About what was most important.

Love and family were everything.

Chapter 34

Niko

I left Vivian with her sisters, as Jack called and said he wanted to meet with me and Chuck Martin. I assumed he had his report regarding the fire at Honey Bee's.

"There he is," Rusty said over a mouthful of hot dog. "You back tonight?"

"Nope. I've got two more days off. Just came to meet with Jack and Chuck."

"How's Vivian?" Tallboy asked.

They'd all been calling and texting nonstop to check on her. "She's doing good. Anxious to find a spot to reopen the bakery."

"Let me tell you what, we're all going out of our minds without the cookies," Rusty said, and Samson punched him in the arm.

"You're such a dick sometimes. We're fine. Happy she's doing okay," he said.

"Her sisters found a place that wouldn't need much work. It's that restaurant next to Beer Mountain that shut down last year. She may be able to get in there and get things going quickly," I said. The owner of the building was an old friend of Jack's and he'd felt terrible about what she'd gone through and offered her a killer deal. It was twice the space as she'd had before, and she'd been busy online pricing out fixtures and equipment that she'd need. The insurance company was being more helpful than anyone had expected, and she was grateful.

"That sounds good. Jada's biting at the bit to get back to work," Rook said as he tipped his chin at me.

"Yeah. I don't think it'll be too long. I'll drop by and see her and Mabel on my way home." I knocked on the table before making my way to Jack's office. The door was open, and he waved me inside. I closed the door behind me and shook Chuck's hand and dropped to sit beside him.

"I wanted you to hear it straight from the source, Niko." Jack cleared his throat. I could sense the discomfort, which immediately had my hackles going up.

"Mrs. Winthrop had installed cameras a few weeks ago outside of Sweet Blooms because she'd had her car broken into apparently."

"Okay," I said, rubbing my hands together because I wanted to know who the fuck did this.

"So, the warehouse fire and the bakery appear to be connected. The teens have all been ruled out. They were caught on camera fleeing the building the night of the warehouse fire, because they were there to graffiti the place. They all had solid alibis the night of the bakery fire, and we've been watching them since that night, and they have given me no reason to suspect them at this point. There was, however, one person spotted on the cameras outside of both places. We couldn't be certain it was him on the camera back when the warehouse fire was set, but after seeing the recent footage outside the bakery I'm very confident both are the same man. Your father."

I pushed to my feet.

I'd fucking kill him.

"That piece of shit," I hissed. "Why the fuck would he set the warehouse or the bakery on fire?"

"Maybe it was a threat to you when he set the first one. Him trying to send a message that he was back? And I'm guessing the bakery was also to get at you, but we don't think he realized Vivi and Mabel had come inside through the front door. We watched the footage of two cameras, one from Sweet Blooms and one from the grocery store across from Honey Bee's. Vivian and Mabel were coming through the front door right when your father arrived at the back door," Jack said, and I didn't miss the anger in his eyes.

"It doesn't matter. He almost killed them both. Vivi and Mabel barely got out of there in time. He burned the warehouse and her bakery down to the ground. Could have killed guys on our team too." I ran a hand down the back of my neck. I knew he was an evil dick, but this was next-level shit.

"Agreed. The problem is, we can place him at both scenes, and we know the bakery fire started moments after he goes out of the screen because we have the time stamp. He's been arrested and he's still denying it, claiming he was at home with your mom. Brady Townsend just had your mom brought in for questioning. If she corroborates his story and gives him an alibi, it's going to make it a lot harder. Right now, we've got him dead to rights, we just need her to back our theory that that's him on the camera. We've got his car. His profile. We need your mom."

Fuck me.

I shook my head. "I don't know if she'll tell the truth. She hasn't before."

"Well, her granddaughter and Vivian were nearly killed in this fire. Hell, you could have been killed as well, Niko," Jack said.

I doubt any of that will matter.

I nodded. "When will we find out?"

"I was going to head down to the station now and see what Brady found out. Hopefully we've got enough to hold him either way. You want to head down there with me? Your mom should be finishing up soon," Chuck said.

I pushed to my feet. I needed to look her in the eyes and see if she told the truth. If she protected the people that she loved over that fucking monster she married, for once in her life. I'd keep my expectations low.

If she lied for him—it would be the final straw that broke the camel's back because there'd be no going back after this. He'd nearly killed Vivian and Mabel.

No fucking going back.

When we arrived at the station, I dropped to sit outside in the waiting area, while Chuck went in to speak to Brady. I wondered where my mother was. Where my father was being held.

The door opened and my mother walked out. She stood in the doorway, her gaze locked with mine. There was a fresh bruise beneath her eye that was almost a plum color. She let out a long breath and walked toward me.

I looked up at her. I couldn't speak because I had so much anger bottled up in me. This man had caused enough pain. If she couldn't see that, there was no hope for our relationship.

"Hey," she said, and she reached out her hand, and I didn't miss the tremble. I moved to my feet and took her hand in mine, and she fell into my chest and hugged me tight. "I'm sorry it took me so long."

I pulled back to look down at her. "What did you tell them?"

"The truth. He was gone the night of the fire. The night of both fires. He had soot all over his clothes the night the bakery went up in flames, and he tied them up in a garbage bag and hid them in the storage shed on the side of the house. I told them everything."

I pulled her back in for a hug as relief coursed through my veins. She'd done the right thing. Didn't matter anymore how long it took her. I'd take hundreds of beatings if it meant she'd finally do the right thing this time. She'd put away the man who nearly killed the two people I loved most in the world. The man who'd stolen my childhood and almost my future.

"Thank you for being honest. He's a bad guy, and he needs to go away."

She cried in my arms, and I just held her there. Neither of us spoke for what felt like the longest time before she tipped her head back and looked up at me.

"You've always been strong, Niko." She swiped at her falling tears. "Brave at such a young age. I was scared of him. Scared he'd hurt you and Jada. Scared he'd hurt Mabel if I didn't let him come home when he got out. But in the end, he hurt everyone anyway. I wasn't protecting anyone."

I nodded. We had a long way to go, but for the first time in my entire life, I felt...hopeful.

"I proposed to Vivian," I said, surprising us both. Hadn't told a soul, but here I was telling my mother.

"It's about damn time." She laughed as the tears continued to fall.

Chuck came out of Brady's office and informed us that they

had enough to hold my father, and the fact that he was on parole meant he'd have no chance at bail. Wayne arrived shortly after and tipped his chin at me as if saying we'd finally gotten him.

I exhaled a breath after everyone walked away, leaving me and my mother alone in the lobby. "We're going to be all right. Let's get out of here. I'll take you over to Jada's and we can fill her in."

"Okay," she said as she hesitantly placed her hand in mine, and we walked out of the station. It's something that should have happened years ago. Her being honest about the monster she married. But I'd given up hope that it would ever happen, and I'd take this small miracle for what it was.

• • •

"So, when's the bachelor party?" Little Dicky asked as he forked his lasagna. We were all crowded around the table as we'd just returned from a call that was ridiculous. Little old Mrs. Weebel, my kindergarten teacher, had needed her battery changed on her smoke detector. She'd called nine-one-one and tried to explain that she'd be killed in a fire if it didn't work, and all they'd heard on the other end was the word *fire*.

So, we'd all gone. Little Dicky had led the charge as he'd really come into his own these past few weeks. Everly Thomas had met with him several times, and none of us knew what was said, but the guy had completely changed and left his fears far from the firehouse. I'd even be bold enough to say I'd walk beside him into a burning building now. The dude was fierce.

I'd changed all Mrs. Weebel's batteries, so we'd be safe from this call for the next while at least.

"I don't do bachelor parties." I bit off the end of my garlic bread.

"Come on. It's tradition. No one thought your ass would ever get married, and we're damn well going to celebrate that," Jace said, and I looked around to see I had no one backing me up on this one, not even Jack.

He shrugged. "It's tradition. You have a few beers and call it done."

"Yeah. We won't keep you too long from Vivian. We know you like to cuddle by the fire and drink hot cocoa like a big fat puss—er, sorry, Cap," Rusty said.

"He's not the only one that finds you offensive, Rust," Gramps hissed, and the table erupted in laughter.

"I've got no shame in my game. I'd rather be with my girl than here with your stinky asses." I shrugged.

"I went by the new bakery today and it looks great," Tallboy said, reaching for his water.

"Yeah. She got it up and running fairly quickly," I said proudly. "And planned a wedding to boot."

Vivian and I were getting married at the Joybills' barn out on the lake. They rented the space out and they'd be catering the event as well from their restaurant. I didn't care much about the details, but I wanted Vivian to have whatever she wanted, so I'd gone to a tasting, which turned out to be damn good because I got to eat just about everything on the menu. Vivian had made us samples of all the cakes we both liked, and we'd concluded that we were keeping it simple. Chocolate and white cake, with raspberry ganache filling and buttercream frosting. The fuck if I knew what any of that meant, but she said it like I should know, and I was going with that. She'd been drawing this cake on paper for weeks and she couldn't wait to show it off at the wedding.

All I cared about was the bride. Marrying the girl that made me whole. The girl who gave me the happiest memories of a fucked-up childhood, and the brightest hopes for the future.

My sister and Mabel had moved back in with my mother, and my father had been sentenced to twenty-eight years in prison for a multitude of charges. He'd been found guilty of recklessness, intention and attempted voluntary manslaughter. With his prior record, they did not go easy on him. It wasn't long enough for me, but I figured I could breathe easy for the next twenty-eight years. My mother had filed for divorce, and we were all moving forward.

The wedding had proven to be a bright light at a dark time. Vivi had wanted a spring wedding, and I just wanted to make her mine, so if it meant waiting a few months I was fine with it.

Since giving up my apartment and not paying rent for my sister anymore, I'd been working on a surprise wedding gift for months.

"You ready to go?" I asked Jack after we cleared our plates.

"You going to tell me where we're going?"

"You'll see." We walked outside and he hopped in the passenger seat of my truck, and I drove through town toward the lake.

Everly, Charlotte, Dylan, and Ashlan stood beside their car at the end of the driveway.

"The girls are here?"

"Yep. All but one." I hopped out of the truck.

They all started talking at once. Asking what they were doing here. Why I'd asked Ashlan to come home from school for the weekend.

"Give the man a minute to speak, you chattery bunch of hens." Jack held his hands up and shook his head.

I barked out a laugh. "I bought the old ranch." I held my hands out to the farmhouse sitting at the end of the long driveway.

"I was hoping you'd help me clean it up, and then I'll hit up the boys at the firehouse to help me paint it before I give it to her on our wedding day."

Everly's eyes watered. "Well, I'll be damned, Niko West, if you aren't the most romantic man on the planet."

"She's always loved this place," Jack said as he cleared his throat. "How'd you pull this off?"

"I've been saving for a long time. Had some luck with investments. And with Jada covering her own bills and just paying half the mortgage for Vivi's postage stamp house which is fairly cheap... I was able to talk old Mr. Clyde into a sweet deal. He wants a family in here, and I promised I'd fill all the rooms. Plus, he's a sucker for Vivi's cupcakes, and I promised him all the baked goods he can eat for free."

"You sappy son of a bitch. Who freaking knew?" Dylan gasped as we all started walking toward the house. "Well, I'll tell you who knew. I knew. I've always known you were a softy under all that broody, arrogant muscle."

Charlotte's head fell back in laughter, and she rubbed her hands together. "This is going to be the best surprise."

Ashlan leaned her head against my arm, and I wrapped it around her as we continued up the drive. "Thanks for making me come home for this."

"Does this mean some of these girls can move in with you now that you have all this space?" Jack teased.

"Maybe Charlie can buy Vivi's house?" Dylan perked up.

"That would be amazing," her twin sister said. "But it's still only one bedroom, so that doesn't solve your problem."

"Guess I'm stuck with you for a few more years until I graduate and find a job." Dylan stuck her tongue out at her father, and he laughed.

"Boys, Niko. Fill this house with boys," Jack said as Dylan jumped on her father's back and Everly punched his shoulder and Charlotte rolled eyes and Ashlan smiled up at me and shook her head.

"He loves us, even if he tries to pretend to be annoyed," Ashlan said.

"I'm certain of it." I squeezed her shoulder.

Because I was.

The girls ran through the house checking out the space, and I took Jack in the kitchen where I'd dropped off a shit ton of cleaning supplies.

"You did good, Niko." His eyes watered and he clapped me on the shoulder.

And damn if it didn't feel like I did.

Epilogue

Vivian

My wedding day was everything I ever dreamed it would be. Everyone we loved was here. It was springtime in Honey Mountain, and the lake was glistening in the distance as the sun was just going down. Niko stood at the end wearing a black suit, sans the tie, as it was a stretch to get him in a dress shirt and coat. He wore black sneakers which I hadn't argued about because I was wearing my favorite cowboy booties beneath my gorgeous dress.

I wore a strapless satin gown, fitted to the waist with layers of tulle that filled out the princess-style dress. My mother's pearl necklace was the perfect addition and it made me feel like she was here with me in a way. Dylan did my hair and makeup. Loose waves fell around my shoulders, and we pinned the front up, before placing the crown of the veil on my head.

My sisters all gushed, and they each wore a satin peach gown with their hair falling in loose waves around their shoulders.

We'd drawn out of a hat years ago, around the time my mom got sick. She openly spoke about our wedding days and said that was the hardest part about her awful disease because she'd be missing all the special days to come. She promised she'd be here in spirit, and I felt her. I really did.

But she made us draw names out of a cup back then and decide who'd stand up at one another's weddings, because she said our dad would never know how to handle that kind of stuff. She'd be right, by the way.

So, Charlotte was my maid of honor. I'd be Everly's. Dylan would have Everly stand beside her, Charlotte would have Ashlan, and Ashlan would have Dylan as her maid of honor. It made it easier knowing that it was already decided.

My sisters were all lined up at the end of the aisle along with Jada who stood beside Ashlan.

Mabel made her way down the aisle dropping peach and pink rose petals in her wake, as her white gown swooshed side to side along the grass. She'd asked me if our dresses could match, and we had a mini wedding gown made for her to match mine. She and I had a bond after what we'd been through together, and I was honored that she was a part of our special day. She made her way over to her grandmother. Shayla had been much more present in our lives since Billy had returned to prison, and I was grateful.

I held on to my father's arm as we strode down the grassy path toward my future husband. His hair was down and blowing in the slight breeze, and those gray eyes found mine. Just like they always had. I had flashbacks of standing up in front of the class in third grade to give a presentation about Abraham Lincoln and finding those same gray eyes out in the classroom that calmed my nerves. Those same eyes that comforted me the day I lost my mother and he held me tight as I cried for hours. The same gray eyes that found me in the midst of a blaze that nearly killed me and Mabel.

When I used to dream about my wedding day, I never pictured a groom. I'd dated Jansen for so long and never once did I imagine him standing at the end of the aisle as I walked toward my future husband. I guess in a way I'd always known there was only one man who truly loved me the way I longed to be loved. I'd been too afraid at the time to admit it was him—but I think I always knew.

Jace King stood beside Niko, and then Rusty, Tallboy, Rook, and Samson finished out his groomsmen.

When we came to a stop, Niko reached for my hand.

"Hold on there, Mr. West. I've got my lines to say first," Pastor Grady said, and everyone chuckled.

Niko's eyes never left mine as he drank me in.

Heat and fire and…forever right there in his gaze.

"Who gives this woman away?" Pastor Grady asked dramatically, and Niko closed his eyes as if he were praying for patience before they opened and settled on me again.

"I do," my father said. "Along with the blessings of her mother."

A lump formed in my throat as my father kissed my cheek and then jumped over the train of my dress which made everyone laugh some more.

I joined Niko in front of the most beautiful floral arch I'd ever seen. Pink and peach and white florals covered the wood frame with the backdrop of the lake behind it. It nearly took my breath away. But it was the man who stood before me that truly stole the air from my lungs. I honestly couldn't tell you a word that Pastor Grady uttered from that point on. All I saw was Niko.

He was all I'd ever seen if I were being honest.

We'd agreed to keep our vows short and sweet, as my future husband didn't believe it was necessary to go on and on in front of our guests, he believed it was about showing each other every single day how much we loved one another.

Niko faced me. No paper. No notes. He held my hands in his as his gaze locked with mine.

"You're my past, my present, and my future, Honey Bee. I promise to love you until I take my last breath and beyond."

I smiled up at him as tears fell down my cheeks. He reached up with his thumbs and brushed them away.

"I think I've loved you my whole life, Niko West. You're my safe place, my heart, and my future. My hero, my prince, and my protector. And now I get to call you my husband—" My words broke on a sob, and he pulled me against him, wrapping his arms around me.

"Damn straight, wife."

He leaned down and kissed me as Pastor Grady had a meltdown beside us until Niko pulled back and everyone watching laughed hysterically.

"Now wait a minute, Niko. You jumped the gun, per usual. Which isn't a bad thing when it comes to fighting fires. But if I may..." He raised a brow at my husband.

Niko motioned with his hand to go ahead and wriggled his brows at me.

"You may now kiss the bride," he said in exasperation, and Niko's mouth was on mine.

Kissing me like we weren't standing in front of all of our friends and family. And I didn't mind one bit. I loved that he didn't care. That he wanted today to be about us. That's all that mattered to him. Not the flowers or the food or the cake.

Me and him.

As it should be.

When we came up for air, Pastor Grady looked at me with one brow raised before turning to the crowd of people who'd gathered here to celebrate our special day.

"Ladies and gentlemen, please stand and help me welcome Mr. and Mrs. Niko and Vivian West."

Pastor Grady continued with directions for everyone to wait before following the wedding party out, but I didn't hear any of it because my husband was whispering things in my ear.

"I can't wait to ditch all these people and get you out of that dress, Honey Bee."

I laughed and squeezed his hand. "Photos. Food. Dancing. Cake. And then you and me."

When we followed our photographer out to the gorgeous field beside the barn where we'd agreed to take photos, he pulled me close to him again.

"I have a surprise for you tonight before we go home." His tongue dipped out to wet his lips and I had to take a minute to process the fact that this was my husband. My forever. I didn't know how I'd gotten so lucky, but I wasn't going to question it.

"Oh yeah? I have a surprise for you too," I said.

He kissed me hard, and we pulled apart when everyone walked over to meet us.

The photos felt like they went on forever, but I knew they were a memory we'd cherish for years to come, so I kept nudging Niko to be patient.

Our reception was everything we wanted it to be. Simple, yet elegant. There were wooden tables and chairs running the length of the barn. A few crystal chandeliers hung above, and Mrs. Winthrop had made the most beautiful floral arrangements which ran down the long tables. Rusty's brother, Leo, was the DJ and he played the list of songs that the guests had requested on the little note card we'd included in our invitations.

I danced with my father. I danced with my sisters. I danced with my friends. And most importantly, I danced with my husband.

I barely ate the chicken dish that they'd served, but I made sure to eat a whole slice of cake. The night was an absolute blur, but I tried to stay in the moment. I knew it would be one of the best days of my life, and I didn't want to forget one single second.

I rubbed my fingers over my mom's pearl necklace as I walked over to check on my dad. He was standing alone in the back corner, watching everyone who'd had a little too much to drink at that point, dancing and singing along to the music.

"Hey, Dad. Thanks for everything today," I said, leaning my head on his shoulder as I moved to stand beside him.

"I'm happy for you, sweetheart. Your mom would've loved seeing you walk down the aisle today. She'd be damn proud of you."

I looked up at him, my eyes welled with emotion, and I nodded. "I miss her. I wish she was here."

"She is, Vivi. I can feel her."

"Me too," I said as I tried to swallow over the lump in my throat. I blinked a few times, stopping the tears that threatened to fall. I squeezed his hand and he turned to kiss the top of my head.

"I think your husband looks awfully anxious to get you out of here," he said with a knowing smirk on his face. I glanced over at Niko. He stood on the other side of the barn, rolling his eyes at Rusty and Tallboy, and holding Mabel in his arms as her head fell back in a fit of giggles. He looked over just then as if he could feel me watching him. The corners of his lips turned up in the corners and he raised his free hand and shook his keys at me.

"You think so?" I said as a laugh escaped.

"Go on, honey. This is your day. These people are going to drink and dance the night away. You go ahead and sneak out."

I pushed up on my tiptoes and kissed his cheek. "I love you, Dad."

"Love you, Vivi girl."

I made my way across the room, glancing over to see Dylan leading the conga line and Charlotte and Ashlan on her heels as every guy in Honey Mountain followed them. I looked to my right and saw Everly off in the corner holding a phone to her ear with a look of concern on her face. I held my finger up to Niko, who was still chatting with his friends and bouncing his niece on his hip, and he nodded, as I beelined over to my older sister. She forced a smile at me and pulled the phone away from her ear.

"Hey, are you sneaking out?" she asked, reaching for my hand.

"Yeah. Everything okay? You looked a little stressed."

"Oh, no. I was just listening to a message. The Lions offered me a temporary job until they decide if they need someone full time."

I squealed. It was something, and I was certain they'd hire her on full time once they saw how talented she was. And she wouldn't be but a few hours away, living in San Francisco. It was much better than the prospects that would take her across the country. "Ev, that's great news. I'm so happy for you."

"It's not quite that simple." She played with the ends of her long dark hair that fell around her shoulders. "Apparently, their superstar is having some major issues. So, in the off-season, they are taking him out of the limelight of the city and the press and sending him home to work on physical therapy and get his head on straight over the next few months. They'll see how he responds and then decide if they want to keep me."

"What does that mean? Are we talking about Hawk Madden?" I asked.

She nodded. "He's coming home to Honey Mountain. They have offered to rent me my own house for the next few months, so I don't have to live with Dad, and I'll be working here, with Hawk, until the season starts. It's not like I have any other offers at the moment, and they've offered a pretty hefty salary to do it."

I tried not to laugh. She looked so panicked, and I knew it had very little to do with the new job, and much more to do with their star player. He was the only boy I'd ever seen my sister be crazy in love with. Sure, she'd dated and had a few long-term relationships since she'd left for college, but she and Hawk had always had something really special.

"You didn't end on bad terms as far as I remember. And it'll be nice to have you at home over the next few months. Not to mention the enormous floral arrangement that he sent to the house when he heard me and Niko were getting married. He said he was sorry he couldn't make it due to the fact that he had a game."

She rolled her eyes. "We didn't exactly end on good terms either. And it's just been such a long time. I don't know how it'll be. I've managed to avoid him the few times he's been home since we left for different colleges."

"Don't let that shadow the fact that you just got hired by a professional hockey team which will probably lead to full-time employment. And if you were living in the Bay Area, we'd be able to see you all the time. This is exciting, Ev."

"I know," she whispered as she chewed on her thumbnail. There was something she wasn't telling me. She never did tell us why they broke up, and she rarely spoke of him after that. We'd all been heartbroken because we were all so close with Hawk. "Now get out of here. Your husband looks like he's about to blow a gasket waiting for you."

I laughed. "I love you, Ev."

"Love you, Vivi. Go," she said, but her smile was still forced, and I didn't like it.

I kissed her cheek and walked toward Niko. He'd just set Mabel down on her feet and she came running toward me. I bent down to catch her in my arms and hugged her tight.

"Thanks for being the prettiest flower girl in all the land," I said as I stroked her little cherub cheek.

"Thanks for making me a bride, Miss Vivi," she said as she reached up and stroked my cheek. "Neek, Neek told me to tell you he needs you to come save him from Rusty."

My head fell back in laughter as I pushed to stand. Mabel ran off to find Shayla and Jada and I made my way to my impatient husband.

"You ready, Honey Bee?"

"I am. I can't wait to see this surprise." He reached for my hand, and we snuck out the back of the barn without telling a soul. Music boomed behind us as we made our way toward his truck. Niko lifted me off my feet and set me on the passenger seat and I started to protest.

"I know you can do it yourself, Mrs. West. But tonight, I want to do it for you, all right?" His face was so close, he rubbed his nose against mine as he leaned over to buckle me in. He pulled something out of his coat pocket and handed it to me.

"What's this?" I asked as I held the silk tie in my hands.

"It's part of your surprise. Tie it around your eyes now, please." He smirked.

I sighed and pulled it in front of my face before tying it behind my head. "This better not be something kinky."

He barked out a laugh before gently kissing my lips as he shut the door.

"You got those eyes covered?" he asked as the truck drove down a bumpy street.

"I do."

"Good. We're almost there."

When the truck came to a stop, I could hear the crickets chirping in the distance and it sounded like water was lapping against the shore.

"Where are we?" I whispered.

"You'll see." He shut his door and came around to my side before lifting me into his arms.

"Are you just going to carry me everywhere tonight?" I chuckled as my arm came around his neck and I settled my cheek on his chest.

"That's the plan." He walked up some steps I think, and then he came to an abrupt stop and set me on my feet. He stepped behind me and untied the blindfold.

My eyes took a minute to adjust to the porch lights and I glanced around. The old Clyde Ranch. It sat right on the lake, with a gorgeous yard surrounding it. Tall pine trees and overgrown grass. It was my favorite house in Honey Mountain.

Always had been.

"What are we doing here?" I asked as I took note of the two potted plants on the front porch with fresh flowers. Someone must have moved into the place. It had been empty for the past few years.

"We're home, Honey Bee." He pulled a key from his pocket and pushed open the front door.

I didn't move. My body was completely frozen as he came to stand in front of me. He bent his legs, so he was eye level with me, and he smiled.

"What do you mean?" I whispered as my hands came up to cover my mouth.

"It's ours. I had quite a bit saved up, and with the money I was using toward Jada's rent, that investment property me and Jace got into together, and what we already pay on the mortgage at your place, it was doable. I wanted to show you how committed I was. This house will be where we start our family. Where your sisters can come hang out. Your father can barbecue at our place any time he wants. And we can renovate the kitchen and you can bake everything you want here."

"Niko," I said, tears streaming down my face as I shook my head. "I can't believe you did this. Now I feel like a jerk. I got you a new canoe for a wedding gift, with our wedding date engraved on the bottom. And you bought me a house?" I snorted.

"I love that you got me a canoe. We can use that every day off our dock. I'm going to pick you up one more time and carry you over the threshold, all right?" he teased as he pulled me in his arms, and I hugged him around his neck.

Once we were inside, he flipped on the lights and set me down. "Welcome home, Honey Bee."

I continued to shake my head in disbelief. "I was already home. Home is anywhere I'm with you."

And that was the truth.

Because Niko West was my husband, my best friend, and my forever.

Bonus Epilogue
Vivian

Niko and I had the weeks following our wedding to work on our new place while we packed up the old place. Everything was working out well, as Charlotte had decided to buy my little house from me, and we'd used the money from the house and the wedding to renovate our new home.

And today we'd officially moved in.

All the guys from the firehouse had come to help us move, and of course my family was here in full force, just like they always were.

"Okay, I'm leaving. I haven't worked this hard—ever," Dylan said, shaking her head with disgust. She had dirt smudged on her cheek and I tried not to laugh.

"Well, you best rest up. You're moving me in next week," Charlotte said with a wicked grin on her face.

"Uggghh. Why you had to buy the postage stamp house, which means I have to stay with Dad, is beyond me." Her twin groaned.

"Hey. I'm still there with you when I'm on summer break," Ashlan said as she gathered the last of the bubble wrap from the kitchen into the garbage bag before tying it closed.

"You're in college," Dylan hissed. "I'm actually a grown-up."

"You're in college too. I mean, sort of. You're in law school," Ashlan said dramatically, and I heard Niko laugh from where he was hanging the big screen TV over the fireplace with Jace and Rusty.

"Will you quit whining, please? You can live with me. The house the Lions got me has a little guesthouse and it's right up the street from here. I'll take you over to see it tomorrow," Everly huffed.

"I didn't know you'd officially signed the contract?" Dylan quirked a brow and studied Everly. I didn't know either. She'd been very mysterious about the whole thing and continued with a few more interviews as she said she hadn't decided yet what she would do.

"They made me an offer I couldn't refuse," she said, crossing her arms over her chest.

Dylan lunged at her. "Praise the Lord, I'm free," she sang out.

"You can stay there too, Ash, until you go back to school."

"Woohoo." Our baby sister fist pumped the ceiling. "I'm only going to be home for a few weeks over summer break this year because of that business internship I got. But I'll take it."

"Do you guys think Dad will be lonely?" I asked.

"Mind your business, Vivi. Dad could use some peace and quiet at his house," my father shouted from the back porch, and everyone laughed.

"I thought you already went home?" I said as I covered my mouth to hide my smile.

"I can't very well cook Sunday dinner over here without hooking up the barbecue, can I?"

"Good point."

My sisters hugged everyone goodbye, and I stood in my newly renovated kitchen. We'd poured all our money and sweat equity into the kitchen and the master bathroom because that's where we figured we'd be spending most of our time. We'd work on the rest of the house over the next few years. There was no rush.

The large white island was covered in dishes that needed to be put away, and I glanced up at the two crystal chandeliers that Niko had hung for me yesterday. He complained nonstop that they were ridiculously fancy, yet he had a permanent smile on his face the entire time he hung them.

The white cabinets had glass doors on the front, so you could see all the pretty dishes that we'd just gotten for our wedding, and I couldn't wait to get it all organized.

We left the original hardwood floors that ran throughout the house, and Niko and I spent a few hours every day after work restaining them. They looked brand new.

My father finished working in the backyard, and Jace said he needed to get home to the girls. Rusty realized he'd forgotten about the hot date he had and hurried out of there as well. Niko and I stood on the front porch watching everyone pull out of our long circular driveway.

"Thank god they're gone," he grumped, and I laughed.

"You're full of it. You love them."

"I love you," he said, pulling me into him and wrapping his arms around me.

"Come on. Let's go walk through the place and see how it looks," I said, pulling away and reaching for his hand as I led him into the large great room. We had a gray L-shaped couch and a coffee table in front of the TV, the farmhouse dining table I'd found and refinished sat in the space between the TV room and the kitchen. Large windows with black panes ran along the entire wall facing the lake, and it was truly breathtaking.

"It feels like home," he said as we stared out the back window just as the sun was going down. "And that canoe you got me makes the place."

I barked out a laugh. "Sure, it does. I honestly can't believe we live here."

We stopped in the downstairs bonus room that we were turning into a workout room for Niko. All the guys from the firehouse were thrilled to have a new place to work out and hang out in. We had big plans to hang a few TVs on the walls and get a little refrigerator to hold drinks. But for now, there were a whole lot of weights and a boxing bag.

We made our way upstairs, stopping in the first guest room that was filled with boxes. We were going to make it a craft room for me, so I could work on things from home, and it would be a fun place to do things with Mabel when she came over.

The next two rooms were extra guest rooms, and we hadn't decided what to do with those just yet. Niko flipped the light on in the room beside ours and took in the boxes.

"What are we going to put in this one?"

"Well, I don't know," I said, moving across the room to the package that sat atop the stack of boxes in the corner. "But I did get you a housewarming gift."

"I thought the house was the housewarming gift?" he asked as his brows pinched together with worry, like he'd blown it by not getting me something.

I laughed. "It is the gift. But I wanted to get you a little something because you've been working so hard."

He took the white box with the black bow and tugged it off the top before removing the lid and staring down with his mouth gaping open.

"What is this?" He pulled the white stick out of the package.

"I'm preggers. So, I thought this room could be a baby room."

His entire face lit up, and he set the stick down on the boxes and pulled me against him.

"I thought we were going to be practicing for a while."

I tipped my head back and looked up at him. "We can keep practicing. Apparently pregnancy can make you real horny." I snorted.

"You did it, Honey Bee," he whispered. His gray eyes wet with emotion.

"We did it," I said, pushing up on my tiptoes to kiss him.

Exclusive Bonus Content

The Nursery

Vivian

We'd had our gender reveal party a few weeks ago, and Niko and I were still both on cloud nine that we were having a little girl. Beth Everly West was going to have the cutest nursery ever, and I couldn't wait to show my husband what I'd been working on while he'd been gone for the last three days at the firehouse.

"Are you ready?"

"I'm always ready, Honey Bee."

There was something about the way that he looked at me that still made me blush. We were married and expecting our first child, yet this man had a way of making me swoon with just a look.

I pushed the door open and walked through, and his big body took up most of the doorway as he paused and stared at the space. I'd spent the last three days getting it set up. My sisters had come over to help me paint the walls in the palest pink color we could find, called dusty rose. We did a coat of glitter iridescent clear paint on top to make it extra sparkly.

My favorite part was the hand painted mural we'd done on the wall behind the crib. Vines with pretty pink roses, in all different shades, trailed along the sides of the wall, creating an arch of flowers over her crib.

Ashlan had found these little hand painted butterflies with colorful wings that we attached to the vines on the walls. We couldn't help but add a couple of honeybees as well, as we'd be calling her Bee for short.

"This is gorgeous, Vivi," he said. "I think it's a little girls dream room."

He kicked off his shoes before walking across the large white textured area rug in the center of the room, toward the window. There were white sheer panels flocked by blush velvet curtains on each side. The natural light flooded the room, and the view out the window of her nursery was absolutely stunning with the large green pasture for miles and the trees that were in full bloom in the distance.

"You think so?"

"Yeah. I think our baby girl is really lucky to have you for her mama," he said, glancing over at the white chenille rocker in the corner with the cozy throw tossed over the arm of the chair.

"Do you recognize the dresser?"

He studied the white antiqued piece of furniture with the vintage silver pulls. "Yes. This was in your bedroom growing up, wasn't it?"

I chuckled. "It was. Charlotte and I put a fresh coat of paint on it, and then sanded it down and got some new hardware. It was actually my mother's dresser when she was a little girl, before she passed it to me."

"And now it's our little girl's dresser," he said, tugging me closer.

"Yep. And these prints are something I painted with Mabel, and I had them framed. I think they came out so cute."

He studied the three prints. One was a honeybee. One was a butterfly. And one was a dragonfly.

"My talented girls didn't miss one single detail." He kissed me, and my fingers tangling into his long hair.

"I'm happy you're home. I've missed you."

"I always miss you when I'm away, baby. Couldn't wait to get home to you," he said, as his large hand settled on my cheek.

"Yeah? What are you going to do about it?"

"Oh, I see how you are. Well, first I'm going to carry my girl out of this nursery, because I can't talk about the things that I want to do to her in my daughter's bedroom."

My head fell back on a laugh, and the next thing I knew, he was scooping me up in his arms and carrying me toward the kitchen.

"Niko, I'm getting to heavy for you to carry around," I groaned, as he set me on the kitchen island.

"Not even close. I will carry you and our daughter wherever you want me to," he said, moving to stand between my thighs.

I glanced over at the bag on the counter. "What is that?"

"I got us dinner on my way home. I don't want you cooking right now. You've been working too hard."

"And you worry too much. I'm pregnant, not sick," I said with a chuckle.

"Baby, you're growing a human in there. Let me spoil you, okay?"

I nodded, as my teeth sunk into my bottom lip, and I stared up at him. My big, handsome man had a way of stealing the breath from my lungs. He was sexy and strong and—he was mine.

"Fine. But I'm not hungry right now. At least not for food."

His lips turned up in the corners, and his hands found mine, intertwining our fingers together. "Is that so?"

"Yeah. I've got other things on my mind." I waggled my brows.

"I've always got other things on my mind when you're in the room. But I'm starving, baby."

I squeezed his hands. "I'm sorry. You've been working so hard. Let's eat now."

He did this slow nod, his smile growing wider. "I'm not starving for food, Vivi."

Before I knew what was happening, his hands moved to my ass and he picked me up off the counter, my legs coming around his waist as he carried me to the couch, and carefully set me down. "I need to taste you right now. I've missed you."

My breaths were coming fast. "I can live with that."

He lifted my skirt to find my white lace panties beneath, and he traced his fingers along the center, and I gasped. My head fell back, and I arched toward him.

"Niko," I whispered.

"I'm right here, baby."

He buried his head between my thighs and my eyes fell closed.

My husband always knew what I needed.

And when I cried out his name, he continued to hold me there so I could ride out every last bit of pleasure. He pulled me forward, his lips glossy with my desire, and he smiled at me. "Now that I've eaten, let's feed you."

"You have a filthy mouth," I said with a laugh as he helped me to my feet.

"And you love it, Honey Bee."

And he was right.

I loved everything about this man.
He was everything I wanted.
Everything I needed.
And he was mine.
Always mine.

Acknowledgments

Greg, Chase & Hannah, thank you for being my biggest supporters and always believing in me and encouraging me to chase my dreams! YOU are the reason that I work hard every day!! I love you ALWAYS & FOREVER!!

Nina, I am so thankful for YOU!! Thank you for listening, encouraging and believing in me. It truly means the world to me.

Caroline, Jennifer, Abi, Annette, Doo, Pathi, Natalie and Lara, thank you for being the BEST beta readers EVER! Your feedback means the world to me. I am so thankful for you!!
Hang, thank you for bringing Vivi and Niko to life with this gorgeous cover! I am so grateful for you!

Sue Grimshaw (Edits by Sue), Thank you for your encouragement, your guidance and your support. I appreciate you so much! I would absolutely be lost without you!!

Ellie (My Brothers Editor), I am so thankful for you!! Thank you for always making time for me and working with my crazy timelines!! Your support and your friendship mean THE WORLD to me!! Love you!

Christine Estevez, I am so thankful for you! Thank you for

all that you do to support me! It truly means the world to me! Love you!

Willow, there are no words to thank you for all that you do for me. Thank you for being on this journey with me!! For reading my words, supporting me, laughing with me, and being the most amazing friend! Love you!!

Catherine, I love you and am so thankful for your friendship!! I love our chats about books and pups and all the things!! I would be lost without you!! Love you!

Mom, thank you for your love and support and for reading all of my words! Ride or die!! Love you!

Dad, you really are the reason that I keep chasing my dreams!! Thank you for teaching me to never give up. Love you!

Sandy, thank you for reading and supporting me throughout this journey! Love you!

Pathi, I am so thankful for you! You are the reason I even started this journey. Thank you for believing in me!! I love and appreciate you more than I can say!! Thank you for your friendship!! Love you!

Natalie (Head in the Clouds, Nose in a Book), thank you for supporting me through it all! I appreciate all that you do for me from beta reading to the newsletter to just absolutely being the most supportive friend!! I am so thankful for you!! Love you!

To all the bloggers and bookstagrammers who have posted, shared, and supported me—I can't begin to tell you how much it means to me. I love seeing the graphics that you make and the gorgeous posts that you share. I am forever grateful for your support!

To all the readers who take the time to pick up my books and take a chance on my words…THANK YOU for helping to make my dreams come true!!

Don't miss any of the sweet and sexy small-town romances of Honey Mountain

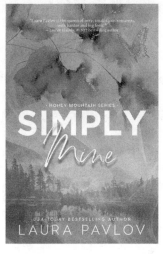

*Don't miss the exciting new books
Entangled has to offer.*

Follow us!

 @EntangledPublishing

 @Entangled_Publishing

 @EntangledPub

AMARA
an imprint of Entangled Publishing LLC